Knowers and Lovers

a novel

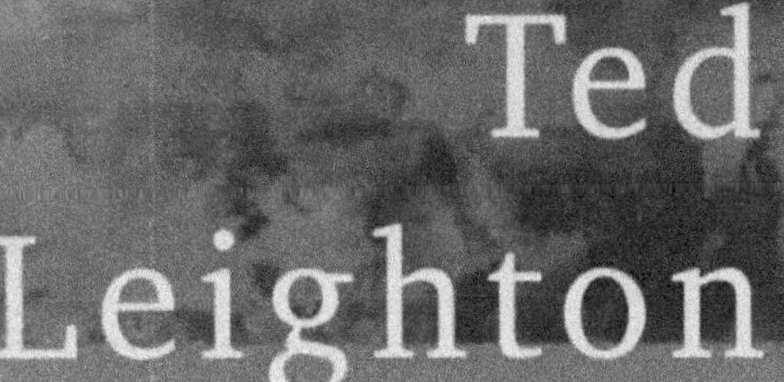

Ted Leighton

Knowers and Lovers
© 2024 Ted Leighton

Cover design: Rebekah Wetmore, using 'The Ghost of Loss (Under a
    Bruised Sky)' 2023 oil on birch panel diptych by Eva McCauley
    www.evamccauley.com
Editor: Andrew Wetmore

ISBN: 978-1-998149-66-7
First edition November, 2024

Moose House Publications
2475 Perotte Road
Annapolis County, NS
B0S 1A0
moosehousepress.com
info@moosehousepress.com

Moose House Publications recognizes the support of the Province of Nova Scotia. We are pleased to work in partnership with the Department of Communities, Culture and Heritage to develop and promote our cultural resources for all Nova Scotians.

We live and work in Mi'kma'ki, the ancestral and unceded territory of the Mi'kmaw people. This territory is covered by the "Treaties of Peace and Friendship" which Mi'kmaw and Wolastoqiyik (Maliseet) people first signed with the British Crown in 1725. The treaties did not deal with surrender of lands and resources but in fact recognized Mi'kmaq and Wolastoqiyik (Maliseet) title and established the rules for what was to be an ongoing relationship between nations. We are all Treaty people.

Also by Ted Leighton

A Ring of Justice – the first Rick Robichaud adventure.

Rick Robichaud abandoned science to stay home and support his wife's career as a veterinarian near the village of Bear River, Nova Scotia, where old ways and new, fair play and foul, generosity and crime weave threads of joy and hatred, contentment and murder.

Robichaud must untangle the threads to reveal startling truths, uncertain justice and the enduring power of friendship.

Ted Leighton casts an intriguing tale of murder and community redemption in rural Nova Scotia as he explores the evil present in some men's hearts. *A Ring of Justice* is a compelling read.

— JM Blais, author of *Working the Blue Lines: lessons learned from hockey and policing*

People of Cove and Woodlot: Stories across 100 years of memory (coming in 2025)

Writings by Ted and his father, Alec, about characters and adventures in and around Smiths Cove, Nova Scotia; extensively illlustrated by Eva McCauley.

The True Vosgian

The people of the Vosges Mountains in eastern France have deep roots and great pride of place.

A Vosgian tests the claim of another with two questions:

Whom do you prefer, your mother or your father?
"Bacon."

The fat or the lean?
"The rind."

To Jack Bower

Wilford White "Jack" Bower, Head of English at The Millbrook School in the mid-1960s, brought wisdom, principles and encouragement to my life at a critical time, and urged me never to stop writing.

This is a work of fiction, imagined by the author on the real landscapes of western Nova Scotia in the first decades of the 21st century. The people, names, homes, businesses, and events not clearly indicated as historical, are fictional. Any resemblance to actual persons or personalities (living or dead), businesses or specific real events is entirely coincidental and not intended..

Knowers and Lovers

Knowers and Lovers

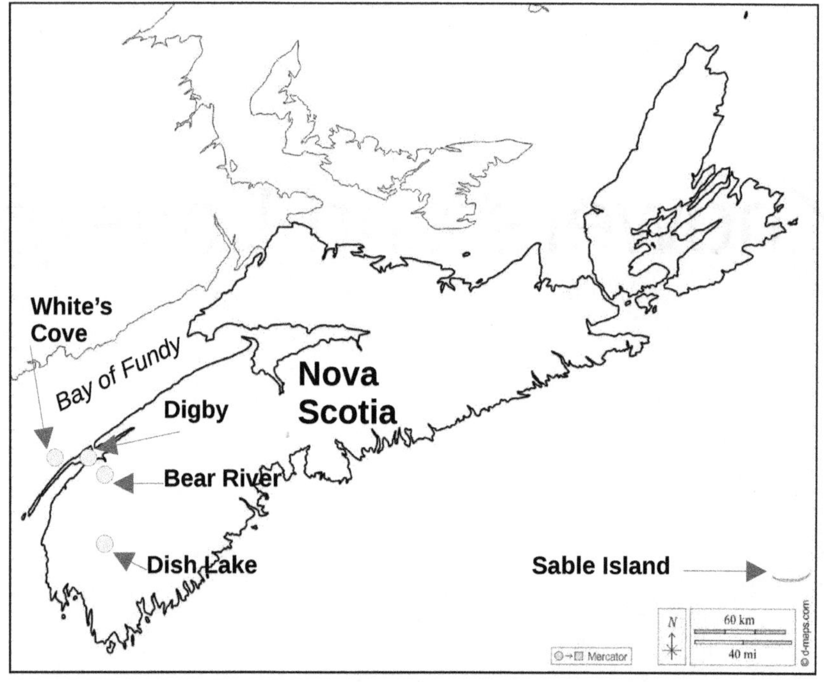
White's
Cove
Bay of Fundy
Digby
Nova
Scotia
Bear River
Dish Lake
Sable Island
Mercator
N
60 km
40 mi
© d-maps.com

Prologue: 1957

"If that doesn't get us a baby, nothing ever will," Sylvie whispered.

She rolled herself onto Robbie's heaving chest and melted into him. They were on top of their own special rock, by the remote little lake they had found once on a map and had decided to come and meet in person. The rock was an unexpected discovery, huge and tall and flat on the top, with a narrow cairn of stones erected at one edge on its highest point, as if to hold a flagstaff.

Robbie had spent an hour cutting and carrying balsam fir bows to fill a low hollow near the cairn, and they were lying there now, on a bed of unimaginable luxury. The perfume of balsam enveloped them completely.

A barred owl cheered them from across the lake, and nighthawks swooped down out of the sky as if to point them out to all creation. The Milky Way was so close and bright they could see its stars in each other's eyes. When they tilted back their heads to follow the arch of the sky, they could see the North Star directly behind them, with two stars of the Big Dipper pointing to it.

"That's the drinking gourd," Robbie said. "It tells us where to go."

They lay there, vibrating to the heartbeats of the universe. Somehow, each knew that no moment in their lives ever would quite match this one.

Sylvie turned to Robbie and held him close to her again, a thin quiver of anxiety running through her arms.

"Robbie," she said, "I'm afraid we might lose this magic some day. I'm afraid we'll get obsessed with stuff, with fancy, and we'll forget that this is the most splendid thing there is. We'll forget, and we won't be able to find it again. Promise me we won't lose this. Promise me we won't ever let ourselves want too much."

1: The road to White's Cove

Spring comes to Digby County, Nova Scotia in fits and starts. What the groundhog may have signalled on February 2nd, or whether a lamb or a lion prevailed on March 1st, makes no difference. Like Jack in his box, a sunny, warm day will pop up unexpectedly and as quickly disappear.

Jack repeats these teasing disappointments chaotically for many weeks until he himself finally tires of hiding, and slowly the earth turns green.

Rick Robichaud and his daughter, Bronwyn, should have been at home, working on cows and cheese at their Lansdowne Highland farm, but they were not. They were playing hooky today because Jack had popped up that morning. It was April, and he soon might hide again.

It was Bronwyn's first glorious spring day as a one-year-old, and it deserved some celebrating!

They had driven all the way down Digby Neck to Whale Cove, and then had walked east a mile or so along the rocky Fundy shore, Bronwyn secure in a backpack carrier. Soon, Rick hoped, they would meet the ATV track that led from White's Cove back to the paved road at Little River, but now it was time for a rest and to savour the wonderful day.

They stopped on the plateau of a basalt cliff high above the Bay. Rick extracted Bronwyn and distracted her with a few grapes while he strapped her into a harness and put her on a short leash attached to himself by a metal clip.

The tide was fully out, and the whole wide swath of green and brown and red seaweeds was on display, the red fringe surging gently up and down in the swells at the water's edge.

Some of the winter ducks were still around, including a small group of harlequins wearing their finest spring colours. The long-tails now were in their dark spring plumage, and the male eiders sparkled black and white.

A black guillemot, standing on his bright red feet on a rock above the high tide line, was rejoicing with occasional high-pitched squeaks. A din of calls from song sparrows, robins and one or two fox sparrows came from the low, bushy forest behind them, as did the sweet smells of damp earth and spruce trees.

Bronwyn found a whole crab shell she could inspect and then balance on her head for a few satisfying seconds, and another old crab claw she could gnaw. The wind was soft, the sky blue, and the dogwood branches glowed bright red. Some early yellow coltsfoot flowers decorated the patches of exposed soil where the forest met the rock edge.

Rick tried to imagine what it had been like when the fish that had kept his family alive and well for 200 years had swarmed in these same waters.

Bronwyn was expanding her zone of exploration to include the muddy edge of a puddle and some pebbles just right for swallowing, so it was time to move on. She squealed as Rick flipped her up over his head, feet first, and dropped her deftly into the backpack, a trick they had practised to perfection over the last month.

White's Cove was just beyond the next rocky ridge, and Rick found a path along the cliff edge that saved him yet another descent down to the beach and the clamber back up again.

The view of White's Cove, when they reached it, was not what Rick had expected. The narrow, winding path over to Little River had become a wide and truck-worthy gravel road, terminating at a small cluster of earth-moving machinery, some temporary house trailers, and some sort of drilling machine.

A long, low, modern building stood on a level site carved out of the forest at the top of the ridge, high above the shore. A sturdy pier, big enough for one or two small ships to use in good weather, had been built as well.

A few cars and trucks were parked beside one of the trailers. A front-end loader was filling a heavy dump truck with large and small fragments of basalt rock recently blasted, it seemed, from the adjacent cliff face.

Rick's first thought was that The Quarry had come to life again. The

Quarry had been a mad scheme hatched almost two decades previously to grind up the length and breadth of Digby Neck in order to pave driveways in New Jersey. David had defeated Goliath in that battle, and the required environmental permits had been denied.

Had Goliath snuck back? *Probably not*, Rick thought, *or he and everyone else would have heard about it.*

But something new certainly was happening in White's Cove.

Bronwyn, who was inclined more toward action than contemplation, gave her horse a kick in the ribs, and they were off down the rocks to the site to find out what it was all about.

"Come on in; I'll be right there."

The voice came from an inner room of the trailer that advertised itself as the site office. Rick recognized the voice as soon as he heard it.

"Hey Trudy, it's me, Rick. Rick and Bronnie."

"Rick and Bronnie!?"

Trudy Denton came out of her office and into the reception area. "My land, Ricky Robichaud, I haven't seen you in ages. And Bronnie, just look at you, so big and so cheery! What brings you here today?"

If you grew up on Digby Neck and the Islands, you knew everyone from Westport to Gulliver's Cove and Rossway, and Rick and Trudy had been acquainted all their lives. They had gone off to university at about the same time, too, but since then had only seen each other at the occasional wedding or funeral.

"We decided to walk over from Whale Cove and then back by the old White's Cove trail. What's this all about, The Quarry, phase two?"

Trudy laughed. "My great grandpa complained all his life that White's Cove needed a good road into it to save the community from disappearing. Well, now, I've finally built that road, but its about 70 years too late. Everyone moved out of here decades ago."

While Trudy was talking, they had walked out onto the little deck that served as a landing for the short stairway up to the trailer's door.

Rick looked around. "So, what's going on?"

"Salmon farming," Trudy said. "Come on, I'll show you."

As they descended from the deck, a large dump truck, heavily loaded with blasted rock, passed in front of them and ground its way slowly up the new road.

Trudy stopped and frowned. "That's not a good road for you to be walking on today, Ricky. Give me your truck keys."

She called out to a man standing beside the now idle frontend loader, "Parker, can you and Johnny take a run over to Whale Cove and bring Rick's truck back here? I'm going to show him around."

After some words of greeting with Rick, Parker and Johnny drove off in a pickup that had been parked by the trailer. Beluga Group was written on the truck's doors.

"That's the owner," Trudy said, "the Beluga Group. They just bought out the company that owned all of the ocean-pen salmon farms here in the Maritimes. Beluga wants to change how they raise fish, switch to land-based fish farms, all green technologies, no effluent. That big building up on top houses the first lot of fish tanks. They plan to build five more tank units like that on this site once the first one is set up and running smoothly.

"That little pier is so they can send the grown fish straight over to their plant in New Brunswick. They'll bring the feed over here that way, too. Beluga Group bought the whole set of properties that that stone quarry company had lined up, so they have plenty of space to expand if they want to."

Rick was puzzled. "How come I never heard of this before? I would have thought it would be all over the news."

"No jobs. They say five people can run the whole thing, so no politicians and photo ops. No government grants, no municipal zoning laws broken, nothing to see from the main road, nothing but environmental kudos. I guess it's a big non-story. This is really my baby, though."

They had wandered closer to the bottom of the cliff, where the truck had been loaded with stone. Now Rick could see that the blasted stone had not come from the cliff face but from a large tunnel, maybe 25 feet tall and wide, that disappeared straight into the cliff.

As they watched, a second frontend loader emerged from the tunnel with a bucket full of stone and discharged it onto the pile from which the truck had been loaded.

"Any civil engineer can build a good gravel road, and probably a small pier, too," Trudy said, "but tunnels are my specialty. That's how I got this job. I'd been doing engineering in mines in northern Manitoba for five years when I saw the ad: same skills, better pay and right here at home! It's all about automated control of the fish farm."

They walked a few yards into the tunnel. "Beluga is bringing in some special, high-tech machinery to install deep in this tunnel. The electronics will monitor and adjust water temperature in every fish tank with geothermal heat exchangers. It will do the feeding and monitor all the water chemistry. There will be above-ground treatment of waste water, and the treated water will be reused. We have sea water from the Bay and all kinds of top-quality fresh water from five drilled wells. At some point, they plan to try using fresh water only. The organic waste from cleaning up the tank water will fertilize the plants in some greenhouses they plan to build."

Trudy seemed pretty pumped about her new job. She had taken it as a two-year contract, she said, but the Beluga Group already had made the job permanent.

"I've got nothing to do with the fancy machines going into the tunnels," she said. "That's all proprietary technology, and what those machines do and how they work are Beluga's little industrial secrets."

Her job, she said, was just to put them very precisely in place and connect them to the fish farm.

"I think they have a central monitoring unit somewhere, maybe over in New Brunswick, and all the monitoring is to be done remotely once everything is up and running. Meantime, Parker and Johnny are doing all the actual fish farm work."

"Who is this Beluga Group anyway?" Rick asked. "I've never heard that company name around here before."

"I hadn't, either. I tried to look them up. It's a private company so there's hardly any public information about it. I think it's just a piece of something much bigger with deep pockets, maybe one of the international food companies. All I can say for sure is that they are fast and professional, and good to work for."

As they stood talking and admiring the mouth of Trudy's precision tunnel, Rick's Lansdowne Highland truck pulled in beside them.

Parker hopped out and returned the keys to Rick with a smile. "Zora was down to Freeport yesterday, Ricky. She brought my old dog back from the dead for the third time. She's a wonder, Ricky, you just tell her I said so!"

Rick said he would. The two women in his life, Zora and Bronwyn, both were wonders, that was for sure.

Trudy said goodbye and walked back to her office. The big dump truck had returned, and Parker got the loader going to fill it again.

Rick looked out once more on the beautiful Bay, the shore now tinged slightly orange in the afternoon light. He could see in his mind where the last herring weir in the cove once had stood, and the houses too, all of them, once, before his time, with cellars full of potatoes and salted herring, enough to see them through to the next summer.

No herring now, and no houses either; everyone had moved away before he was born. Now, some foreign outfit had arrived to grow salmon in big tanks where the houses and gardens and the cemetery once had stood.

Well, he grew grass and cows, and sold cheese where a forest once stood; was it really any different?

Bronwyn had found tunnels and existential philosophy equally boring, and had fallen asleep on Rick's back. Rick sighed. Unscheduled nap, late to bed, and another long night, all par for the course when you play hooky from the daily routine.

He eased Bronwyn off his back, out of the carrier and into her car seat. She needed a clean diaper, but that could wait. There was no point in trying to wake her up now.

It was Friday, Rick and Zora's pizza and movie night. Bronwyn could just join in this time around.

The pizza dough should be just about right by the time they got home. There would still be enough time to get it oven-ready before Zora turned up, unless she'd gotten stuck doing a Caesarian or something else veterinary and unplanned.

The new gravel road out to the pavement was indeed a fine piece of work. Kudos to Trudy.

2: Vaduz

Liechtenstein is the best choice for private meetings. In Switzerland, there is too much visibility. A private estate near Vaduz is preferable.

Eight people had gathered there now, in well-managed seclusion. None carried a cell phone or a pencil. Their names were not known to the magazines that praise and rank the rich. Each controlled at least 100 billion American dollars.

The topic of the meeting was war, and the necessity that there must be more of it to ensure the continued growth of their wealth. Several points were raised with respect to supply, demand, territory, and collaboration, each discussed according to the speaker's current position in their hierarchy of power and mutual loathing. None believed what the others said, but each could discern the truth. Their businesses were free of ethical concerns, and thus were simple and transparent.

The last item on the day's agenda was of great concern to all. Nuclear deterrence was working too well and, overall, nations were spending less than they otherwise would on conventional weapons. What could be done? Coercion, debt, tribal hatreds and natural disasters all had been invented, manipulated, and exploited to good effect to promote high consumption, but it was not enough. Sales had slowed.

A lady accorded deference by the others rose to speak. She was dressed and styled in the silvers and greys of bullet-proof steel and looked both older and younger than her 60 years.

"Perhaps," she said, "we have not given enough attention to the market potential of a perceived nuclear threat, for example, the belief that a rogue state has acquired nuclear capacity and might soon hold other states hostage. If this imaginary threat could be elevated to the level of a perceived international conspiracy, then rich nations would spend lavishly to spy on the many potential rogues by every possible means, to acquire large stocks of modern weapons, and to develop new weaponry through large research and development contracts with our corporations. If magnified strategically, such an apparent conspiracy could stimulate an arms race among practically all nations, as all political ideologies would seek to gain an upper hand."

There was a brief discussion, and the proposal was adopted. It would cost only some hundreds of millions of dollars, a trivial amount.

As was their custom, the member who proposed the project would be responsible for its implementation and administration. Olga Alexandrovna O'Grady, the speaker, nodded her consent.

To avoid any misunderstandings, Olga Alexandrovna stipulated that a single code number would identify all items and transactions related to this project. It was March 14th and the code would be 3141593.

No one present would forget this; they all were very good with numbers. One or two might find the choice of number amusing. Her daughter, Juanita, certainly would take note of it, if it ever crossed her desk.

Money always buys more in dictatorships. Thus, it is best to conduct business in such places, where hope and morals are in short supply. It is there that, for example, a long-forgotten administrator might find it convenient to set aside a few tons of expired nuclear warheads for a well-filled account in a western bank.

Olga Alexandrovna enjoyed inventing such strategies, knocking off pawns and cornering kings, and enriching herself. She looked forward to these personal pleasures.

Perhaps she also could find a way to engage her reticent daughter in some aspect of the plan, to find some crack in the wall that Juanita had built between herself and her mother's affairs.

3: Some Coloured Ashes

"We're going to use the title of the novel as the title of the film too," the director said. "*Some Coloured Ashes*. It's a great title and the novel is well known. We'd be crazy to call the film something different, and we'd be crazy not to shoot it right here in Bear River, where the novel takes place."

The director was speaking over morning coffee to the astonished patrons of the café. This was the first anyone had heard that a big Hollywood movie was to be made in Bear River, and the news and excitement were spilling out onto the streets and into social networks at a frantic pace. The actors in the cast were well known, some of them big stars. However, none of the patrons could remember ever hearing about the novel or its author, Louie Penny.

"Actually, the filming is mostly done," the director said. "We filmed 80% in studios. We're here to get all the outdoor shots and to capture the background scenery. We're going to need some help from you folks, too."

Rory was listening from his favourite writing spot at a corner table. He thought that maybe he once had heard of an author named Louie Penny, but he couldn't place him. Since he was connected to wifi, he made a quick online search while the Hollywood buzz in the café continued, and there he was: Louie Penny, well-known author of stories, plays and poems.

The list of published works was short, but his accolades were impressive. They included two off-Broadway plays, the Templeton Prize in 2008 for his body of work and a Griffin Poetry Prize in 2000 for his only published collection of poems.

Biographical information was appallingly thin for a writer of such distinction: born in 1935 in western Nova Scotia, where he lived out his life until he died in 2010, a carpenter and writer. Nothing more.

On reflection, Rory thought that maybe he had read some of Louie Penny's poems, probably in a literature class: sonorous, bittersweet meditations on love and loneliness, as best he could remember them. He had never heard of *Some Coloured Ashes.*

On a whim, he walked a few doors down the street to George's eclectic used book store, a long-standing feature of the village, and went looking for Penny in the fiction section.

The alphabetical organization of books by author last name was only notional on George's shelves, but luck was on Rory's side, and on the edge of the T-U-V section he found an old hardcover edition. He took it to George to ask the price.

"That's a Templeton Prize winner, Rory, it'll cost you thirty bucks," George said.

He turned the book over in his hands.

"It's in kind of rough shape, though; I'll give it to you for fifteen."

As Rory paid, he asked George if he knew the book was being made into a movie right in the village.

"That news was old ten minutes ago," George said. "If I had remembered I had this copy, I would have put it in the window, priced at $100."

He winked and turned back to his boxes of books.

Rory returned to his writing spot in the café. The director and associates had left, and the place was quiet again. He decided to read a few pages, just to get a flavour of Penny's apparently famous book.

When the café closed late that afternoon, he was half way through it, and he finished it at home just before midnight. It wasn't really a thriller, but it had gripped Rory's mind and turned it inside out.

The story was simple:

> A boy from a poor, rural family escapes into the world and returns to his home town of Bear River a wealthy man. He and his wife set about using their wealth to better the whole community. After what seems like a good start on a well-conceived plan, everything goes wrong, and the community begins to tear itself apart over money.
>
> The wife is killed as a bystander in a related turf-war shooting and, in his grief, the rich man re-examines everything he ever thought or believed about material wealth.

The man organizes an elaborate mid-summer celebration of his wife's life, centred around a bonfire with fireworks.

Special bonfire boxes designed to burn brightly in different colours are provided to every household, school, organization, business and community group in and around the village so that each can ceremonially throw a box on the bonfire in her honour.

The man liquidates all his financial holdings, collects it all together in cash over several months, fills the gift boxes and a hundred more with the bills, presides over the public incineration of his fortune, and then disappears.

Only during the cleanup of the bonfire site the next day does the village discover what it had done the night before. All the money that was to make everyone in the village better off, rich perhaps, now is gone forever.

After a period of grieving, the village resumes normal life. It gradually becomes a happy place again for the first time since vast wealth had been brought to it.

Rory could see that a movie based on this novel could have some exciting scenes and plenty of action, but the story delivered a very heavy load of inconvenient and unpopular ideas.

He awoke in a sudden panic that resolved, mercifully, into the jarring ring of his own alarm clock. Lisa must have set it for him, so he could sleep in as long as possible without missing his work shift at the café.

Always the sweetheart. She herself had left for her first house call at 8:00 am.

He stumbled to the kitchen and made himself a Jeremy breakfast special, thick with crunchy peanut butter and with his own personal twist: pineapple juice.

Early spring was in the air, and the half-hour walk down to the café was a delight. The sun was warm, and the sides of the road were partially covered in the yellow faces of coltsfoot flowers mixed in with blue violets wherever the soil was damp. A few of the leafless branches in the tangles of bushy shrubs along the road bore clusters of the tiny fuchsia flowers of wild Daphne, and the buds on all the trees and bushes were swollen.

Buckets to collect sap hung on several of the sugar maples along the way, evoking the pleasing prospect of new maple syrup. A mourning cloak butterfly had staked out his territory at a cluster of pin cherries along Middlesex Road, confident that both females and tree leaves soon would appear.

Lunchtime at the café was a total madhouse, and Rory was run off his feet for a good three hours. In addition to the regular diners, a dozen or so of the Hollywood crowd had come in as a group, followed by a posse of local groupies.

By mid-afternoon, they all were fed and had departed, and Rory was alone at the counter when Henry Wambolt came in.

Henry was Rory's favourite conversationalist and philosopher, a local of Hessian Loyalist stock from Waldeck. Henry had studied in Oxford and Paris, and had taught at Bishop's University and Yale, but he had cut that short because what he really wanted to do was to live on his own home turf and write poems and songs.

Henry ordered his usual espresso and then motioned to Rory to join him at his table. He had a proposal to make. Walt Whitman's birthday was coming up on May 31st. Since they were both serious philosophers, Whitman fans and song-writers, he proposed that together they should write a song that would capture the essence of Whitman's *Leaves of Grass*, and that May 31st should be their deadline.

"I don't know, Henry," Rory said. "I'm not sure two poets can write a poem or a song together. I was in a creative writing class that tried writing a play together one time. It was a disaster."

"So, what did you write for your part?" Henry asked.

"A nasty guy with a touch of Hamlet in him had become the main character, and he was about to answer an existential question. I had to write his answer."

"What did you have him say?"

"I had him thump out a few rhythmical and mysterious phrases with no discernible meaning, like a Harold Pinter character, and then conclude that 'life is but a drop of urine, trickling down the leg of time.' I left the existential question of whether or not to wipe that drop away to the next author." "I like it," Henry said. "I think we'll work well together." Henry had a plan. He had come across an upbeat gospel song called *Don't Knock,* by Roebuck Staples and Wesley Westbrooks, written back in the 50s. It had terrific rhythm, tune and tempo, just right for *Leaves of Grass*. Henry had a version by The Staples Singers themselves on his phone, and he set it playing for Rory.

Part-way through the song, the café door swung open and Purley Jordan walked in.

"Professor Henry! How the hell are you?" Purley came straight over to Henry's table and sat down. "Rory, I need three of them 'lattay' things and a real coffee for me, all for takeout."

Purley turned to Henry. "These movie guys are quite the task masters, Henry. I got a few days work with them while they're in the village, showin' em around, and they just never stop. They sent me up here for coffee while they figure out some camera angles down at the bridge. Did you ever hear of this guy Louie Penny, wrote that book they're followin'? No one I've talked to ever did, but he sure musta' known this little town. Sometimes they read me descriptions out of the book, and I can just see right away what house or road or view Penny is describing."

"You know," Henry said, "once, long ago, I played a part in one of Louie Penny's plays, in an amateur theatre troupe. I read his book of poems, too, but I never knew Penny had anything to do with Bear River.".

The coffees were ready and Purley was out the door.

"Okay, Henry," Rory said. "Let's do it. We've got six weeks. That's not a lot of time. We should have started in January."

Well, I did," Henry said. "I took a shot at a first chorus, just to see if Whitman would work with this tune."

"Let's hear it."

There was no one else in the café. Henry spread out a bit of paper from his pocket on the table, started tapping out a driving rhythm with one foot, and sang out in his best gospel-choir voice:

> *You don't knock, you just walk on in*
> *That door to everything.*
> *There's love and joy for you,*
> *And hope to carry us all time through.*
> *There's a vast similitude to guide us to infinitude.*
> *You don't knock, ring, pay out gold,*
> *The rolling earth is just a-waiting for your soul.*

You don't kno…ock, you just walk on in.

Greg, the café owner, came in from the office in the back to cash-out the till, since it was almost closing time. "That's a kick-ass song, Henry," he said. "Let's hear the rest of it."

"Gotta write it first, Greg. That's our next project."

"Rory's next project is to close this place down for the day! But don't rush off. It'll be a good twenty minutes before he'll have to lock you out."

As Greg turned to go back to his office, Purley Jordan burst in again.

"Greg!" he said, "That movie crew don't want to go back to town for supper, want to get a few more hours of work done and look around at some locations after dark. They'll make it worth your while to give them a meal in about an hour's time, if you'll do it. They said $35 a plate for soup and sandwich would be okay with them. Those probably are American dollars. Thirteen people, including me."

Greg thought for a moment, then turned to Henry and Rory in the poets' corner. "Rory, are you good for two or three hours' double overtime, starting right now? How about you, Henry,—a bit of sous-chef at the same rate?"

Rory and Henry were on their feet.

"Two well-paid poets present in Bear River on the same day! It's unheard of, it's historic!" Henry said.

They headed for the kitchen.

4: Vet in the water

Never before had Zora seen a sea pen salmon farm from the inside. Now, here she was, 30 feet down in the cold water of the Annapolis Basin, at the bottom of a net pen where, in principle, 30,000 Atlantic salmon were circling, circling, circling.

She had decided to invest in some SCUBA gear and training just for this purpose, and already it was paying off.

Only some of the fish were circling normally. The bottom of the pen was littered with dead fish in various stages of decay, something you can't see when you look into a pen from the top. A few dead fish floating in each pen every day was the norm in salmon farms, and in her work as a newly-minted fish vet, Zora saw plenty of such retrieved dead fish.

However, she needed to observe the living as well as the dead. So, here she was, watching the dead fish and the still-circling fish, already able to discern many fish that swam less well, or differed in colour, or had red spots on their skin.

Six months ago, Zora had decided to educate herself about health and diseases on fish farms, and to add that work to her veterinary practice if she could. She didn't much like salmon farms, especially open-pen farms like the one she was in right now. They seemed wrong in every way, miserable for the fish and terrible for the environment.

But the fishing families she and Rick had grown up with were fishing families no longer. All the wild fish were gone. Some of Zora's friends and relatives had found work on local salmon farms, and she hoped some good fish-health advice could make the salmon less miserable, reduce environmental harm, and support people who, like her and Rick, were trying to make a living in rural Nova Scotia.

Zora bagged up a few of the freshest of the dead fish at the bottom of the pen and made her way up out of the water. She was chilled to the bone.

Jon Apt hurried over to help her out of the pen and lifted off the heavy air tank. He hosed down Zora and her equipment with water and then with disinfectant. He put the bag of fish in a big cooler and hosed it down, too.

Jon helped Zora into the warm cabin of the farm's boat, where she could get out of her wetsuit and into warm clothes.

"What's the good word, Doc?" he said when she re-emerged.

"Not good, Jon," Zora said. "I think you've got ISA in that pen. Get these dead fish off to the lab today to find out for sure, but tell your boss to prepare for the worst."

Those poor fish. Zora was sure all 30,000 of them soon would be headed for a landfill, and probably the fish in the other eleven pens in the farm would go, too, and those in the pens of the other salmon farm in the Annapolis basin.

Zora wanted a hot bath as soon as she got home, and Rick decided she should have Bronwyn as well, to share the bath and brighten her spirits. Before long, a din of giggling and splashing filled the house. Even Engelbert the cat had to come see what was going on.

It all had to be cut short, however, because they were invited to Marie's for dinner, and dinner with Marie they did not want to miss. "I'm doing Chinese, and I need some hungry opinions." Marie had said.

Lisa and Rory would be there, too, and, of course, Jeremy. Whenever Marie got serious about preparing a meal, you knew it would be the best meal you had ever eaten.

~

When they arrived, Marie was on her deck, wearing a colourful dress, her red hair in a bandana, her turquoise-nailed feet in sandals. She ushered them in and put glasses of Kir in their hands in exchange for Bronwyn, whom she cuddled and bounced around the kitchen until Bronwyn saw Jeremy across the room and made frantic motions in his direction.

Marie summoned everyone to the table. It was laid out with 15 or so different dishes. "I'm trying to work out a few culinary details for a contract," she said, "so I need your opinions on these dishes. I'm trying to balance out a few ingredients for a restaurant group in Chicago. I want you to tell me the dishes you like most and least."

As expected, it was the best meal any of them could remember. The conversation dove deeply into flavours and textures.

As they ate, Rory wondered where all this came from. Why did Marie want their opinions on her amazing food just at this time, and what did she mean about this "Chicago group?" He and Lisa had known Marie pretty well for a few years now, but she still held some mysteries.

"What is it you actually do for that restaurant group in Chicago?" he asked. "You can't really be their chef and still live here."

"I design restaurants and their menus," Marie said as she circled the table, filling wine glasses. "That was my job for twenty years, but I quit; it got boring and paid absurd amounts of money. I only do it now when some company begs hard enough, like this Chicago crowd I used to work with. Here's to their health." She raised her glass and took an appreciative sip.

"I'll work on this project off and on for about a month here at home and then spend two weeks with them in Chicago, and they'll pay me $100,000. It's nuts. I turn down three or four of these jobs a month. Jerry, come and eat something so I can play with Bronnie."

Marie wanted to know the diners' judgments. Zora offered the closest thing to a criticism when she said that the Szechuan-style eggplant and scallops had just a touch too much chili pepper for her, although she would gladly suffer the pain to get to all the other wonderful flavours.

"It's too hot for me, too," Marie said. "I'm going to tone it down a notch. What did you like best of all?"

Zora immediately pointed to the dish in which nothing at all remained, thanks to its general popularity. "I liked that one the best, but I don't know what it was."

"Do you want to guess?"

Zora thought for a moment. "Somehow, I think you must have started out with clams," she said, "but if you did, they are so enveloped with other flavours that the whole thing goes way beyond any one of its ingredients. It's the most amazing dish I have ever tasted."

Marie clearly was both pleased and impressed. Clams indeed were the starting point, and hours had been dedicated to its creation. "What about the rest of you?" she asked.

But it was unanimous. The clams were tops, no doubt about it, even if no one had known what they were eating.

"Zora, what made you think it was clams?" Lisa asked.

"I don't really know. My grandfather was a clam digger. He sold them for fish bait in those days, but he brought lots home to eat, too. Those were happy times, with my grandpa. Maybe I picked up a taste that was lingering inside those good memories."

There was a knock on the door and Melvin Prime stepped in. "I thought I might find Jerry here," he said. "I'm spending the night at his place so we can be off at dawn tomorrow."

"Off to where?" Rick asked.

"Spring camping back to Whitesand Lake, with Jeremy and Sandy McEwan. Sandy just got home last night and he's raring to go."

Sandy was the son of Mel's life-long friend Billy-Jean McEwan, an elder and one-time chief of the Bear River First Nation. Sandy was an air traffic controller who did ten-day shifts at the Halifax airport, but otherwise lived in Bear River, close to the forest.

"April is the best canoe-camping month of the year," he said, "not a blackfly in your ear, not a pismire in your sugar. We're gonna go in the old way, from Lake Joli down the chain to Sixth Lake, down Sixth Lake Stream, across Fifth Lake, and up Whitesand all the way. The water will be high, and the trout will be hungry, and Jeremy and Sandy are going to lug all the heavy stuff across the carries."

5: IMO 3141593

"*Slocum Warrior,* Westport, IMO 1769093"

Rick and Bronwyn were admiring the big letters and numbers painted on the stern of Wolf Wiley's brand-new ship. This one-of-a-kind boat had been launched at Meteghan River that morning, and now was tied to a pier in Yarmouth harbour, awaiting some fine-tuning.

Wolf was Rick's childhood hero. He already had left Westport before Rick was born, heading out to sea for the storied privateer adventures of distant-water fishing when he was only 15. By the time he was 18, he had seen too much, and committed himself to putting an end to that larcenous fishery forever. He got his captain's papers, signed on with others equally dedicated to saving the seven seas, and began hunting them down, ship by illegal ship, chasing and harassing them into the hands of the national and international law.

He was christened Clarence Outhouse, but had taken on the buccaneer moniker of Wolf Wiley. Even his mother called him Wolf now.

He came home to Westport from time to time, for a month or two, and his stories had burned into ten-year-old Rick the passion to save all the fish in the sea. Rick felt a twinge of guilt and regret that he himself wasn't doing much along these lines now. Wolf still was his hero.

A week ago, Wolf had telephoned excitedly to tell Rick that he was coming home to pick up a new ship. He wanted to connect with Rick and Zora, and to show them his marvellous boat.

So, Rick and Bronwyn had come to Yarmouth to find Wolf and bring him back to their Lansdowne Highland farm for an overnight visit.

To Rick, the *Slocum Warrior* looked way too wide for its length, stump-nosed and portly, like the new lobster boats. It was completely decked over in the manner of a rescue vessel or a submarine. All available surfaces were studded with built-in solar panels.

Wolf ran down the gang plank, hugged Rick like a long-lost brother and took Bronwyn in his arms before she had time to resist. She was trending toward loud complaint when her attention was caught by the splendid black and yellow sea snakes in spiral tattoos along Wolf's marvellously thick, bare pirate arms. These she began to trace and explore with a probing finger.

"I thought you would have built some kind of destroyer," Rick said. "This looks more like a tugboat."

"We're in the 21st century, Ricky," Wolf said, "Not so much Captain Nemo now; more like Captain Kirk. World opinion mostly has come around to our side, and the oceans need critical care on a whole new scale. This boat is not for ramming speed; this is mission control."

Inside, the wheelhouse looked like the flight deck in a Hollywood version of a modern B-52 bomber: screens, dials, lights, knobs and switches everywhere. The *Slocum Warrior* could stay at sea for up to three years, at the poles or in the tropics, plugged in to all the satellites and surveillance technology of the world, including a lot of military networks.

"Those things on the decks that look like cannons are cameras, powerful like space telescopes, and there's a lot of electronic detection stuff. We'll hang out at sea anywhere we please, move in on strategic targets to fully document offences, and track the offenders until they come to port or scupper themselves as a last resort. Either way, they will be put out of commission."

The rest of the ship was equally remarkable. Rick had never even seen a fuel cell before. Living spaces were small and efficient, but appeared comfortable, even inviting.

It was time to head home. Rick gave Wolf a forty-pound wheel of the best Lansdowne Highland cheddar to stow in the ship's food locker, then changed Bronwyn and bribed her into her car seat with half a banana. They were off to the farm for a long-awaited visit.

Zora had been busy getting a good evening meal together, to give Rick a break and because she liked to cook when she could find the time. As a rural vet, she benefited occasionally from the local barter economy. The slices of home-smoked bacon she had received in exchange for castrating Elmer Potter's eight piglets had furnished the key ingredient today to her favourite augmented version of beef Wellington, just now turning golden brown in the oven as Rick's truck pulled in.

A plate of Lansdowne Highland cheeses was on the table, with a few bottles of five-year-old Lucie Kuhlmann, of which the vintner had given her two cases for resolving his horse's long-term lameness.

Wolf swept in and swept her up in a pirate's embrace. It had been years, too long, but she looked the same Miss Universe she always had, according to him.

They had so much to catch up on, to tell each other after five years apart, that it was hard to know where to begin. Back then, they had only just moved to Bear River, Zora had only just started being a vet, Rick had only just walked away from academia and into Lansdowne Highland farm. Bronwyn was still two distant meiotic cell divisions away.

Fascination with Wolf had caused Bronwyn to miss her afternoon nap. A quick meal and a bath, and she was off to a deep and peaceful sleep.

The three friends talked through cheese and wine, an exceptional dinner, and a seemingly endless evening sipping through Wolf's gift of tequila añejo.

Zora and Rick were happy to fill Wolf in on their lives, but mostly they wanted to hear of his adventures. Not everyone you meet has put himself between a whale and a harpoon gun, chased rogue fishing boats to ground, or been sprung from jails around the world by international opinion and philanthropy.

Wolf could tell stories for hours and especially now, when he was with people who loved him and he could express how he really felt about things. All these adventures also had been personal traumas that had left their marks.

"I've come to think that violent confrontation for conservation isn't what's needed, probably a waste of resources," he said.

Zora looked at him quizzically. "That seems like a big shift for you," she said. "What's changed?"

Wolf settled back into the sofa. "It was the last big chase we did. We were way down in the South Atlantic off the Falklands when we found a boat we had wanted to locate for years, the very worst of the bad actors. It had no flag, no name and no number. All the conservation groups called it the *Grim Reaper.*

"When it saw us, it took off, and it was empty so it could go as fast as we could. It steamed north for 25 days, 8500 miles, to the edge of the Grand Banks, then east to Norway and north to Russia, another 12 days and 3900 miles. It disappeared into Kola Bay, probably headed for Murmansk. The whole Atlantic fleet of the Russian Navy is in that bay. Its a poor place to try sneaking into Russian territorial waters! So, 40 days and 13,000 miles and we lost it."

"What would have happened if you had caught up with it?" Zora asked.

"Sometimes those pirates sink their ship, so that all the evidence against them goes to the bottom. Then we end up having to save the crew and take them to a port somewhere. Sometimes they get out guns and start shooting at us. A good video of that can get a conviction and cause the nearest navy to come take charge. You never really know what's going to happen until you get there."

"So, was that long chase worth the effort?" Rick asked.

"I guess we stopped the *Grim Reaper* from fishing for those 40 days," Wolf said. "No, we didn't really accomplish much. The landscape is changing, too. There are some impressive new international agreements against this kind of illegal fishing, and various navies and port authorities will arrest and prosecute these boats if they know who they are. That's where the *Slocum Warrior* comes in."

Wolf wanted to know all about Rick, the hot-shot scientist turned farmer, and how Zora actually could make a living as a country vet in western Nova Scotia in the 21st century. There was a lot to tell and to explain. Wolf probed and queried with the genuine deep interest and concerns of the elder brother and uncle they felt him to be.

As the tequila mellowed out the world, Wolf's thoughts turned back the *Grim Reaper*. "You know," he said, "that *Grim Reaper* actually came back to haunt me."

"How did that happen?" Zora asked.

"About a year and a half after it disappeared into Russia, I saw that ship sail into a harbour in the Faroe Islands. I was in the main town, Tórshaven, meeting with local groups about their pilot whale hunts, when I saw the *Reaper* sail in and tie up at the commercial wharf. I knew it was the *Reaper* from some odd bits of its design, but now it had a Russian name, which a sailor told me meant 'White-tailed Eagle', a Russian flag, and IMO 3141593. It no longer was rigged for fishing, and it started unloading some cargo onto the wharf and onto a small freighter that had come up beside it. The small freighter was named the *Cahow*, Majuro, IMO 3141593."

"Isn't that the same IMO number you said was on the Russian boat?" Rick asked.

"Yes, the same number, on both boats, and both numbers incorrect, too."

"How do you know when an IMO number is incorrect?" Zora asked.

"The check digit," Wolf said. "It's a trick, but not a secret. The check digit is the last of the seven numerals of an IMO. The International Marine Organization assigns these numbers to boats when they're built. They're like serial numbers. The first six digits are just randomly-assigned numerals, but the final one is calculated from the other six and can only be one number. I guess it's intended as a kind of verification or something. If you can do a bit of arithmetic in your head, you can figure out whether the last digit is correct. If it isn't, the number is either a mistake or a fake."

"How do you calculate the check digit?" Zora asked.

Wolf called for paper and pencil. He wrote out the fake IMO of the former *Reaper*: 3141593.

"The check digit '3' is wrong," he said. "To calculate the check digit, you multiply each of the other six digits by 7 or 6 or 5 or 4 or 3 or 2, according to their position in the IMO number, like this, and then you add them up."
He wrote out in large print:

$$(7\text{x}3) + (6\text{x}1)) + (5\text{x}4)) + (4\text{x}1)) + (3\text{x}5) + (2\text{x}9) = 84.$$

"The check digit is the right-hand digit in the sum, '4' in this case. On those two ships, the check digit was '3' – incorrect. Also, no two boats are assigned the same IMO number. It would be easy to make a fake number with a correct check digit, but most people don't know check digits even exist, much less how to calculate one."

Zora and Rick glared at Wolf's confusion of explanatory numbers and arithmetic for a while. Finally, Rick said, "Okay, let's try this."

Wolf wrote down a number: 1769090. Rick started working it out on paper while Zora just kept glaring at it.

"Three," she said, after about half a minute. "That last number should be three, not zero."

"That's right," Wolf said, in a voice tinged with surprise and disap-pointment.

Rick glared at both of them, while Zora basked in a brief triumph. Then she turned to Rick.

"You do this kind of thing way quicker than me, Ricky, always. Just put that pencil away and focus on the numbers. Let's try another. How about. . .684373. Go!"

All three closed their eyes, remembering, multiplying, adding, for-getting, starting again. Finally, more or less in unison, they each said, "9!" Indeed, the arithmetic added up to 149 and the check digit thus was 9.

They giggled with their shared accomplishment and had another round of tequila. Four more IMO numbers and they'd had enough for the time being, but they figured this was a winner as a party game, at least at the right party.

"Was that the last you saw of those fake-numbered ships?" Rick asked. "You have to wonder why they were faking their IMOs"

"I did wonder that," Wolf said, "and I kept wondering during the two days I spent in Tórshaven. I checked the marine traffic websites. The old *Reaper* had sailed directly to the Faroes from Murmansk and had its ship identification transceiver going all the way. The *Cahow,* on the other hand, had arrived in Tórshaven with no trace of the route it had taken to get there. It must have disabled its transceiver and snuck in somehow without that being noticed. It left within a few hours of taking on cargo from the old *Reaper* and headed west 3300 miles to Bermuda, transceiver on all the way. The old *Reaper* left three days later and headed north the way it had come, but the transceiver signal disappeared about 300 miles out."

Wolf said he'd contacted the marine traffic agencies, and all had as-sumed the boat had sunk, but could find no weather or other reasons to explain the sinking. Since it was a Russian boat, NATO had been fol-lowing it too, Wolf learned later on, from unnameable sources.

The old *Reaper* had sunk in just a few minutes and no lifeboats had been left behind. To the NATO observers, it had appeared to be some kind of accident or sabotage.

"I figured that, whatever those two ships were up to, it probably had nothing to do with destroying the fish in the sea and I decided it was best just to ignore them. I had too much else to do. But I learned some new things about modern ship surveillance from trying to figure out what had happened to the *Reaper* and talking to an officer with NATO. That set me off on the path that has led to the *Slocum Warrior*."

The *Warrior* was to leave Yarmouth the next day for a shake-down cruise to Annapolis, Maryland, at the head of the Chesapeake Bay. There, some final installations and training would take place with the help of the US Navy. And then…?

Wolf would come home whenever he could, and tell them.

6: Nothin' worse than me

Sandy switched on the receiver while Jeremy put on the headphones and lifted the antenna high in the air, as Sandy had shown him. He slowly turned to the right in almost a full circle, but then stopped and swung the antenna back to the left a few degrees, then right again, then back to a steady position. He began to walk forward in very slow paces.

"Do you have a signal?" Sandy asked excitedly.

Jeremy made no reply, but continued his slow advance, moving the antenna slightly from side to side as he went.

They were on the shore of Whitesand Stream, near the mouth of Dish Lake Brook. Two years ago, a biologist friend had put a radio transmitter on a big Blanding's turtle a mile or so downstream, just below the stone dam. The turtle team had named her Maeve.

The site was too remote for regular monitoring, so on this camping trip, Sandy had agreed to try to relocate her. He had spent a day in the field with the turtle people to learn what to do.

In early spring, the turtles are near their over-wintering places, usually in deep pools in narrow side channels. Yesterday, the three campers had set up their tent on an old cabin site across from the Dish Lake carry, and today was their day to track down the turtle, if they could.

After negotiating safe passage across the stone dam with an aggressive pair of Canada geese, they started their search about half a mile below the dam and worked very slowly upstream to their present location, scanning for the radio signal along both shores and in all directions, but finding none. Now, perhaps...

Walking in a straight line across the small delta of the brook required careful footwork. The dry sedges of last summer were tall and tough, and they hid treacherous logs, rocks and channels. Jeremy stepped high and carefully, but kept on a straight trajectory while Sandy and Mel followed as best they could.

A few early swamp sparrows were trilling in the leatherleaf bushes on the stream bank and a sapsucker was flitting among the birch and maple, calling and drumming.

Jeremy's path led across two yard-wide channels which he stepped over nimbly. A few yards beyond the second one he stopped, closed his eyes in concentration, and slowly turned in a circle, pointing the antenna straight in front of himself as he did so. Then he turned 180 degrees and walked back along his own path, listening intently all the while.

He crossed the first channel he came to and stopped at the edge of the second, leaning the antenna left and right and down toward the water. He set the tracking gear aside, lay prone at the edge of the channel and reached into the cold brown water up to his shoulder.

After some vigorous groping in the depths, he pulled himself gradually up and off the ground, and held out to Sandy a ten-inch-long turtle with a small black box attached to its shell. "Maeve," he said.

All four participants looked at each other with mutual surprise, Maeve perhaps less surprised than the others since she, at least, had encountered human beings several times before. Neither Jeremy nor Sandy nor Mel ever had seen a Blanding's turtle.

Except for a speckling of dull-grey spots, the shell was a plain, colourless dark grey. However, the underside of the chin and neck and parts of the legs were a spectacular bright yellow, and on the bottom shell, patches of the same yellow formed a large-tile mosaic among other patches of a rich dark brown.

Well, well, thought Mel, *Who knew?* He had canoed this stream probably thirty or forty times, yet had no idea such turtles lived here.

Sandy's mission, should he find Maeve, was to bring her radio back to use again on turtles elsewhere. Removing the radio from the shell took some time and care.

Once liberated from her burden, Maeve lingered on the edge of the brook channel for a minute or so and then, unhurriedly, crawled into the water and swam down out of site. A mate was next on her to-do list.

~

The campers were on their way back home after four days on Whitesand Lake, but they were in no hurry. They had set up their big wall tent on the old cabin site. The cabin itself had been burned down by the authorities a few decades ago when the Tobeatic Wilderness Area had been expanded and leases for cabins on Crown lands in the expanded zone had been terminated.

Mel agreed with the strict protection now applied to the Tobeatic, but he wondered if destroying all those cabins really had been necessary.

He was musing on this over their supper when Sandy asked him what he knew about the old cabin.

"I don't know much about it," Mel said. "Different people seemed to use it. Most times when I travelled this way, it was empty."

He paused to sprinkle a thick layer of black pepper over his plateful of rice and sardines. "There was a fellow, Robbie MacAlisdair was his name, lived in it for a while, back in the 90s. He invited me in for tea and a chat one time when I was going by. He was mostly spending winters out here, he said. Those must have been long, lonely winters. He'd done a lot of carpentry on the inside, really top-quality work."

They were only half way through their spring camping trip, but Sandy and Mel had had enough of trout fishing, at least for a while. There is no better meal than fresh brook trout rolled in corn meal and fried with a bit of fat-back pork. However, after four days of perfect trout for breakfast, dinner and supper, it had lost its lustre. Now, they just wanted to lounge and putter around their stream-side camp until Sandy's job beckoned and they really had to leave.

Jeremy had shown no interest in trout fishing. Mel had tried to get him into it on day one, but when it came time to impale a worm on a fishhook, Jeremy was having nothing to do with it. He'd gone out once with them while they fished from the canoe, but after that he stayed ashore and did his own thing.

He had discovered a small brook near their camp, filed with big fish on their spring spawning run, and he spent one whole day gently lifting up one silvery sucker after another as they passed, admiring each completely, and releasing it back into the water again.

Another day, he had tied a bit of raw bacon to the end of a length of string and thrown the bacon end out into the lake. Every hour or so he tugged on the string cautiously and gently pulled it in if it felt heavy. In this way, he coaxed to the surface and into his view a horned pout, an eel and a snapping turtle before each spat out the bacon and swam away.

As dusk descended now on their streamside camp, the air became chill, and the campers clustered around a blazing campfire. It was time for stories.

Sandy's family had travelled and lived in these woods for countless generations, up until about his grandfather's time. However, until very recently, Sandy himself had experienced the forest only through his own imagining of the stories he had heard from his elders. The stories he remembered mostly were about a hilarious pair of trickster spirits who usually appeared to people as a rabbit and an otter.

There were always a few cautionary tales about scary monsters, to keep the kids from wandering off, but the stories mostly made the forest seem lively, happy and safe.

"Lively, happy and safe. That's how the forest feels to me, too," Mel said. "But most of the folks I grew up with are afraid of the woods, terrified. They absolutely do not want to be here after dark. Quite a few of them make their living in the woods, but hardly a one would ever want to live here."

Mel watched the stream flow past in the waning evening light. Maybe it was the conversation or just old happy memories, but his mind turned to the camping spot he had found as a teenager on the Big Bend deadwater and had made his special place, and of meeting Joe Ashton out there.

"There's a lot of stories about bad things and bad people in the woods," Mel said. "You don't want to be too quick to believe them. You take Joe Ashton now, 'course he's been dead for thirty years."

"Joe Ashton!?" Sandy exclaimed. "I've heard of him. Folks don't forget people like that. They say he was a terrible drunken thug, likely into murder and thievery. They don't even want to say his name."

"Well, that's sure what people say," Mel said. "There's always a few like him around to talk about, fellas that are poor and hated and feared by everyone else. They're always to blame. The stories keep going no matter what they really do."

He poked at the fire absentmindedly with a stick, and scooped into it some of the ends of the sticks that were too far out on the edge to keep burning.

"I sure never wanted to meet Joe Ashton. When I was going camping as a kid out on the Big Bend, not so far from where Joe lived, more than a few people told me never to go anywhere near him and to run away if I saw him coming. But one fall evening around suppertime, Joe Ashton walked out of the woods right into my camp, carrying nothing but a big axe."

"How'd you get away?"

I didn't. There was nowhere to go. He stood for a while looking at me with his terrible eyes. I just stood there too, trying to look back. Finally he put down his axe and looked around.

"Do I smell coffee?" he said.

He did smell coffee, because I had just made some, and suddenly I was falling all over myself trying to get a cup of it in his hands as fast as possible.

"Sugar?"

I started apologizing, making excuses because I'd used all mine up that morning, but he cut me off.

"It don't matter."

He took a first sip. "Where's yours?" he said, nodding toward my empty cup beside the fire.

I snatched up my cup and splashed some coffee into it. Ashton grunted, sat down on a log by the fire and sipped his coffee. I just did the same thing.

After a long silence, he asked, "What you doin' here?"

"Fishing," I said. I could see he had noticed my frying pan on the other side of the fire with a few small trout in it.

"That all you got for supper?"

"I guess I'll be having a can of beans too," I said.

"Me, too," Ashton said.

It was night by then and I had to grope around in the dark to find a second can of beans, open both, heat them beans in a pot and serve them evenly into two bowls. All that while Ashton just sat savouring his coffee.

Once we got eating, though, he started to make the odd comment. He said he lived about three miles away as the crow flies, was checking out the lakes and streams all around to see if there would be any beaver to trap in the winter. He used to live with his brother, but he died a few years back—cancer. Nothing much to eat at home now, not much work around, would I happen to have a spare can of those beans he could take along with him?

As we sat there, a loon out on the deadwater made a long, loud call.

"It's gonna rain soon," Ashton remarked.

He stood up, and in the firelight, I was struck by how small and thin and frail Joe Ashton really was, despite his fearsome reputation.

He picked up his axe and my last can of beans, turned his back to the fire and to me, and walked off into the forest.

I called after him. "Wait!" I said, "you can't walk home three miles through the woods in the pitch dark! Who knows what you might meet up with? You'd better stay here 'til morning."

He turned back toward me. I could still see him in the fire-light.

"Ain't nothin' in these woods worse'n me," he said.

Sandy pulled Mel back into the present by asking him what he knew about Dish Lake and whether maybe they should take a side trip there before they left.

"My granddad once told me that he went there a few times with an American kid about his own age," Sandy said. "Great granddad had been hired as a guide to take the kid camping, and granddad went along as a sort of companion. Granddad said you could walk from Dish Lake a few miles straight south to a really huge rock; he called it 'Flagstaff Rock' because there was a cairn of stones built up on top of it looked like it could hold up a flag on a pole. He said it was rough bushwhacking to get there, no trail to follow. He said he and the American kid liked climbing up on top of that rock. They could see for miles. He said it was just magical."

"If the first carry is still open enough to follow, it would be an easy trip to Dish Lake," Mel said. "I'm not interested in trying to find that rock, though. That country used to be all barrens, but now it's grown up in trees. Good luck finding that rock in a forest."

Mel rose and yawned, and he and Sandy headed for the tent, leaving Jeremy alone by the dwindling fire.

7: Alcohol and leukemia

The body on the autopsy table looked the same as that of the many other overweight, middle-aged, alcoholic men that Dr. Pyotr Nikolaevich Anichkov had examined during his two decades as medical examiner for the city of Ozyorsk. *How alike we all are in body and soul*, he thought, *our differences really only the smallest of details.*

Now Leonid Semchuk lay before him. Dr. Anichkov had met him once: a Ukrainian from Chernobyl who had come to work at Lighthouse P. A. twenty years ago. *Out of the frying pan and into the fire, so to speak.*

How had they met? He could not remember. Around soccer, perhaps, on a spring day like today, when their boys were small.

Now he was dead, and the safety committee of Lighthouse P. A. wanted to know why. The awful nuclear disaster at Ozyorsk had happened 50 years ago, and the region had not been dangerously radioactive for at least two decades. But memories are long, and the disaster had been horrific, and Lighthouse P. A still produced plutonium warheads.

Leonid's cheeks had the prominent blood vessels associated with too much alcohol, but this is not a reliable sign. With a thin needle and syringe, Anichkov withdrew a few millilitres of aqueous humour, a fluid in which blood alcohol levels still could be measured in the recently dead, from the anterior chamber of each of Leonid's eyes.

He placed the syringe on the bench, and turned on the ever-present Geiger-Müller counter to scan Leonid's skin, hair, and fingernails for radioactivity, just in case.

The counter buzzed like a rattlesnake the moment he touched the power button.

Anichkov froze; he had not yet even picked up the probe. He

backed away from the table, removed his apron and protective coveralls, and vigorously washed his hands, face and neck in the laboratory sink. He then removed his own clothes completely, put on a radiation-resistant suit kept in the autopsy suite in case of need, donned a self-contained breathing apparatus, radiation-proof gloves and a heavy lead apron, and approached the autopsy table once again.

Why is the Geiger-Müller registering such high radiation?

He picked up the probe from its holder on the side of the instrument and moved it toward Leonid's body. The machine went silent.

As he returned the probe to its holder, the machine buzzed alarmingly as the probe passed over the syringe of aqueous humour on the bench.

He brought the probe to the body again and moved it over all surfaces. There was no signal.

With a speculum, he gently opened Leonid's mouth and inserted the Geiger- Müller probe. The machine buzzed loudly.

Anichkov removed the probe, turned off the machine, covered the cadaver with its shroud and called on the intercom to tell the staff outside that the autopsy suite now was under quarantine, and no one was to enter. He scrubbed himself vigorously for 30 minutes in the shower in the change room, and then called the Chief Coroner.

The verdict, when it finally came, was murder, but it was never uttered outside the executive meeting room of Lighthouse P. A.

Under his skin, Leonid Semchuk's body was so radioactive that it had to be disposed of as toxic waste. The radiation was from polonium, a deadly poisonous element ingested by Leonid, it seemed, since it was confined to the inside of his body.

The dose had been very high and his death rapid. A search of Leonid's apartment had discovered half a bottle of vodka that could be safely retrieved only by a person in radiation-proof clothing and a lead container to enclose the bottle and the empty glass beside it.

The source of the polonium was Lighthouse P. A. itself, according to the chemists who examined the vodka. It was produced by them only in tiny amounts for special purposes, such as fuelling some instruments that would be sent into space.

The family would be told that Leonid had died of alcohol and leukemia, of loneliness and a lifetime of exposure to radiation. They would not find this surprising.

However, the director of the Lighthouse P. A. was determined to find out how the theft of polonium had been achieved and by whom. Security had been breached.

His resources for investigations were few but, perhaps, sufficient.

8: A fire in his head

Jeremy awoke suddenly before dawn, feeling hot and anxious, even a little frantic. He scrambled out of the tent and down to the stream bank, quivering with a strange exhilaration. The stream was calling to him.

He squatted beside a shrub on the bank and broke off a large branch that partially blocked his view. Its bark was finely mottled, and a few small, open nutshells decorated its upper branches.

He broke off the side branches and peeled away the bark until he held a twisted wand of pure white wood. With this, he probed the water and the bottom of the stream.

A blanket of teaberry grew on the stream bank beside him, with a few round, red berries among its shiny green leaves. He picked one and rolled it around in the palm of his hand for a while.

He rose then, and took from his backpack the bit of string he had used to pull a horned pout to the surface at Whitesand Lake. He tied one end to his pole and the other tightly around the red berry and dropped the berry in the stream.

It floated along with the current as far the string and pole could reach, and then Jeremy swung the berry upstream again.

As the berry floated past this time, a fish swam up and took it into its mouth.

Jeremy pulled the line in slowly and gently, expecting the fish to release the berry at any moment, but it did not. As it came near, he could see that it was a large brook trout. The trout held fast to the berry and Jeremy slowly slid it out of the water and laid it on a patch of wet grass on the shore.

The trout released the berry and lay still.

Jeremy was mesmerized by its beauty. The many-coloured spots, orange fins and total lustre filled him with an overwhelming desire to become one with this fish, to blend himself with it completely.

He ran to get a fire going just as Mel wandered out of the tent to relieve himself.

"That's the most perfect trout I've ever seen, Jerry," Mel remarked in passing.

There were a few coals still glowing from the night before in the ashes of the campfire. Jeremy covered them with thin strips of birch bark and a few small sticks, and as he blew on them, they began to flame and crackle. He dashed back to the stream bank to bring the trout up to the fire. But the trout was gone.

A faint dawn light was giving a ghostly illumination to the morning mist over the stream, and the last of the night's early spring moths still were on the wing.

Jeremy searched desperately for the trout in every direction near where it had lain, until his eye caught a flicker of light on the far shore of the stream, a glimmer that pulsed once into a distinct patch of brightness and then faded to nothing.

Jeremy was standing where the trout had been, looking across the stream, when Mel wandered back toward the tent.

"Where's that fine trout, Jerry?" he asked.

"She's gone," Jeremy said, to himself more than to Mel. "She's gone, but I'll find her."

~

Mel himself thought that another hour or two of sleep would be the best way to start that day, and he crawled back into his warm sleeping bag. As he was dropping off to sleep again, he heard a splash, and in the first of several pleasant dreams he imagined the indignant beaver that was slapping its tail to get Jeremy to go away.

Mel and Sandy needed some time, and a few cups of coffee, that morning to conclude that Jeremy had taken off somewhere on his own. That splash had not been a beaver. Jerry's fresh tracks went into the water on their side of the stream but did not come back out again.

This caused them neither surprise nor consternation. Jeremy could never really be lost in the forest. Probably, he could walk straight through the woods to Halifax and back again if he wanted to. Wherever he had gone, he had taken no food and so would almost certainly be back within two days and probably sooner, like tonight, around supper time.

After a breakfast of pancakes and bacon, it was easier for Sandy and Mel to consider where he might have gone and what, if anything, they should do about it.

Sandy wondered if he or Mel had said something the previous evening that might have disturbed Jeremy, something in the Mi'kmaq stories or about Joe Ashton. However, Mel had seen Jeremy through some very tough times and knew he was unlikely to be troubled by stories about a lurking man-bear or a long-dead villain. Something might have been going on with that big, beautiful trout, but he probably just had decided to let it go for some reason. What else?

"That rock!" Mel exclaimed suddenly. "Sandy, you told him about that rock, what was it? Flagstaff, bushwhacking two miles south from Dish Lake. That's it! You put a fire in his head with that story and I'll bet you that's where he's gone, dollars to doughnuts."

~

Sandy still was trying to get this head around Jeremy. This camping trip was the first time they had spent any serious time together. He had discovered there was a lot of substance to Jeremy underneath all the unexpected behaviour. He was just starting to get the hang of Jeremy now, but he also had come to like him, both in spite of, and because of, the surprises.

"So, what should we do?" Sandy asked.

"Jeremy's gone overland to that Flagstaff Rock," Mel said, "and there's no way we're gonna try to follow him through those five miles of woods and bogs. How about we do a little parallel play? Let's go to Dish Lake for the day, check out the old carry. We might meet up with Jerry and we might not, but Dish Lake is worth seeing, either way."

"Great idea!" Sandy said. "The trail there holds some of my own family's history, too."

There was a square of white plastic nailed to a tree just across the stream from the campsite, the usual backwoods marker for one end of a carry. At least they would know where to start.

Sandy carried the canoe and Mel carried the sandwiches. The trail was just barely discernible. They went up hills and down into hollows, and from time to time they had to check Sandy's GPS to be sure they were headed in the right direction.

It took them a good hour to get to the deadwater, but in the end they felt triumphant.

As they paddled down the deadwater, the bog laurel at the water's edge was just starting to display its fuchsia blooms, and the leather-leaf was pushing out masses of flower buds. A pair of otters huffed and puffed at them from a safe distance, seemingly half curious, half annoyed.

Some beavers had been busy, and they had to lift over a beaver dam part way along. A few wood ducks and a pair of hooded mergansers added dashes of colour to the brown spring landscape still waiting to turn green.

They carried over into Dish Lake proper and made a complete circumnavigation, all around the island and around Little Dish Lake, too.

They lunched on the south shore of the lake and napped for half an hour on the sun-warmed beach.

They awoke to find Jeremy seated near them, muddy, bedraggled and, it seemed, bursting with self satisfaction.

"How did you find us here, Jerry?" Sandy asked.

"Noise," Jeremy said.

"Where have you been?" Mel asked.

Jeremy was beaming, there was just no doubt about it. Mel had never seen such an exuberant, happy countenance on the usually dour and silent Jeremy.

"The Rock!" he said, with his eyes all a-twinkle. "She brought me there!"

He smiled and looked down at a white flower he was fiddling with and tossing from hand to hand.

"Who brought you there?" Sandy asked.

"She's gone, but I can find her now," Jeremy said.

He cut short any further interrogation by jumping up and putting the canoe in the water. He took his usual place, seated on the bottom in the middle, and waited for Mel and Sandy to grab the paddles and climb aboard.

9: Lunch with Frankie

Even paradise has its dark corners, where some of those assumed to be saved in truth are lost and forgotten.

Lisa Willson was sure she had found one such corner now, as her GPS navigator directed her to turn left off the almost-impassable dirt road she had been following onto an even less-passable one, and then, a mile further on, left again onto a faint trace of wheel tracks down a grass-grown lane without power poles.

A few hundred yards in, the lane forded a small brook, and one of the two ghostly wheel tracks became a footpath that led from the brook to a shack covered with a patchwork of tar paper and odd-shaped sheets of plastic.

It was a cool day, and a wisp of wood smoke rose from a rusty metal stovepipe protruding through the roof. Mr. Gully was at home.

Richard, the pharmacist in Digby, had asked Lisa if she, a home-care nurse, could somehow pay a visit to Mr. Gully. He had a prescription for beta-blockers to treat his heart failure, but he had not turned up at the pharmacy for the renewals that he certainly would be needing by now. Gully lived alone, and the address on the prescription seemed to be way off in the middle of nowhere.

Richard had given Lisa a year's supply to pass along to Gully if she could, or to return to him if she could not. Well, here she was.

The house had no front door. At the back, Lisa found a door into a shed attached to the house.

Knocking on this door produced no response, so she pushed it open and advanced through the shed to an inner door to the house itself. She knocked, waited, knocked again, and put her ear to the door to improve her chances of hearing something.

Gradually, she discerned an occasional moist choking cough and a faint, mechanical scraping sound. An unpleasant smell wafted to her in the air seeping out around the loosely-framed door.

Lisa gently turned the handle and opened the door slightly, and immediately recoiled from the full effect of the stench in the indoor air. She paused to get a grip on herself. After all, she was here on business.

"Hello? Mr. Gully? Good morning, Mr. Gully. I'm Lisa Willson. I'm a nurse. I have some pills for you, from Richard, at the pharmacy." As she spoke, she slowly stepped into the single room that was Mr. Gully's home.

Gully was standing at his wood-burning cook stove, stirring a steaming pot, and turned part way around to look at her. He stared at her without evident expression for ten seconds or so, then said, "I guess that's your car," and turned back to his cooking.

The room was sparsely furnished, with a mattress on a bed frame along one wall, a small table with two chairs, two oil lamps, some firewood beside the stove, two buckets of water, a plastic basin and several good-sized boxes of cardboard and plastic that seemed to contain food items, clothing and personal affects. Gully was dressed in several layers of heavily-worn clothes, but his feet were bare and the skin around his ankles was puffed and swollen. His breathing was laboured, and he coughed frequently.

"I've brought you some medicine, Mr. Gully, the heart medicine you were taking. Do you still have some? I brought you some more."

Gully nodded his head. "Frankie said you'd likely come today."

Lisa looked around for Frankie as she took the packages of pills from the bag she was carrying and placed them on the table. She checked the prescription on the package and extracted a daily dose.

"Where is Frankie now?" she asked.

"Just having a nap there on the bed," Gully replied.

Lisa looked again at the empty mattress. She walked over to the water buckets and used the dipper in one of them to scoop up a half cup or so.

She held out the day's pills to Gully with one hand and the dipper with the other, encouragingly. "Frankie will want you to have these before he wakes up," she ventured.

Gully looked at her and at the pills with a countenance announcing suspicion, but then he nodded again and swallowed down the pills and the water.

"He'll want you to do that once every day," Lisa said.

Gully nodded yet again and turned back to his pot.

It had become clear to Lisa that the stench in the house was emanating from Gully's pot on the stove. It contained small white and brown bits suspended in some liquid that was slightly yellow.

"Are you eating well, Mr. Gully?" she asked.

"Me and Frankie is doing okay for food. A lady comes by about once a month with a basket, from the Lions she says. Our potatoes all froze in the winter, but there's some bits of them still you can eat. Frankie found a deer killed up on the road around Christmas time. It's still not too bad. I got some of that deer here in this pot."

"Is that old meat and potatoes still really good to eat?" Lisa asked, her voice filled with doubt.

"Well," said Gully, "Frankie and me is just finding that out now. This here stew, it's come back up twice, and if comes back up again, we're gonna throw it all away."

Half an hour later, when she found Zora waiting for her at the café in Bear River as they had arranged, Lisa was still trying to gain control of her emotions. She felt guilty and sad, but mostly furious.

"How can we just leave these people to die by the side of the road, all our Mr. Gullys?" she blurted out. "We pretend they don't exist. We hide behind words like 'neurodiversity' and mental 'health' as if real mental illness doesn't matter. These really ill people should be first in line for care, with real psychiatrists and the best treatments and life-long follow-up. They'll never get better on their own. Except for the Lions Club and people like Richard, our Mr. Gullys have only their Frankies to turn to."

"Lisa, tell me what just happened," Zora pleaded.

"I don't want to ruin your coffee and pastry."

"Try me," Zora said, "I'm a vet!"

After learning about Mr. Gully's stew, Zora needed some time to get back into her lemon Danish, but finally she did, and Lisa also slowly pried herself loose from the jaws of guilt and failure. With her phone, she filed an emergency report, demanding urgent help for Mr. Gully.

10: Robbie MacAlisdair

Marie was late in joining Lisa and Zora at the café, but not too late. By chance, neither had any appointments until after lunch.

Marie had been delayed by a great idea. She ordered an espresso at the counter from Rory, and sat down.

"Lisa!" she said. "You need an electric car, and there it is!"

She pointed out the window. The electric four-wheel-drive sedan she had been nurturing into superior mechanical condition all winter was parked in full view.

"Marie, that's your special car; that's your baby. You can't give that away!"

"Yes, I can, and I just did. I've got another one in the shop right now. You drive your rounds every day and come home to roost every night; that's perfect for an overnight battery charge. I've got someone coming to install a charging station at your place tomorrow, on me. Humour me. Try it for a week or two."

Her mission accomplished, Marie relaxed into the general conversation. The café was empty, in the pause between mid-morning coffee and lunch, and Rory was able to join in, except for an occasional take-out order.

Some trucks and vans of the Hollywood film crew were making a din in the street outside. Marie mentioned that they also were working at an old house up the road from her place in Morganville.

"Marie," Rory said, "did you know about this author, Louie Penny, and his novel about Bear River before the film crew turned up in town?"

"Of course," she said, "I've read everything Robbie wrote. You do that for your friends, you know, when they write books."

"Robbie?"

"Yes, Robbie. Robbie MacAlisdair; that was his real name. He used a pen name to keep fame and fortune away. He found a pottery jar at an old campsite on Lake Joli one time and 'Louie Penny – His Jar' was written on it. He liked the name."

Rory was flabbergasted. "Not even Wikipedia knows Louie Penny's real name or anything much about him. What else do you know about him?"

"What's not to know? My house used to be Robbie's house. He gave it to my aunt forty years ago and she left it to me. Robbie came back and lived in it with me for his last two years, when he couldn't manage on his own any more. He's buried in Morganville."

How is it possible to keep such things secret? Rory wondered. Aloud, he asked, "Does the film crew know that your house once was Louie Penny's, or that his grave is just down the road?"

"I don't know," Marie said, "none of them has ever stopped in to ask."

"You seem pretty doubtful, Rory." Marie said. "Let's drive out to Morganville right now and visit Robbie's grave. Lisa, Zora, you'd better come, too."

Lisa and Zora figured they would have just enough time, and Rory begged an hour off from Greg. They headed for Morganville in convoy.

The cemetery was small, and most of the stones were old, their lettering partly weathered away. The MacAlisdair stone was among the newest. 'Robert MacAlisdair' was the second name on that stone, and under his name was written: '1935-2010. Carpenter, Philosopher, Author (under the name Louie Penny).' Above his was another name: 'Sylvie Saulnier MacAlisdair, 1936 – 1960, Teacher, Partner, Muse.'

"Sylvie was Robbie's wife," Marie said. "She was a school teacher here back then. She was killed, hit by a truck, right in front of the house. They'd only been married for three years. Robbie never got over it. He took her ashes away somewhere and never came back to the house until his last two years with me. He probably didn't want a gravestone for himself either, but I did, and I put this up for both of them."

"Why did you call Sylvie Robbie's muse?" Zora asked.

Marie sat down, leaned her back against the gravestone, and gazed down the hill that sloped gently away toward the West Branch of Bear River. All the winter's snow had melted, even from the shadiest nooks under low spruce branches, and the stream flowed a twisting path, laughing and bubbling between mossy green banks toward the sea. The overhanging red maples were in bloom, their blossoms animated by a gentle breeze into yellow-legged pixies with red skirts, dancing among the branches.

"I think Sylvie was Robbie's principal axis all his life, the source of his greatest joys and sorrows, and the inspiration for his writing and philosophy. For ten years, my aunt spent every summer at a place down near Yarmouth run by Carmelite monks, and Robbie was in the cabin beside hers. He was the carpenter and maintenance man, and had to do all the work without power tools because silence was the key feature of the place. My aunt said she watched Robbie's grief over Sylvie gradually find expression in poems and in some compelling thoughts about material wealth. She was really impressed, and she found an agent in New York interested in publishing his work."

Marie said that Robbie earned his living as a carpenter his whole life, mostly working on cabins back in the woods without electricity or roads. He would live in these places as he worked on them, in all seasons. Sylvie's family down in Clare received his mail, and kept his whereabouts to themselves.

"According to my aunt," she said, "Robbie believed that, above a small amount, material wealth is poison to contentment, and he agonized over what to do with all the money that came to him as Louie Penny. Eventually, he arranged to have all of it go to some agencies inside the United Nations, and none at all to himself."

"That sure fits with the themes in the novel they're making into a movie," Rory said.

"It's the way he talked too," Marie said. "When he was living with me, he told me he'd read that when paper money is destroyed, the value of all remaining money of the same kind increases in value by a very small amount so that everyone benefits, but not very much. He'd decided that the least harmful way to dispose of excess wealth was to destroy it. He told me that most of his life, he had saved up the money he earned but didn't need as hundred-dollar bills and, once or twice a year, he would travel out to a little lake where he and Sylvie had gone camping for their honeymoon, and he would compost those paper bills in an urn he kept there. He was pretty near his end when he told me that story. I'm not sure I believe it."

"Marie, I think you don't really want the movie-makers to know what you know about Louie Penny," Lisa said. "Am I right?"

"I don't. If Robbie were here now, I'm sure he would not want to be discovered. He would have disappeared somewhere until the movie-making was done. I respect that."

"*Fugit irreparabile tempus*," Rory announced. "Pardon my Virgil, but I gotta get back to work. Greg'll be desperate."

He took off in his and Lisa's old beater.

Zora headed home to prepare for five hours of in-clinic pet appointments. Her newly-hired, super-qualified veterinary nurse, Amanda Anaittuk, would be with her for the first time that afternoon, too, and Zora was hoping this would be the start of a whole new practice adventure. If she was quick, she might get in a half hour with Bronnie and Rick too.

Lisa took the pilot seat of her new electric car, and glided away with Marie, to drop her off at home and then make her monthly call on Jeremy Franklin, her wondrously neurodiverse home-care client. She had not checked in on him since he'd returned from camping with Mel and Sandy, and it was time.

Jeremy had no important health problems. He only needed a little monitoring to ensure he did not neglect important matters, like vaccinations and eating well. Lisa's first inspection always was of his fridge. Marie made sure that many good things went into it. Lisa searched through the opened packages and leftovers at the back to root out any potential food poisoning.

When she arrived, Jeremy was playing with Rosie the cat in his kitchen, and after a few general inquiries and confiscation only of a bowl of chili with blue-green hair, her visit was complete.

Lisa was not in a hurry, so she asked Jeremy about his camping trip, just in case he felt like doing some talking that day. Most days, he didn't.

To her surprise, he had a lot to say about how wonderful it had been: the colours and the smells and the sounds. He was most excited about following a bright light or an idea or something to find a huge rock that Sandy had said was called Flagstaff Rock. It was clear he'd had a wonderful week in the woods.

"Rory and I have been talking about going canoe camping this summer," she said, "maybe for four-five days. Where do you think we could go?"

Jeremy did not hesitate. "The big rock. Dish Lake, and then the rock. It's that way," and he pointed his arm very precisely toward the south corner of the room.

When Lisa got home that evening, she pulled out the local topographic maps she and Rory had collected. She found the location of Jeremy's house on Lake Joli Road, and traced a line south from there in the direction Jeremy had pointed. Her moving finger soon found Dish Lake and, a little further south, a tiny lake clearly labelled Flagstaff Lake.

"Rory," she called out, "we have a plan!"

11: Seven weeks from Sinpo

The *Slocum Warrior*, Westport, IMO 1769093, was on its first deployment in the middle of the North Atlantic Gyre, latitude 28.563, longitude 59.333.

It seemed a good place to test things out. No ships came this way, partly because it was not on the route to anywhere and partly because it was in the Bermuda Triangle and subject to the myths and superstitions that govern so many of the practices of ships and sailors.

No boats came here if they could avoid it. If they did, they would not know the *Warrior* was lurking there, equipped as it was with the latest anti-detection equipment from the French navy.

Four volunteer conservation warriors, two naval intelligence officers contributed by the British and French navies, and Pedro, the first mate, made up Wolf's crew, working eight-hour shifts at the monitoring stations and sharing in cooking and general maintenance.

Since arriving a week ago, the *Slocum Warrior* had identified and monitored the movements of 26 potential illegal, unreported and unregulated fishing vessels, IUUs as they are known to authorities, across the North and South Atlantic. Twelve were moving in ways that suggested they were headed for a port or a rendezvous with another ship to off-load their catch, and all of these now also were being tracked by national military authorities with the intention to intercept and capture them.

At the end of his watch one day, a volunteer from Norway, a retired fisherman from Lofoten, showed Wolf a dot on one of the surveillance screens and said, "That boat is setting illegal long line for tuna and swordfish. It goes downwind slowly, about eight kilometres, waits a few hours and then goes upwind even more slowly. I am sure it is setting and then retrieving baited lines."

This suspect long liner was 500 miles south of Greenland. The

Warrior's crew found a Canadian research ship about 100 miles west of the suspect vessel, and its captain agreed to sail toward the suspect and try to identify it.

However, as soon as the research ship was clearly on a route toward it, that suspect vessel began to sail south at full speed. The research ship had to give up pursuit and go back to its work.

Over the next five days, the suspect long liner pursued a course that eventually brought it to Corvo Island, the outermost of the Azores, where the alerted Portuguese authorities boarded it and arrested captain and crew. The hold was indeed filled with whole frozen bluefin tuna and swordfish, all illegally obtained.

A week later, as Wolf was relieving Pedro and resuming his captain's duties, Pedro pointed to a marker he had dropped on a point on the GPS map screen about 30 miles north of the *Warrior*.

"Watch that spot," he said. "There's something there that only shows up on radar as an occasional flicker, and these two other ships not far away seem to be heading for it. One of them is a gill-netter from North Korea."

Wolf said he would keep a close eye on them, and settled into his busy shift.

The identification transceivers on the North Korean vessel and on a ship coming in from Bermuda were active and they were easy to follow. The third vessel was mostly invisible to their usual radar, but could be seen on a special anti-interference radar the Swedish navy had given the *Warrior* to try out, and which Wolf now switched on. The mystery vessel's transceiver was turned off.

Marine traffic databases showed that the Korean gill-netter was ancient, 40 years old, and had voyaged non-stop for seven weeks from Simpo to its present location. Wolf looked up its name: the *Taeyang-Wang*, which the Internet told him meant the *Sun King*.

The ship from Bermuda had made a short direct voyage south from Hamilton. He looked up its name too: the *Cahow*! *Well, well, well, we meet again!*

As the Korean and Bermudan boats came together and were seemingly side by side, the third boat remained about three or four miles away. There was some radio traffic coming from the general direction of this cluster of boats, but it was unintelligible.

Near the end of Wolf's watch, the *Cahow* turned off its transceiver and headed back toward Bermuda, and the *Taeyang-Wang* headed southeast, skirting the Sargasso Sea, probably on its way back home. The third ship departed on a westward course, moving fast, but quickly was lost to all of the *Slocum Warrior's* surveillance electronics.

Wolf was eating and catching up on paperwork when the crew member on watch called him up to the bridge. The *Taeyang-Wang* had just disappeared off the surveillance screens. It had been steaming along with its transceiver active and a good signal on the *Warrior's* radar, but then had just disappeared, poof, no more transceiver signal, no spot on the radar screen.

So, Wolf thought, *the Bermuda Triangle takes down another ship.*

Almost anything could sink an ancient, rusted-out ship like the *Sun King*. Perhaps some mishap on board had sent it to the bottom.

The *Cahow*, on the other hand, showed up clearly on satellite imagery and on over-horizon radar, and the *Warrior* tracked it all the way back to Hamilton.

The *Slocum Warrior* was stationed far offshore because it was equipped to communicate directly with civilian and military surveillance satellites. The ship could receive and decode images and other data in real time and do the same with recently-recorded information. By being more or less under the orbits of the satellites transmitting information of interest, they could receive those data quickly and at high resolution. This is what the designers of the boat had hoped would be the case and, so far, it had proved to be so.

The two naval intelligence officers had quickly improved the ship's surveillance capacity even further. Wolf was quite sure that, in addition to being expert with the electronics, they also had some passwords to French and British satellite data not available to Wolf himself. That was okay with him.

Not quite four decades ago, the French foreign service had blown up the *Rainbow Warrior* because it was campaigning so successfully against nuclear bomb tests in French Polynesia. Now, a French naval intelligence officer was on the *Slocum Warrior* campaigning to ensure that there always would be fish in the sea. Maybe one day they would even trust him with a password or two. Sending the *Warrior* officers who knew those passwords, and a lot more, was even better.

12: Inventories

To arrive at the headquarters of the International Atomic Energy Agency in Vienna, you must turn your back on the old city and travel east across the canal and the railways, and, via the Reichsbrücke, across the wide and once-blue Danube, three miles through the fabled city to its International Centre.

The IAEA is the vanguard for all uses of atomic energy to the betterment of human kind, and the safeguard of humanity against nuclear harm, be it from bombs, pollution or terrorism.

Its remit regarding terrorism falls to its Division of Nuclear Security, which engages all IAEA member countries in security practices to achieve tight control of the global inventory of high-grade fissionable material, and to prevent its theft and black market sale. A terrorist group able to put together a dirty bomb might hold cities and countries hostage, or choose to irradiate fatally tens of thousands of people, terrorizing and causing mayhem in a target population, even if they could not create a great explosion.

On this day, the international technical committee of experts on nuclear terrorism opened its annual spring meeting in the Division offices, to review the events of the first four months of the year. Members quickly reviewed several hundred incidents of attempted theft and sale detected during the previous year, and received updates on investigations into incidents that posed substantial threats to regional or global security.

Under "new business", members presented to the Committee recently-documented or suspected incidents.

Bulgaria reported the arrest of a woman long-suspected of seeking a market for a small quantity of enriched uranium stolen from the power plant at which she worked. An IAEA team working in Russia reported a single positive signal during a three-week period when they had used the latest in radiation sensors to scan trains passing through Volkhov on a main rail line east from St Petersburg. The signal had come from a car in a container train. The train had gone north toward Murmansk, and it seemed most likely that one of its cars carried some imperfectly-packaged uranium destined for the Kola power plant. No investigation was warranted. Pakistan had welcomed an inspection by IAEA staff regarding a reported theft of enriched uranium by the Taliban. It had provided documentation of its total nuclear inventory sufficient to show that no such theft had taken place.

There were some more troubling new developments, however. The data reported regularly from Russia's nuclear reprocessing plant in Ozyorsk contained irregularities that could not be reconciled. As much as 1000 kg of outdated plutonium warheads received at Lighthouse P. A. for reprocessing seemed unaccounted for. Ozyorsk is closed to all foreigners and thus also to inspection by IAEA. An unofficial inquiry would be initiated.

In another case, a white-supremacist group based in Copenhagen was reported to be under close surveillance because of intelligence reports that it was planning to steal uranium fuel from the Doel power plant near Antwerp. A sting operation to counter this plan had been put in place.

A Committee member from China reported the most disturbing new development. China's intelligence service had determined that the Democratic People's Republic of Korea recently had obtained 25 units of the most advanced ballistic-missile guidance systems, units produced exclusively for the United States military. China had no information on how North Korea had acquired these exceptionally-sensitive armaments.

The Committee member from the United States challenged this assertion immediately and forcefully. She said that it was impossible for such top secret materiel to be acquired by anyone outside of the American Armed Forces. She was incredulous, then, when the expert from China passed to her a copy of the top-secret technical instruction manual for installation and use of these guidance systems, a document which China's intelligence service had obtained in North Korea.

"Our countries have many differences, Colonel Lindenmayer," the

Chinese expert said, "but neither of us wants any deployment of nuclear weapons."

This newly-reported event was so significant that the Division director adjourned the meeting for two weeks to give IAEA time to seek verification and further information.

Col. Lindenmyer hurried to IAEA's secure communications centre and directed a staff officer at the Pentagon to verify the integrity of the manufacturer and the military's inventories of these missile guidance components.

An hour later, she was greatly relieved to learn that the two inventories matched and were complete. She had the presence of mind, however, to ask for assurance that manufacturing records also were identical to the inventories. This information would require a day or two to obtain. She would be in Washington herself by then, to receive the answer.

On the same day, three hundred miles west, across Austria, another meeting was taking place in Liechtenstein, because of its discretion and convenience. The munitions cartel had gathered to review progress on their project to instigate a global arms race.

There was a hint of satisfaction in the otherwise passionless voice of Olga O'Grady as she spoke from the head of the table. "Thus far, all has gone according to plan and is on schedule. One thousand kilograms of warhead-grade plutonium have been secured from a facility in Russia. The cooperating manager has died of radiation poisoning, an unfortunate workplace hazard. IAEA soon will conclude that the plutonium has been stolen."

She surveyed the others for questions or comments, but there were none.

"Two thousand kilograms of highly-enriched uranium have been secured from military sources in North Korea in exchange for missile guidance systems obtained from an American military contractor. This information has been leaked to the Chinese intelligence service. The accuracy of the first missile test that makes use of such a guidance system will verify the information and cause grave concern around the world. The ships and personnel involved in these transactions no longer are security threats."

She surveyed the room again.

One member posed a question. "How will our nuclear material be secured against detection?"

"The material soon will enter secure storage in a remote location in a non-nuclear western nation under cover of an unrelated regional enterprise. One insecure employee essential to the final phase of the project soon will be eliminated. A trusted associate will provide site management through the transition. Security will be maintained by indentured mercenaries supplied by Verdi. They, too, are disposable."

She concluded the meeting with an admonition. "In the next six months, we must anticipate large orders for all manner of conventional weapons, and exceptionally large research contracts for improved weaponry and defences. Demand will increase quickly. Supply-chain shortages must be anticipated and overcome. Basic materials should be sourced immediately. We must not fail to deliver. This opportunity may last only a few years."

13: Slippery as eels

She had sat down beside him in the movie theatre in Annapolis Royal, had actually chosen to sit beside him. There were lots of other available seats, but she had selected the one next to him deliberately.

She had smiled at him as she took her seat, and said hello, and that her name was Anita, Anita St-Pierre.

She had a captivating smile and an inviting twinkle in her eyes when she spoke. She said she was really looking forward to the film. She was a big fan of Benedict Cumberbatch, and had heard that his version of *Hamlet* was spectacular.

Henry was thinking that Anita St-Pierre's version of herself was spectacular—gold and silver hair in a classic Dutch braid, a face that might launch a thousand ships, an aura of Venus herself—but mostly because she actually seemed to want to talk to him, leaning in a little as she did so.

"You're Henry Wambolt, aren't you?" she'd said, "I live in Bear River, too, now, on Purdy Road. I've seen you around, here and there."

The lights dimmed and the film came on. Henry mostly watched Anita watch the movie, attracted like a moth to her warm light. Did she notice? At one especially moving segment of the play, Anita reached over and touched his arm, as if to steady herself. There was no ring on that left hand, nor on his.

Henry's heart had nearly burst.

For the past several years, Henry had lived alone, cast off and left to sink or swim by a former spouse. Loneliness had inspired his writing in some powerful ways, but only if he wrote about sadness and misery. Slowly, he had allowed his eunuch's life, solitary and loveless, to seem normal. Anita had just shattered that new normal.

Since that evening, Henry had never felt so intensely alone, nor so hopeful. A few days later, he'd met Anita at the grocery store and, somehow, they were still talking after 15 minutes. Yesterday, they had coffee together and she asked to read some of his recent song lyrics. She said she was a documentary filmmaker.

Henry wanted to know, had to know, more. He had to know everything there was to know about Anita St-Pierre. He tracked down Purley Jordan.

Purley was an afternoon regular at the café if he wasn't on a job somewhere, and Henry found him there having an animated conversation with one of the manager-types from the movie crew, who were just packing up the last of their equipment after finishing their filming.

"We want to get this film out the door pretty quick," the manager was saying. "It won't take long to edit in the scenes from here. It's going to do well; we're sure of that. We hope for a prize or two at TIFF, but it'll be in theatres this fall. We're pre-booked already."

Purley was adamant. "You just make sure the first theatre gets that film to show is here in Bear River! This village just went crazy helping you out, and now we're all excited to see it. We shouldn't have to drive to the big theatres in Yarmouth or New Minas; it should be shown right here, in the Oakdene and then at King's in Annapolis."

The manager said he would pass along that proposal as best he could.

Purley shrugged as he saw the movie-makers out the door for the last time, and then turned to Henry. "They're a good bunch, them fellers," he said, "but slippery as eels."

He pulled up a chair at Henry's table. "I guess we'll see that film eventually. I did my best. How's the professor today?"

Henry got right to the point. "I need to know everything there is to know about this lady Anita St-Pierre, and then I'll need to know some more on top of that. No one knows better than you do what's going on in Bear River. I need a full account."

He offered Purley a biscotti to dip in his coffee, by way of encouragement.

Purley paused to assemble his personal database on Anita, and then held forth. "This Anita St-Pierre seems to come from up by Antigonish somewhere, but was in Montreal a long time before she come to Bear River. Blanche, out in Greenland, is from up that way and she remembers the family. Anita bought that old place no one would touch for falling apart, across from the new vineyard on Purdy Road, bought it two years ago, real cheap according to Angie, and she'd know for sure. Anita really fixed the place, lifted her up, tore the old cellar out of the ground and put her back down on a new basement. Denny done the work, and he's the right man to do it. Nice small house on a nice bit of land, with a fine view, if you don't mind always looking out on them O'Connors on the other side of the river.

"They say she did film work for a living, and some say her stuff was on TV a few times, mostly whales and nature and the like. Blanche is pretty sure she has some grown kids, so there likely was a husband or two at one time or another. No husband now, professor. They say she's about 60, just like you, but if you ask me, she looks more like 40."

Purley signalled to his daughter Marlene, the barista that afternoon, to bring him another biscotti. "It don't seem she's retired, but probably workin' from home mostly, according to the neighbours. Nice lady, they say. Not many visitors. I see her out running on the roads early some mornings. She seems to have taken a shine to you. Marlene, there, tells me Anita was in here the other day, and she got Rory over to her table and quizzed him about you just like you're quizzin' me."

Henry's heart leaped up and danced around the room a few times before landing squarely on his sleeve. He couldn't help it. In spite of himself, he was daring to hope.

Henry and Rory had missed the deadline to have their song ready for Walt Whitman's birthday, and they weren't any closer now. It was mostly Henry's fault, he knew. He'd been adrift in the doldrums and could find no spark of inspiration that produced words worthy of Whitman.

But Whitman's birthday had been a watershed moment anyway. Anita cooked up a Whitman birthday dinner, and baked a cake. Lisa and Rory came, and when they departed and it was Henry's time to be the last to leave, Anita had stopped him at the door to say that maybe he didn't have to go home tonight, and maybe not the next night either, and that there was an empty bureau for clothes in the bedroom, and his cat might like the place, too...

Once they'd caught their breath, life had a new energy for both of them.

Over the previous year, Anita had spent hours and hours watching and filming the water flowing past the town, the mud flats being covered and revealed and covered and revealed, hoping to discover some inner theme of meaning, but really finding it all about as interesting as, well, mud.

Now she saw interest and video possibilities everywhere. Where were the fish that used to be in the river? Should the tidal power causeway stay or go? What about those Blanding's turtles? What about those clearcuts? How do people make a living in rural Nova Scotia?

In two weeks, she'd made five pitches and gotten two contracts.

Henry was back on task as a writer, too, but he also had found new employment as Anita's chief grip, script writer and sound engineer.

14: Travel logs

It was in a small restaurant in Omsk that the Director of Lighthouse P. A. first learned, from a discrete representative of IAEA, that there might be gaps in his company's inventory of old plutonium warheads. He had hurried back to Ozyorsk to check the records against actual stored material, and now he was in Astana, the capital city of Kazakhstan, to report his findings to the IAEA Committee.

He preferred to hold such unofficial meetings outside of Russia, and also outside the habitual gaze of the rest of the world. Astana was a wonderful city—modern, well-planned, where everything worked—and where, conveniently, the headquarters of the world's largest uranium production company was located, a genuine reason for him to travel there.

It was the polonium, not the plutonium, that had been the Director's first and greatest concern, and he himself had begun a low-profile investigation as soon as he had learned how Leonid Semchuk had died.

On the pretext of retrieving any documents that might pertain to the company, he was authorized to search Semchuk's apartment once it had been declared safe with respect to radiation. There he had found, tucked into the frame behind a photo of a man who looked as though he could be Leonid's son, a hand-written note: a word that seemed to be in German, "Rausfinanzbank"; and a number, 3141593.

From the Internet, the Director learned that the word was the name of a Swiss bank. Through a discrete inquiry made by a business partner in Basel whose company depended heavily on medical radioisotopes supplied by Lighthouse P. A., he learned that an account of that number had been established about six months previously, with a deposit of two million Euros.

The deposit had come from a numbered company in Barbados and could not be traced. The balance had been withdrawn, and the account closed, ten days after Leonid had died.

The Director could not imagine why Leonid would have been in possession of such information. Perhaps it explained his murder in some way, but it was not clear how.

Only four people had security clearance to enter the laboratory that produced polonium. The Director had access to the recordings of all the company's security cameras, and he spent many hours watching the recordings from the camera that monitored the only door to the polonium lab. During the week before Leonid was poisoned, the four workers came and went at regular hours, and nothing happened in between.

Of course, the polonium could have been stolen weeks or months before.

The Director did not himself have the time to review months of camera recordings, but he also did not wish to alert anyone to his investigation. As a shortcut, he tried comparing each day's images of the laboratory door just after the lab closed for the day and then just before the first worker arrived the next morning, to see if he could detect that something had changed after hours.

In one such comparison, three days before the murder, the door handle had changed position by about 15 degrees between the two images. The Director sped through the video recording of the hours between that closing and opening to find the moment when the change had taken place. It was 2:49 in the morning.

Looking carefully at the surveillance recording in the twenty minutes that preceded that moment, he discovered a period of fourteen minutes during which the surveillance camera image had frozen, and the camera had ceased to record. In the first unfrozen image after these fourteen minutes, the door handle was at the new angle.

The company's security apparatus of cameras, card locks, pass codes and personal tracking devices was controlled by its own central intelligence unit. Only eleven people worked in this unit, and all had the required security status. All had worked in the unit for at least five years.

The Director brought to his screen the personnel files of each of these people. The file for Anya Ivanovna Skryabin quickly attracted his attention. She had not come to work the day that the fourteen minutes of surveillance had been blocked in the early morning, and she had not signed in to work since then.

The Director quickly learned that Anya had disappeared from Ozyorsk on the day Leonid Semchuk had been found dead. She had lived by herself, and her small social circle had no idea that she had planned to leave or where she might have gone.

Anya perhaps was a murderer, but she was not an important security risk. Her unit provided security only for the company, which, in truth, no longer had anything of importance to hide. To track down Anya would necessitate bringing the cold hard eyes of the Kremlin—or worse—down on the company. She would be safely out of Russia by now anyway, he was sure, enjoying, perhaps, the two million Euros she had been paid to murder Leonid.

But why?

The Director had been less concerned about the potential problems IAEA had identified with the company's inventories of plutonium. He was quite sure the problem was not lost plutonium but, rather, human incompetence. The old Soviet-era joke that "We pretend to work, and they pretend to pay us," was still the case for many state-run organizations in the new Russia, including his own company. Always there were too many old warheads to re-process and little real urgency in supplying the new ones.

His interest in the plutonium increased however, when his own unofficial assessment showed that there was much less plutonium in storage than was on record, and it increased further when he had traced the responsibility for inventory control back to the desk of the late Leonid Semchuk.

Now it seemed possible that Semchuk had diverted a quantity of plutonium out of Lighthouse P. A., for which, perhaps, he expected to be paid two million Euros. Well, now he never could confess.

Perhaps Anya Ivanovna Skryabin could explain it all, if she could be apprehended, but she now was out of reach, and perhaps also silenced.

The meeting in Astana was short and efficient. The Director confirmed that about 1000 kg of warhead-grade plutonium intended for reprocessing apparently had been transported out of Lighthouse P. A. without authorization by a now-dead staff member.

"You must track down this missing plutonium quickly, as your most urgent priority," he said to the Committee. "But I myself can do no more. I have no authority or capacity to take actions outside of my company. To do so would draw attention and create difficulties."

Several Committee members recalled the report by Russian engineers of a single distinct radiation signal captured from a rail car that had passed through Volkhov from the west and on to the north. It now seemed possible that the signal had come from a container on the train that held the stolen plutonium.

A Committee member from Rosatom, Russia's civilian nuclear agency, said it would be a mistake at this stage to engage Russia at a political level or to seek help from the military. All subsequent investigations then would be done in secret and would be classified, so that neither IAEA, nor Rosatom nor Lighthouse P.A. ever would learn the outcome. She said she herself could authorize and direct an unofficial investigation of this plutonium shipment, and that she would report back to the Committee within a few weeks.

So it was that the Director found himself at IAEA in Vienna two weeks later, much sooner than he had anticipated. Rosatom had completed an investigation that was impressive in its speed and scope.

The train that had included the railcar from which the prototype detector had recorded a radiation signal had been identified by number and date, and its transport records had been reviewed. Three days before the detection at Volkhov, a truck from Ozyorsk had delivered a six-meter-long metal shipping container to the railyard at Yekaterinburg for shipment to Murmansk. It had been placed on a flat-bed railcar with other consignments for Murmansk, and that railcar had been joined to the main train to Murmansk at Nizhny Novgorod.

In Murmansk, the container from Ozyorsk had been picked up by a local trucking firm and delivered to a pier in the city's fishing port. Rosatom had located the driver, who said he had used the crane on his truck to lower the container onto the deck of a small ship that might once have been used for fishing, but was not rigged for fishing at the time of his delivery. The driver did not know the name of the ship. All shipping costs had been paid to the trucker's company through a commercial bank in Murmansk. The money had arrived at the bank through an electronic transfer from a bank in Switzerland.

Rosatom had reviewed the records of ship traffic in and out of Murmansk and had determined that the ship with the container on board was named *The White-tailed Eagle*, and had been cleared to sail for the Faroe Islands with unspecified general cargo destined for one of the large salmon farming companies there.

The Danish marine traffic agency had confirmed the arrival of this ship at Tórshaven four days later and its departure again a few days after that. When it was about 300 miles north of the Faroes, *The White-tailed Eagle* disappeared from routine ship tracking screens and its transceiver ceased transmitting. The Danes assumed the ship had sunk for some reason, but no distress signal had come from the vessel. No company in Russia reported the vessel missing in the days that followed.

"What happened to the shipping container?" the Director asked. "Did it end up on the Faroes or at the bottom of the sea?"

"We have tried to determine the fate of the container, but it is uncertain" the Rosatom officer said. "Fish farm companies are competitive and secretive, and do not provide information. In Tórshaven, *The White-tailed Eagle* delivered cargo to a company called Styrja, which recently acquired a large salmon-farming business on the Faroes. Styrja loaded cargo of some kind onto a small freighter the same day that *The White-tailed Eagle* arrived. This freighter was named the *Cahow*. It sailed immediately to Bermuda, where it discharged cargo at a merchant wharf. The *Cahow* made one additional voyage, south from Bermuda about 500 miles and back again, and then went into dry dock in Hamilton.

"In Bermuda, we lose track of the container and the ship," she said. "An obituary for a man said to have been the captain of the *Cahow* was published in the *Royal Gazette* newspaper a week after the *Cahow* returned to Bermuda from its last voyage. According to international shipping records, the *Cahow* has not sailed again."

The Director listened to the report from Rosatom with a grave countenance. So it was true, 1000 kg of weapons-grade plutonium was stolen from the Russian military while awaiting reprocessing by his company, under his watch, under his nose. If, or when, this news were to reach the Kremlin, he would surely end his life in a cold work camp in Magadan.

But more was at stake than his personal risk. The stolen plutonium was as much a threat to Russia and his people as it was to the rest of the world. He looked across the table at the Rosatom officer and saw the same fearful dismay in her eyes.

"Our first priority must be to determine who has organized and paid for this theft," the Director said. "The risk to the world lies in their capacities and motivations to steal from the stockpiles of a major nuclear power. We must discover who they are, how they have achieved this theft and where the plutonium is now."

15: Paper money

"You're just the best ever," Lisa whispered to Rory, snuggling even closer to him as their breathing returned to normal.

They were bedded down high on the top of Flagstaff Rock, looking up at a night sky so filled with stars that it seemed impossible. They could just see each other in the soft starlight, and when they tilted back their heads, they could see the north star high in the sky behind them.

They had followed through on their plan to spend a few days camping on their own in the deep woods, and they had taken Jeremy's suggestion of visiting Flagstaff Rock as both a good plan and a challenge. They had plotted their route on maps with Mel's guidance.

Rain had fallen heavily the week before, and the water was high in the lakes and streams they planned to follow. It was July, the spring clouds of black flies were gone, and everything was in leaf and in bloom.

Mel had dropped them off at Lake Joli early on a Friday morning, and promised to pick them up again Monday evening. The mouth of Ninth Lake Brook was choked with pickerel weed bearing a few early blue flower spikes, and with yellow cow lilies and white water lilies, and the urn like leaves and tall flowers of pitcher plants crowded the wide boggy shores. Turtles plopped off their sunning spots ahead of the canoe, ripples in the water marking their quick escapes.

A beaver swam smoothly ahead of them for two or three meanders of the brook until it dived quietly at a beaver lodge hidden in a side channel. At the head of the brook, they carried across a forestry road and managed to find the ancient trail through the tangled clear-cut and over the low height of land to tiny Ninth Lake, a headwater of the Sissiboo. By then, the magic of the backwoods was fully upon them.

They paused for lunch at Sixth Lake Stream and arrived at the carry to the Dish Lake deadwater at about 5:00 in the afternoon. They shared that carry with a curious bear for half a minute, until the bear had had enough and bolted away.

When they finally reached Dish Lake, they paddled across and into Little Dish Lake, where they found a good place to make camp along its southern shore, the closest they could get by canoe to Flagstaff Rock.

The next morning, they set off on foot to spend one night at Flagstaff Lake and search for the rock. Sandy had lent them a GPS unit, and it guided them unerringly on a one-and-a-half mile trek through dense and pathless forest to the tiny lake.

Jeremy and Mel had warned them that the big rock might be hard to find, and it was, but late that afternoon, after several hours of searching, they found it!

The rock was sheer and steep on all sides, but on one side there was a place where they could scramble up and stand with their heads level with the surrounding tree tops. The upper surface of the rock was irregularly flat, with a wide, shallow hollow near the middle filled with a lattice of thin, dry tree branches.

These old branches gave Rory the idea of making a bed of boughs in the hollow and spending the night high up on top.

They piled a thick layer of new balsam boughs over the old branches and made a surprisingly soft and comfortable bed. From that bed, they had watched the sun set, the stars blaze, and the sun rise again, enveloped in the perfume of fresh balsam and the songs of thrushes.

In the morning, they swam in the lake, then returned to the rock to savour their success at its rediscovery before making the hard trek back to their canoe.

Along one side of the rock, the vertical wall was undercut, creating a long, narrow crevice big enough to crawl into and filled with dry leaves.

Lisa decided to explore it. Against the inner wall, where the crevice was tallest, her crawling hand touched something smooth and hard under the leaf carpet. After brushing away the leaves, she could just see in the dim light that it was a large vessel of some kind, half buried in the soil. She gently rocked it loose and carried it out into daylight.

It was an old earthenware jar with tapered sides, about a foot tall and eight inches wide, with a slightly narrowed opening and an out-turned lip. A word was painted in small, worn letters on one side: "Sylvie." The vessel was nearly full of light, dry material.

They emptied the jar slowly onto a space they cleared on the ground. First to emerge was what seemed to be chunks of very thin layers of a paper-like material, tightly packed together. The content deeper in the jar graded slowly into a soft grey substance without structure. Some of the top-most layered material was dry enough that they could peel away each thin sheet from the one beneath it.

Several layers in, they began to discern a faded pattern on the surface of both sides of each layer.

In one very thick wad, the patterning on the middle layers was better preserved than elsewhere, and as they carefully separated the delicate layers, they were surprised to discover that each was a piece of a one-hundred-dollar bill.

They could hardly believe what they held in their hands. The jar must have contained at least a hundred of these bills, maybe several times more.

They sat in silence for a few moments. Rory was first to speak.

"Louie Penny," he said. "It's his jar."

"It's the urn for his wife's ashes," Lisa murmured. "It's the jar Robbie MacAlisdair told Marie about just before he died, where he'd take money to destroy when he had too much. She wasn't sure it was true."

They sat in silence a while longer. "What should we do?" Rory asked.

He paused and then, by way of answering his own question, began scooping the material back into the jar. Lisa watched for a moment and then helped him until everything they had removed from the jar was back inside again. The jar would stay at Flagstaff Rock

They took with them two small fragments of the decaying money to give to Marie. To her, these would be Robbie's own signature at the end of his last story.

As they put on their backpacks to walk back to Dish Lake, Rory said, "Robbie MacAlisdair really believed that wealth is harmful. That's what his book is all about. I don't know if destroying the money you don't need is the best way to avoid that harm, but I think he really was generous and brave to try."

Lisa looked up at the rock and put her hand gently against its cool grey side. "When we have more than we need, Rory, I want us to be as brave as Robbie. Let's work just as hard as he did to make sure it doesn't harm us or other people."

16: Cargoes

The White's Cove fish farm had moved ahead swiftly under Trudy Denton's direction. Excavation of the tunnels was complete. Water treatment and recycling systems passed all the required pre-use tests. The first fish farm building and its infrastructure of tanks, water pipes, feed lines, geothermal heat and controls was complete, and half of the tanks were filled with sea water, ready to receive the first shipment of young salmon that would test the system fully.

A temporary control panel in the fish tank building controlled the farm, pending the arrival and installation in the tunnels of the automated systems. From the farm building on top of the ridge, Trudy bored a 12-inch-wide channel 300 feet straight down into the back of the tunnel below, so a sea water pipe and fibre-optic cables could run from the farm buildings down to the control centre and water intakes. She was proud that she had hit the tunnel at the right place on the first try.

Parker Churchill and Johnny Tidd had stayed on as employees to run the farm manually for the time being and to build the floors, ceilings and cross-walls needed in the tunnels.

Trudy told Zora all of this as she gave her a brief tour of the tunnel entry ways and the small, sturdy wharf, and then walked her up to the fish farm.

Zora was surprised to find herself making so much of her income these days from fish. She hoped that new farms with small herds of goats, sheep, pigs and poultry would continue to increase in number locally, as was the current trend, and that she and her veterinary nurse, Amanda, could expand their work in that direction, too. However, at the moment, she was much needed as a fish farm vet.

The recent epidemic among the local sea pen salmon farms had run her off her feet. Now Beluga was after her again. "They liked the way you worked them through that sea-pen disaster," Trudy said. "It's no surprise that now they want you on their team for this new on-shore farm. I guess this is your first official visit as our vet, 'Dr. Cromwell.' Let me show you around.".

The farm was right up to date in every respect, as far as Zora could see. She reviewed the protocols established to monitor water quality and to keep records of the readings and related information, and she took water samples from several of the tanks to send away to verify the on-farm monitor readings.

"When are the first fish going into the new tanks?" Zora asked

"Right now." Trudy said. "The supply boat from Blacks Harbour is just coming in. You can see it there approaching the wharf. It's got smolts for the tanks and feed for the smolts. Let's go see."

They walked back down to the wharf and out to the supply vessel. Zora took photos of the unloading process to document the handling techniques in use for the containers of live fish. She took samples of the water in the transport tanks and asked the crew how they monitored the fish in the tanks during this tricky time of transportation. Everyone she talked to seemed well informed and competent.

The supply boat was named *Wagamama*, Blacks Harbour, IMO 5247873. Zora stared at the number, paused, closed her eyes…check! The last digit was correct.

She giggled to herself. What an obsession to have acquired; but then, she didn't see ships and their IMO numbers every day, so it qualified as a special occasion. Happily, Trudy was busy talking to the captain and hadn't noticed.

Another ship, larger than the *Wagamama,* also was tied at the wharf and was using its freight crane to hoist large metal boxes out of its hold and place them gently on a pallet on the wharf. Parker picked each one up carefully with a pallet mover, and drove it slowly away toward a tunnel entrance.

Trudy and Zora walked over to the larger ship. "The special control equipment for the farm is in those boxes and that sea container on the deck," Trudy explained. "For this stuff, my responsibility ends at the tunnel entrance. It's all secret industrial electronics, and only Beluga's own technicians are allowed anywhere near it."

"Doesn't it bother you not to know how it is all supposed to work?" Zora asked

"Nope. I'm a civil engineer, not into electronics. My job is to build and maintain the tunnels, and to keep the temperature cool and the humidity right. That's enough for me".

The larger ship was named the *Nightingale*, Majuro, IMO 3141593. Again, Zora couldn't help herself. She closed her eyes and churned through the arithmetic.

This time, try though she might, she just couldn't get the check digit to come out right. She felt mathematically defeated. She decided she would sort it out with pencil and paper when she got home; she was out of practice.

She snapped a photo of the stern of the *Nightingale* so she would not forget the number, and walked back to her truck.

17: Jeremy Special

"Melvin Prime, that's about the nicest *erythema migrans* rash I've ever seen!" Lisa exclaimed.

She was admiring the broad expanse of Mel's right buttock, on which was displayed a two-inch-wide patch of rosy-purple surrounded by an inch-wide circle of pale pink and then an outermost inch-wide circle of bright red.

Mel was too sick either to accept the praise or to feel embarrassed. He hurt all over and had a fever, and if Jeremy hadn't turned up, he might have forgotten even to drink water.

But Jeremy *had* turned up, walking into Mel's house about midnight two days after Mel was supposed take him out to his camp but hadn't done so. After a visit of an hour or two, Jeremy left Mel and had returned just now, with Lisa.

"You've got Lyme disease, Mel. We'll get you tested to make sure, but I am putting you on doxycycline right now. Take this pill, another tonight, and then morning and night, every day for 10 days. We'll go four days more if you're not way better after ten. Nineteen times out of twenty, the pills do the job and you'll soon be back to your old self. Now, I need some blood."

Mel was not a fan of needles, but he was too weak to protest or make a fuss.

"I've got to get this sample to the lab in Digby right away, or they'll insist that you come in yourself," Lisa said. "Jerry, can you stay with Mel for a few days? Marie can look after Rosie, I'll call her. Mel needs water all the time and some food, too. Water, energy and rest, Mel, that's what your body needs right now. Get Jerry to make you one of his breakfast specials when you start feeling hungry again, but keep the tea and toast going down in the mean time."

Those pills did do the job, but it seemed to take forever. Five days in, Mel still was sore all over, but not too sore now to do a little some-thing.

He got out his accordion. He hadn't played in years. He always was just too busy with other things, and the people he used to play with had died or moved away or had just given up playing for some reason, kind of like him.

But now he had the right kind of time on his hands. The old bellows still worked, no leaks, and all the buttons still produced clear notes. He started out on a few of the easy polkas he used to play, but gradually, more and more tunes came back into his head and into his fingers.

Mel was playing *John Ryan's Polka*, just about up to full dance speed, when Henry walked in to check on him.

"You never told me you played the box," he exclaimed.

Mel made excuses, hadn't played for years, was in a little ceili band once, just remembering a few tunes now.

Henry was having none of it. "You just keep playing. I'll be right back."

He was back in twenty minutes, bringing a guitar, a mandolin and Rory Willson with him.

"Sandy will be here soon, after he picks up some beer," Henry said, as he tuned his guitar and Rory got out the mandolin. "Rory plays the fiddle, too, you know, but he wouldn't bring it, and Lisa plays flute like you wouldn't believe. Too bad she's working. Strike up a tune, maes-tro!"

Mel gave *Maggie in the Woods* a go, and Henry and Rory were fully into it before he even got to the first turn. When they'd played the tune three times, Mel's fingers just took off into *John Ryan's* like in the old tune set, without him even thinking about it. Then Rory went right on into *Dennis Murphy's*, and Mel's fingers remembered that one, too.

Sandy arrived with a six-pack while they were well underway, and he got his Irish drum going about half way through the set. All eyes were on fire. Holy cow! A real house session, with Mel, the new-found dynamite box player!

They toasted the moment enthusiastically with Sandy's beer. It felt like a new beginning.

"Anything else you've been keeping from your friends, Mel?" Henry inquired. "Maybe you're this Louie Penny person everyone's wondering about, or the fella that thought up the Internet?"

Mel said he'd thought he was a crack shot with a rifle before he met Jeremy Franklin, but otherwise he'd done nothing much except be kicked by horses, pound hot metal and dig clams. Henry and Rory had played together a few times as part of their song-writing collaborations, and Rory and Lisa played together a lot, but only at home.

Henry had had no idea that Sandy played the Irish drum. "I hope you didn't trade in that gorgeous ceremonial drum of yours for this colonial aberration."

"No trade-in, Henry. I've got'em both. They're for different things. I heard an Irish bodhran in a pub in Halifax a few years ago and I liked the sound so much I took some lessons. It's my drum for tunes. The other one's my heartbeat."

After two weeks of pills and another week to let all those regular bacteria in his gut get back to normal, Mel felt as good as ever. He knew that it was the antibiotic that really had done all the work, but he figured the five music sessions in his house while he was sick must have done some good, too; kept his immune system energized and invincible, or something.

Lisa had come back for a check-up and another blood sample after two weeks. Today, she swept into the café as he and Jeremy were celebrating his return to good health with coffee and pastries, and told him that her backup MD had closed off Mel's case as "acute Lyme disease, now cured."

As Lisa dashed out again, Purley Jordan walked in and joined Jeremy and Mel. Greg, the café owner, was seated at the next table, trying to work out some clever change in menu items to improve the food side of his business.

"Didn't know you was home with Lyme disease, Mel," Purley said. "I got that last fall, but it was three months before I felt good again. I should'a went to Lisa first, or to the hospital, instead of that homeopath."

Greg was mumbling to himself over his scribbler of notes and menus.

"Are we in for a big menu change?" asked Rory, as he stood up to go back to work.

"Nope," Greg said. "I just need to confront the V-word in a small but rigorous way."

"V like Vegetarian?" Mel asked.

"V like Vegan. 'Vegetarian' food is impossible to make because every vegetarian is different: eggs yes, eggs no; dairy yes, dairy no; fish yes, fish no. Vegan, however, is absolute, and also includes nothing to offend the lesser vegetarians. Vegans eat no items of animal origin, full stop, not even honey because it's bee vomit. I need one more item that could do for breakfast or lunch, tastes really good to everyone and is vegan 100 per cent. Right now, we've got some honey-free granola and a lunch rice bowl. The pastries are all full of butter, and most other items are polluted with a bit of cheese or a crumb of bacon."

Mel got thoughtful for a minute and then turned to Jeremy, who seemed to have paid no attention to any of the conversation since they had arrived.

"What was that breakfast stuff you made for me last week, the one you eat with a spoon out of a glass, and you had to make me a second one because the first one was so good?"

Jeremy looked at Mel, but made no response.

Mel snapped his fingers with sudden insight and turned to Greg. "That's it! That's what you need in this café, a Jeremy special! Jerry, go out to Rory in the kitchen; he'll find you what you need. Make one for Greg and Purley to try."

Jeremy rose slowly and walked to the kitchen, from which a low mumbling chatter soon arose.

A few minutes later, he and Rory emerged, with Rory carrying a tray of two parfait-style glasses filled with a swirly mix of golden brown and blue. He placed one ceremoniously in front of Greg and then in front of Purley. "Your Jeremy Specials, gentlemen," he said.

Jeremy had stopped half way from the kitchen to the table and was watching Greg and Purley.

"After you, chef," Purley said. "Wouldn't want to influence your judgment."

Greg looked his over. "Nice presentation." he said. "What's the blue swirl?"

"Blueberry jam," Rory said, on Jeremy's behalf.

Greg picked up a spoon, gouged out a good mouthful, and tried it. After some internal contemplation, he took a second spoonful, and then a third.

"Is this really vegan?" he asked. "What's in it?"

Rory looked at Jeremy to see if he would answer, saw he would not, and answered for him again. "Toast, peanut butter, jam and orange juice. No butter on the toast."

"I bet a few food companies out there wish they could come up with a breakfast cereal that tastes like this," Greg said with admiration. "It's a sweet and sour peanut butter parfait."

Purley was tired of waiting, and spooned into his like a trencherman. When he had eaten just over half, he was ready to pronounce judgment. "Now, this is some good! I'd have this for breakfast any day or for lunch, too, and maybe for both on the same day. Must be easy to make; it only took you about five minutes. How do you make it?"

Rory gave a quick explanation.

"Did he say that right, Jerry?" Purley asked.

Jeremy gave a single affirmative nod and sat down at his place at the table.

Purley turned practical. "So, let's see now, in one of these you got three pieces of bread, not too fancy but maybe brown bread for health. Then you got two layers of peanut butter and two layers of jam, and maybe you serve it up with a bit more jam to get that swirl, and you got half a cup or so of orange juice and five minutes' labour. Might cost you two dollars and fifty cents to make, Greg. You could sell these for at least six bucks. Upgrade the whole thing to organic and it'll cost you three-fifty, and you can charge eight."

"Rory," said Greg, "you've got a college education. What's the right way to spell it out on the menu: a Jeremy Special or Jeremy's Special?"

18: Captain Singh

In fair summer weather, the best place to be on the Tiverton ferry, the *Petite Princess,* Halifax, IMO 9308259, is on one side or the other of the loading ramp at the forward end.

Bronwyn had no words to express how wonderful it was to see the upwellings and currents and eddies of the swirling tide, and the cormorants and eiders and guillemots letting the ferry pass close by, and the great thrum of the engines, but her arms and face told the story. Her face also told the story of the ice cream she and Rick had shared at East Ferry while awaiting their turn to cross.

Captain Surinder Singh had enjoyed some ice cream with them too, while waiting, and now he was sharing with them the too-short passage across this rippling, surging marvel of nature.

Rick and Bronwyn had met Surinder in the line-up at the ice cream window, and had discovered that he was the captain of the *Nightingale*, currently docked at White's Cove, and was in search of a cargo to take away with him when his boat would sail in a few days' time.

Surinder was on the tall side, about six feet, neither fat nor thin, with short black hair. Rick guessed his age to be about 35. He was hoping to find up to 200 tons of frozen lobster, and was headed to a potential supplier in Westport It was not the usual season, but he hoped there might be some unsold product still to be had for a good price. The *Nightingale* had large freezer units in the hold and the ship's owners were in contact with potential buyers in Boston and New York.

Surinder had no car. Johnny Tidd had taken him to East Ferry and told him just to ask on the ferry for drivers headed for Freeport and he would have no trouble getting there and on to the Westport ferry. Surinder already had made some deals with suppliers in Centerville and Meteghan, and hoped he could find enough lobster in Westport to make up a full load.

Rick invited Surinder to ride with them if he could squeeze himself into the mini-crew cab seat behind Bronwyn. They were headed for Westport, too, and probably could bring Surinder back to White's Cove at the end of the day, if they timed things right.

With an hour spent on the ferries and a slow half hour drive across Long Island, Bronwyn, Rick and Surinder had time to get to know each other. Rick was delighted to have a newcomer to tell about Digby Neck and Islands, and especially about Westport, his childhood home.

Bronwyn at first kept a close watch on the stranger with the deep voice who was facing her over the back of the seat, but soon she relaxed and shifted her attention to her collection of toys.

Surinder said he had grown up in Bermuda, but his father was Canadian, and so Surinder had dual citizenship. His parents ran a small import business in Hamilton, mostly food. Boats always had been his first love. As a teenager, he had worked as crew on sailing yachts during school vacations, and had done so full-time for three years after that, while using shore time to study for seaman and officer credentials. He had been an officer on some big container ships for five years, and also had managed to get through a university degree by correspondence during the long, lonely hours off duty.

During the past four years, Surinder had been captain on a few big sailing boats. This really was his favourite work. His last such command was six months on a three-masted barque similar to the *Endeavour*. These jobs were hard to get, though. On a visit home recently, he'd heard that the *Nightingale* needed a skipper, so he had taken a contract for a few months. The ship had been in dry dock for paint and repairs when he had signed on. This delivery to White's Cove was his first voyage in it.

It was just after ten o'clock in the morning when they drove off the ferry at Westport. They agreed to meet again on the ferry that would leave Westport at 4:25 that afternoon. Rick and Bronwyn were headed to Rick's family for a visit, a diaper change and a nap.

Captain Singh walked off to cry the town for lobsters. Rick figured Surinder likely would attract a ship-load of attention from all the women in town, too.

As far as Rick's parents were concerned, Zora, Rick and Bronwyn never could visit too often. The last visit had been in June, a month ago, so there was lots to catch up on.

Rick's mother loved to be with Bronwyn on her own, one on one, so after lunch he and his dad drove out to the western lighthouse to stare and marvel at the broad Atlantic, and then back through the village, to greet people and accumulate news and gossip. All the Westporters knew Rick, so their progress was delightfully slow.

"Well, there's Ricky. Did you bring some cheese? The store's right out of it."

"You're looking good, Rick, but not as good as you lovely wife. Where's Zora? Bring her along next time."

"Where's Bronnie? Home delighting grandma, I'll bet. We need her, too. Be sure to stop in with her before you leave."

The love of a whole community was a wonderful thing. Rick was glad he and Zora had chosen to live close to home.

Brad Henshaw came up to the truck and leaned in the open window, wide-eyed with excitement. "There's a ship's captain here buying lobsters! We thought he was just looking for a few to eat, but he said he wanted fresh-frozen and that ten tons might not be quite enough! He's doing the rounds with Aaron Thurber right now."

Surinder knew how to do business, it seemed. In a small village like Westport, any money that comes in nourishes the whole community. No wonder Brad was excited about a big sale.

By 4:25 that afternoon, Rick had taken Bronwyn on a tour among friends, and they were in the line-up for the ferry to Freeport. Surinder was having a final conversation with Aaron Thurber, and he scurried on board just before the ramp went up and the propellers surged.

Once the ferry was underway, Rick, Bronwyn and Surinder gathered at the forward end as they had on the two morning crossings. They exchanged greetings, but Surinder seemed preoccupied with his own thoughts.

The ferry steamed south close to the village before turning into the tide surging toward the Bay of Fundy. Surinder pointed to a medium-sized house near Church Street. "Do you see that house?" he said, pointing carefully.

Rick zeroed in on the house Surinder was indicating. "That's the old Thurber place," he said. "I had a crush on Jenny Thurber when I was 13."

Surinder smiled. "I bought it this afternoon," he said.

Rick was too stunned to speak.

Surinder looked at the house again, then turned back to Rick and Bronwyn. "I've never really felt at home in Bermuda. The sea is the only anchor I ever found there. I'll be at sea for the rest of my life, I suppose, but today I'm sure that this is the place I want to come home to."

Rick was surprised but rather pleased. He liked Surinder already, and would be glad to get to know him better. With this news, that friendship now seemed a real possibility.

On the way to White's Cove, Rick told Surinder something about Lansdowne Highland and Zora's veterinary work, and suggested he come for a meal and a visit some evening before the *Nightingale* sailed away.

"That must have been your wife Zora I saw on the wharf yesterday," Surinder remarked. "She was checking on the fish coming off the supply boat."

When they reached the wharf at White's Cove, Surinder extracted himself from the narrow back seat and out the driver's door, shook hands with Rick, and went around to Bronwyn's side. "I'm pleased we met each other today, Ms Bronwyn," he said. "You chose the ginger ice cream ahead of me, and so I chose it, too, and it was the best I ever had. I hope we meet again before I sail away."

Bronwyn seemed to get the gist of Surinder's farewell. She reached out and touched the tip of his nose with her finger, a sign of approval.

Surinder ran up the gangplank of the *Nightingale,* and Rick and Bronwyn headed for home.

19: Fine old steel

Rick and Zora had stumbled into bed, trying to ignore their colds and exhausted well beyond the usual, when Bronwyn awoke to a full-blown ear infection.

Rick spent that long night holding his suffering daughter, spelled off a few times by Zora, who herself had both a cold and an 8 o'clock appointment in the morning, and then four hours more in the emergency department at the Digby hospital to get the required medical attention.

Now, three days into the antibiotics for Bronwyn and mostly recovered from his own cold, Rick was just beginning to feel that he no longer was sleepwalking 24 hours a day.

He had mostly forgotten about Captain Surinder Singh, but then Surinder called him to say there were some substantial delays in his departure from White's Cove and to ask if his invitation to dinner still was open. A bit of adult conversation with someone he found interesting was an occasion Rick decided he could rise to. He checked with Zora and then said that the next evening would be a good fit.

Zora was delighted that she finally would meet this Captain Singh Rick had taken a shine to, and she proposed they also invite Henry and Anita, since they had not seen Henry for ages, and she wanted to get to know Anita better.

Pizza would do for everyone. If Rick could make up the dough, she could do the rest.

Rick arrived at White's Cove to pick up Surinder at five o'clock the next evening. As he drove up and over the ridge, he could see that the fish farm was growing. Some new tank buildings were going up, and land had been cleared and graded for several more.

He drove down to the wharf beside the *Nightingale*, and Surinder soon walked down the gangplank, carrying a heavy box. He plunked the box into the back of the truck with a pronounced thud.

"You told me you had a blacksmith friend," he said. "I brought some pieces of fine, old steel I thought he might like to play with. Let me show you something on board before we go."

Surinder led Rick up the gangplank and around to the far side of the ship, and pointed up to the top of the bridge.

"Look what that Aaron Thurber brought me!"

A large wooden dory, maybe 18 feet long, built in the Lunenburg style with wooden knees, was roped upside down to the cabin roof. It was painted traditional 'dory buff' yellow, and looked in perfect shape.

"That's what the Grand Bankers used to fish from," Surinder enthused. "I remarked on a dory like that when Aaron was driving me around Westport, and he up and brought me this one two days later. I'm going to take it with me to mess around in whenever my ship is in a port. It's a beauty, don't you think? I got the oars tied inside and it even has a small mast and sail."

Rick looked the dory over with admiration. He had rowed boats like that all over Westport harbour when he was a kid. A big one like Surinder's could hold a ton of fish. He'd love to have one himself.

On the way back to Lansdowne, Surinder explained the delay in his departure. The Beluga Group technicians had insisted on unloading the ship themselves. They were especially careful, but nonetheless had managed to drop the twenty-foot sea container into the hold from a height of about fifteen feet.

It really wasn't their fault. The ship's generator suddenly had failed, and the winch lost power at a critical moment.

The container had broken open. About twenty-five metal barrels were inside, held in place by 2" by 2" steel bars welded together into a grid. Only one barrel had toppled out, but the container was too damaged to use to hoist out the rest.

The ship's crew had cut through the steel two-by-twos with a torch so the barrels could be taken out one at a time.

"Now, I have to get the generator fixed before we can get those barrels out of the hold."

A company from Yarmouth was coming to do the repairs tomorrow or the next day.

"That steel we had to cut away is wonderful heavy, solid stuff.

That's why I saved some of it. Once the barrels are off the ship, the technicians want us to hoist the broken container out of the hold and dump it overboard as far from the wharf as the ship's crane can reach. They figure that's the easiest way to get rid of it."

Rick said, "Mel will be pleased as punch with such an unexpected gift."

Before the pizzas went into the oven, Anita asked Zora for a quick tour of the cows and la fromagerie, and of her veterinary clinic at the back of the house.

As they toured and talked, Anita found Zora and Rick's enterprises to be inspiring. Imagine creating a classy cheese business from nothing but an idea and a few grassy meadows, as Rick's Uncle Gilles had done and Rick and Zora had continued, or making a mixed animal practice succeed in remote Bear River.

"Your businesses here are exceptional accomplishments," she exclaimed over the rhubarb and strawberry desert. "I'm working on some documentaries about life in western Nova Scotia in these changing times. Zora, how would you and Rick feel about being included in a documentary about the new economies that are developing here?"

Bronwyn suddenly howled from her crib, and Rick excused himself.

Zora, left to answer the question, said, "We would not look forward to being on TV. If you really think there is value for others in telling these stories, I suppose we would try to help. We don't want to be portrayed somehow as being special people, though, because we aren't. Uncle Gilles and the farm might be the best topic to start with."

Rick had advised Surinder to bring along his toothbrush and pyjamas, because Rick did not fancy driving him back to White's Cove at two o'clock in the morning.

The next day, while they were at breakfast, the repair crew for the ship's generator called Surinder to say they would arrive about 10 o'clock. Before Rick and Bronwyn left to bring Surinder back to his ship, he stowed the box of 2" steel bars in the storage room that served both the house and the clinic. The bars could stay there until there was an opportunity to give them to Mel.

As they drove back to White's Cove, Rick asked, "Where will your ship head after you leave here?"

"My instructions are to load up with frozen lobsters and take them to Boston or New York, the actual destination to be determined by the ship's owners once we are under way. I've never worked for these people before. The company seems to be a piece of a larger conglomerate. They seem kind of fickle to me. I won't be surprised if my instructions change a few times."

20: Worth their weight in lobsters

Zora sat down with pencil and paper, and began calculating that annoying check digit that had defeated her. She had forgotten all about it, but it had come back to haunt her after Surinder's visit and all the talk about seafaring and ships.

She was glad they had not tried to play the IMO game that evening. She wanted to get her confidence back first. She was doubly annoyed, really—annoyed at the defeat, yes, but even more annoyed that she was being so silly and obsessive about the stupid number! But she was.

Zora did not remember the IMO number on the *Nightingale*, but she knew she had taken a photo of it the day she did her first inspection of the White's Cove fish farm. She scrolled through the photos on her phone and finally found it, mixed in with some photos of the supply boat unloading salmon smolts.

There was the stern of Surinder's ship: *Nightingale*, Majuro, IMO 3141593.

Okay, she thought, *how does this work? (7X3) + (6x1) + (5x4) + (4x1) + (3x3) + (2x9) equals 21 + 6 + 20 + 4 + 15 + 18 equals ... 84.*

The check digit should be 4. But it wasn't; it was 3. How was that possible?

She did the calculation again, and then made herself do it in her head. It came out to 4 each time.

She was supposed to be doing her weekly financial accounts while Rick was doing the laundry, and here she was playing the IMO game instead.

She went in search of Rick, to make sure that he would get the same answer as she had, and folded diapers and entertained Bronwyn while he stared at the number for a minute or two.

"The check digit is wrong. It should be 4," he finally said. "Where did this number come from?"

"It's the IMO painted on Surinder's ship," Zora said. "I saw the IMO on the supply boat and just had to play the game. It came out right. Then I tried Surinder's, but I couldn't get it to come out right. I thought it was just me. I meant to work it out on paper as soon as I got home so I took a photo to record the number. Then I forgot all about it until last night, when Surinder was here talking about ships."

She showed Rick the photo. There it was, plain as plain.

Rick said slowly, "Why does Surinder have a false IMO on his ship? Does he even know? Would he know a false check digit if he saw one? Do captains pay attention to this sort of thing? Didn't Wolf say he'd found the same number on two different ships, the old *Reaper* and another one?"

They stared at the photo together. Rick noticed the big sea container chained to the deck of Surinder's ship. It was old and rusty, but there was a bright white patch on one corner.

He zoomed in the photo, and they could see that the white patch was a bar code of some kind.

~

Surinder was impatient to get his ship underway again. The generator was fixed, and the fish farm cargo was off-loaded. The freezer compartments were down to -20°C and were ready to receive frozen lobster.

However, the ship's owners had not yet paid for the lobster cargo he'd found for them, telling the suppliers please just to hold on to the lobsters while payment was arranged.

Surinder and his crew spent their down time well, however, reviewing the state of maintenance on board, doing repairs and painting, servicing the many electric motors and doing general clean-up.

As the delay continued, he and the crew turned to reviewing their safety equipment: fire extinguishers, fire hoses and pumps, connections, valves, emergency shut-off switches, backup bilge pumps, and hatch seals. They reconnected the marine transceiver that seemed have come unplugged at some point, ran through all the safety checks on the big, self-deploying life raft, and tried on their new survival suits.

Ships like the *Nightingale,* registered in countries of convenience, don't often carry survival suits for the crew, but Surinder prided himself on always having them ready to use on his ships. He would bury their cost somehow, and owners seldom noticed.

Aaron Thurber had looked around and found some used suits for him, in serviceable condition and complete with fitted life jackets. Their certifications for "262"—survival for at least six hours in water as cold as 2°C—still were valid. "I figure they're worth their weight in lobsters," Aaron had said, "and that's how I'll charge them to the owners in the lobster manifest.".

And still they waited.

The next morning, the *Wagamama* pulled in and docked behind the *Nightingale.* Five passengers eventually emerged onto the wharf. Four seemed to be 30-something men of military bearing, and the fifth was a woman of greater but uncertain age who clearly was in command of the group.

She went directly to Trudy Denton's site management trailer, and then to the tunnel entrance into which she was admitted and into which she ushered the four men.

Ten minutes later, she left the tunnel, accompanied by two of the resident technicians, and came directly to the *Nightingale* and up to the bridge.

Surinder greeted her. "What can I do for you?"

"I am the Beluga Group," she said. "We own this ship. A damaged container was dropped over the side of this ship after unloading it. It is not acceptable. It must be retrieved and placed back on this ship. These technicians will retrieve it. I will inspect also the place in the ship where the container was dropped and spilled its cargo. Take me there now."

The woman did not seek Surinder's agreement, only his service as a guide. She was wearing a grey pant suit and practical shoes, and carried a leather bag that might have been her purse.

She had no trouble with the steep companionway stairs. She demanded the details of the accident and the rescue of the barrels from outside and inside the container. She placed something that looked like a cell phone on the floor at the place where Surinder said the one barrel had tumbled out. After several minutes of further inspection, she retrieved her device, looked at it's screen, and put it back in her bag.

She turned to Surinder. "You will be sailing soon. You must keep the damaged container on the ship until we send you instructions on what to do with it."

With that, she climbed up out of the hold and onto the wharf.

The crew of the *Nightingale* helped the Beluga technicians retrieve the damaged container. The warm summer nearshore water was turbid, but the ship had not moved since the container went overboard and it did not take long to catch hold of it with two grapnel hooks and to winch it back to the surface and up onto the deck of the ship.

The woman watched from the wharf until the broken container was retrieved. "Chain it down well," she said, and walked back to the tunnel entrance.

The walls of the container had collapsed like a cardboard box with its sides partially cut apart. Surinder helped the crew secure it in place.

On the inside of one of the container's walls, he noticed that a word he did not recognize had been written but then lightly painted over, so it showed through weakly with fuzzy edges. "МАЯК" it said.

On Russian nautical charts, that means a lighthouse, he remembered. *Everything is being recycled these days; why not rusty old containers that once served lighthouses?*

While the damaged container was being retrieved, the crew of the *Wagamama* had offloaded a few pallets of fish feed and a small collection of suitcases and duffel bags. The four men who had arrived on the boat came from the tunnel entrance, picked up the luggage, and headed for the residence trailers that had been installed for the technicians. At about the same time, the original crew of technicians, whose last job had been to unload the *Nightingale*, emerged from those trailers carrying their own suitcases, walked to the wharf and placed them in the net to be lowered down to the *Wagamama*.

A change of personnel, Surinder thought.

Trudy had come out on the porch of her office trailer and seemed to be saying farewell to the departing crew and chatting with the new arrivals, who also were watching their departure. The grey-suited woman left the tunnel, walked to the *Wagamama* climbed aboard, and the supply boat departed.

~

Olga O'Grady's surpassing wealth and influence were due largely to her understanding of the risks posed by evidence and how to dispose of those risks. Her dosimeter had detected very little radiation in the hold of the *Nightingale*, but there should have been none.

She had anticipated this potential problem, however, and its solution. The technicians could go back to their regular work, and the mercenaries now were in place, temporary foreign workers secured by chains of financial need and criminal documentation. There was a contract for the engineer. Overall, the project was on schedule.

The first delivery of frozen lobster came early the next morning. Surinder had been notified only an hour before.

The three suppliers sent truckloads, and by evening the freezer compartments of the *Nightingale* were full. The ship was due in Gloucester, near Boston, at mid-day two days hence.

Surinder received word he was to add some fuel to his reserves while in Nova Scotia and then depart. The diesel arrived the next morning and the *Nightingale* departed at noon.

Surinder had hoped to visit Rick and Zora again, but it was not to be.

Once he was in the shipping lane and his course was set, Surinder telephoned Rick to express his regrets and say farewell until his next visit to Westport. They chatted for a while and then Rick remembered the error in the IMO number he and Zora had discovered.

"Do you know that you have an incorrect IMO number on the back of the *Nightingale*?" Rick asked.

"What's wrong with the IMO?"

"The check digit is wrong."

"The what?"

. Rick explained that he and Zora had learned a kind of check digit game from their friend Wolf Wylie, and that they really had no idea how IMOs were used in the shipping world.

"I never heard of the check digit," Surinder said. "No one except maybe marine traffic control officers pay much attention to IMOs, and they get them from the transceiver signal, not from the stern of the ship."

Surinder seemed to be in a mood to chat. Bronwyn was napping, so

Rick could relax and enjoy the conversation.

Surinder gave Rick a full account of the visit by the authoritarian woman from the Beluga Group who had made everyone snap to attention, the change over of technicians, the dredging up the broken container from the seabed, and how he had found the Russian word for lighthouse on an inside panel, painted over but still evident.

"Like some kind of palimpsest," he said.

"Like a what?"

"It means something that's been covered up, but you can still see some part of it. It's a great word. That college degree I got by correspondence was in English literature. *Gnomon* is another great word, starts with a 'gn.'" He laughed, "Look it up."

He told Rick that everything started to happen as soon as the Beluga woman had departed: lobsters, instructions, fuel, as if she had snapped her fingers that it was time for his ship to leave. All good, as far as he was concerned!

"Rick, that western light is astern now. I had better get back to running my ship."

They agreed to keep in touch.

"The internet is so important to marine commerce now," Surinder said, "that even small ships like mine have a good connection via satellites. So we can easily communicate, no matter where the ship is."

After Surinder took his leave, Bronwyn was awake again and ready for action. They needed to inspect the re-seeded hay meadow to see how the new mix of grasses and legumes was growing. Lansdowne Highland had high hopes that they might be able to grow hay with a very high nutrition density, and this was their first attempt.

As he changed Bronwyn and gave her a snack of milk and peanut butter on bread, Rick tried to picture the steel-grey woman from the Beluga Group whom Surinder had described. He always had imagined that the company had taken its name from the little white whale that had become such a cultural icon for children in Canada.

This seemed a poor fit now. He mused that perhaps it was the fish, not the whale, that this company had named itself after, the great white sturgeon of the Volga River, nearly extinct from human greed, the world's largest predatory bony fish, whose caviar sold on the black market for $5000 a pound.

21: Text Lisbon

Portugal? Seriously!?

That was indeed what the new message from the *Nightingale's* owners said. The ship was only two hours away from its destination in Gloucester when Surinder learned of this change in plan. His load of frozen lobster now was to be delivered to an agent in Portugal, 3000 miles east across the Atlantic.

"Yo ho ho! the wind blows free; Oh, for the life on the ro-o-olling sea," he sang to himself. Change always was in the wind.

In truth, it mattered not at all to him. A bit of shore time in Lisbon was a pleasing prospect. With the fuel he had taken on in Nova Scotia, he had more than enough to get there, and plenty of food and water, too.

He charted a great circle route to Lisbon and turned the *Nightingale* 45 degrees to port.

For the next thirty hours, the *Nightingale* had to keep a sharp watch for small craft and fishing boats until it reached deep water at the edge of the continental shelf. There was thick fog along the way, too. Surinder put a crew member right at the bow as a lookout and another on radar full time until the *Nightingale* was well beyond the fishing and shipping zones of the Northeast Channel and Brown's Bank.

It was about two o'clock in the morning when the ship reached a location 100 miles beyond the continental shelf, and the high vigilance against possible collisions could be relaxed. They were in a zone of clear sailing now, and everyone could get some regular sleep again.

Surinder called the crew up to the bridge to reset the watches and the work schedule for the next ten days. The ship's owners had instructed him to send a text message to the Lisbon office once the ship was well out into international waters and headed across the Atlantic.

While the crew made their way to the bridge, he looked up the text number he was told to use, keyed it in, typed a short confirmatory message about his estimated time of arrival in Lisbon, and pressed the send button.

The *Nightingale* exploded.

The sabotage had been planned by experts. Explosive charges blew four large holes in the hull below the water line, and the ship immediately began to fill and sink. The engine room flooded within 30 seconds, and all power was lost. No distress signal could be sent.

When the crew deployed the life raft, it flew apart in fragments.

The temperature of the surface water at their present location in the Labrador Current was just below freezing; a vigorous swimmer might survive in it for twenty minutes. The seabed was two and a half miles down.

Within fifteen minutes, the ship was being prevented from sinking only by the air retained in the hold, and the cables of the hold covers were starting to snap.

Few plans are perfect, however. The saboteurs had not anticipated the presence of survival suits for captain and crew, or the 18-foot wooden dory lashed to the roof of the wheel house.

When the ship exploded, Surinder had no idea what had happened, but very quickly understood that his ship was sinking fast. The survival suits were in the chart room on the bridge, and he ordered everyone into them and their life jackets. He knew immediately that their only chance of survival lay with his old fishing dory.

He ordered the crew to the roof of the bridge to prepare the dory for launch. He donned his own survival suit and vest, grabbed what food and water he could see on the bridge, and forced open the outer door against the rising water. He rushed up the ladder to the roof as the sea rushed in to claim the wheelhouse.

Surinder ordered his three crewmen into the dory while he and the engineer frantically cut away the remaining rope lashings and attachments. They were waist-deep in water when the dory finally was completely free, and they clung to its gunwales as the roof of the bridge sank beneath their feet and the *Nightingale* began its long and final journey to the ocean floor.

The crew hauled Surinder and the engineer aboard, and they all sat in the dory in silence, shocked and bewildered, trying to assimilate what just had happened.

There was only a light breeze, and the ten-foot ocean swells were so widely spaced that the ocean surface seemed almost flat. Light, ghostly fog drifted past, just barely visible in the light of the waning gibbous moon. Each man sat expressionless, lost in imagining when and how each of them now would die.

Surinder was the first to break through the spell cast on them by their near-death experience. He looked around the dory. Their total of life-saving supplies was the three bottles of water and two boxes of crackers he had found on the bridge.

There were no leaks in the dory. Somehow a plastic bucket had made it on board; it could serve as a bailer if needed; and a toilet, too, he supposed.

He thought about his childhood hero, Joshua Slocum. What would the great captain do in a mess like this? Slocum would find some way to get himself and his crew to shore alive, that's what he would do. But how?

Surinder snapped to full attention. Their dory was not the only object floating on the nearby ocean. Sections of the torn-apart life raft were scattered around them. That raft would have contained enough food and water for eight people to survive for ten days.

Surinder was on the forward seat, the usual rowing seat for a fishing dory. He took up one pair of oars, put the thole pins in place, and shouted, "All hands, look alive. Debris to starboard. Bring it alongside." He began rowing the dory toward the nearest raft fragment.

The crew, startled out of their despair, slipped mechanically into their roles as crew members doing the captain's bidding. When they reached the first piece of life raft, Surinder told them to search through it for anything it might contain.

It was hard work twisting and hauling and tearing and cutting a way into what had been the inside compartment of the raft, but the first items retrieved were 5-gallon containers of water— four of them.

This unimaginable treasure brought with it a first real glimmer of hope.

It took two hours to search through all the raft fragments they could locate, but they were rewarded with another twenty gallons of water, a compass, a first-aid kit, eighty military day rations, and two fishing lines with some hooks and lures. The old dory had not held such a good catch in many a year.

All five survivors sat quietly and pondered the same question: *What now?*

Dawn gradually brought full daylight and made the shifting fog banks visible. Soon, however, the fog lifted entirely, and they could see the vast expanse of the Atlantic Ocean extending forever in every direction.

Surinder nursed his own thoughts for a long time, and then finally broke the general silence. "We were scuppered. I don't know why, but nothing on the ship could have exploded like that. But we're okay, and we are going to stay okay. Your ancestors could navigate a thousand miles between Pacific islands they couldn't see by keeping track of the waves on the sea and the stars on the horizon. I guess we ought to be able to navigate 150 miles straight north to Sable Island in a seaworthy dory with the North Star and a compass to help us. There's a coast guard station and a national park office there. We've got rations for two weeks, but we can get there in one."

The crew did not know they could be so far off shore yet so close to apparent safety, and their spirits changed from dark foreboding to quiet determination. Two men could row at once and they could keep that up night and day by taking turns.

At that moment, there was a moderate southwest wind. "Let's try that little sail," the engineer said.

As they set it up, they discovered it was a bamboo-battened sail of the kind used on Chinese junks and the like, practically unheard of in Westport Nova Scotia, but wonderfully easy to use and practical for an open dory. They set one oar in the socket carved into the stern railing for steering, fastened the stays of the short mast to the risings, hoisted up the small sail and slowly gathered headway due north on a broad reach.

Surinder settled into the stern seat for the first steering watch, the oar under one arm, the small compass tied securely to the seat beside him. He was deeply worried for them—so much could happen between here and Sable Island—but he also felt that he was living a page out of one of his hero's stories. He was leaving a wrecked ship with his crew alive and well, being pulled by a battened sail toward safety.

He thought of Joshua Slocum again, and wondered if he had measured up to The Captain's expectations. In Slocum's honour, he decided to name his dory the *Liberdade*.

22: Two miles down

The *Slocum Warrior* had been on station at the edge of the Sargasso Sea for almost three months. Today, the crew were tracking seven suspect boats off the west coast of Africa while also scanning the whole north and south Atlantic for anything that might be illegal fishing.

Of the original crew, only Wolf remained on board. Two weeks ago, a British navy frigate on a training voyage had provided transportation for a crew change to and from the Bahamas.

On his shifts at the surveillance consoles, Wolf occasionally would focus his instruments on the Bay of Fundy as a way of feeling in touch with his old home. The ferries from Digby and Yarmouth always provided some action to watch, and there was modest commercial shipping to and from Saint John.

Today, a new transceiver signal popped up off the tip of Digby Neck, moving west. Wolf was surprised he had not seen it sail into the Bay, but there it was, sailing out. He looked up the ship in the transceiver directory and had a second surprise – it was the *Cahow*!

There was no record in the marine traffic databases of the *Cahow* sailing away from Bermuda in the past month, but sometimes those transceivers stop working or aren't turned on when they should be. What was the *Cahow* doing in the Bay of Fundy? Wolf decided to keep a watch on it.

The *Cahow* sailed southwest well off the New England coast, as if headed for Boston. Before it got there, however, it suddenly turned and headed straight east, as if bound for Europe instead.

Wolf's watch ended as the *Cahow* was part way across the Gulf of Maine. His next turn at the surveillance screens was at midnight the following day. An hour later, after he had run through the inventory of boats currently under intense surveillance, he decided to check in on the *Cahow*. He found it about 450 miles out on its eastward course, heading right into the deep Atlantic. *Eight days to Europe in good weather*, he thought.

He turned his attention back to rogue fishing surveillance, replaying and analyzing the movement of a big vessel his crew believed to be a factory ship processing fish for an off-shore fleet of smaller boats from China, all working off the coast of South Georgia Island, six thousand miles to the south. The tracking data available to the *Warrior* for that part of the ocean had suddenly gotten much better when the new British naval officer had joined the crew, and it was very clear now that the fleet was fishing illegally in a British economic zone that was closed to all fishing.

Whether anything could be done to stop it, at that remote location, was another matter. It was August, and those boats would be catching lots of adult king penguins, too, if they were setting gill nets, which they surely would be. It made Wolf sick to think of all that drowning. He turned back to check on the *Cahow*, to give himself a break.

But there was no *Cahow*. The signal was gone.

It was pitch dark at their longitude and the weather maps showed intermittent fog for the area where the ship should have been. The satellite images he had access to would be of no use in fog.

He woke the French officer who had access to surveillance data that even the British couldn't match. She needed a few minutes to wake up and understand Wolf's concern.

"Yes, we track everything within 500 kilometres of French territory," she said, "including from St-Pierre-et-Miquelon. Let me see."

It took twenty minutes for her to gain access to the information she was looking for, but finally she said, "Yes, there it is. 01h30 Atlantic Daylight Time today, a small ship is here."

On the map on her screen, she pointed to a spot off the continental shelf of Nova Scotia. "The name of the ship is *Cahow*, for IMO it says only 'unknown or error.' It is registered in the Marshall Islands. At 02h00 it is seven kilometres further east. At 02h15, it is no longer present."

She typed on her keyboard again. "It is an iceberg zone, but no ice bergs are in that area now."

Wolf was perplexed. Here was yet another mysterious disappearance of a ship, first it was the *Grim Reaper*, then the *Taeyang-Wang*, and now the *Cahow*. There was not much he could do about it; his boat was 2000 miles away.

"Can you report this disappearance in an official way, so it will get some further attention?" he asked the officer.

"Yes, right now, to our French Navy. They will respond in some way, but I don't know how."

Wolf sighed. He had to leave it there. Drowned penguins and the pillage of the seas were on his mind.

He powered up the engines and set the *Slocum Warrior* on a course out of the Sargasso Sea and south toward the Antarctic convergence, 7000 miles away.

23: Pigs

At six o'clock in the morning, Bronwyn announced that her day had begun. Rick and Zora could hardly believe it. Bronnie had been asleep for ten hours straight. Both grandmothers had told them that this moment would come, but they never had imagined it really could be true.

Zora fetched Bronwyn to their bed in the hope that she could nurse and cuddle her into another hour of rest for herself and of sleep for Rick. At 6:30, however, Bronwyn demanded action.

After breakfast, Zora was off on her first veterinary calls. Rick whisked Bronwyn up onto his shoulders and out to the dairy barns to begin a busy day.

A quick consultation with Jérôme Weaver about hay, and a drink of Lansdowne Highland's finest milk, fresh from the pasteurizer, and they headed off to Clarence in the old truck, Bronwyn's favourite, for a load of newly-made hay that would supplement what Lansdowne Highland grew for itself. What with loading the bales, and a stop to play in a park in Paradise, the round trip took three hours.

Bronwyn kept busy cycling through the box of toys attached to her seat and listening to Rick sing along to her current favourite collection of Woody Guthrie songs. "Put your hand on your head, on your head..."

Timing was critical today, because Rick had agreed to an interview with Anita St-Pierre at two that afternoon. As it turned out, Bronwyn had just drifted off into her afternoon nap when Anita knocked at the door.

They set up with a voice recorder and coffee at the kitchen table, far enough from Bronwyn's room that their conversation would not invite her curiosity, but close enough that she easily could call attention to herself if need be.

Anita knew the basic story of Lansdowne Highland, built up by

Rick's Uncle Gilles with his big lottery win, and passed on to Rick as sole owner and proprietor only a few years ago, when Uncle Gilles had chosen suicide among his beloved cows over living a few additional years with increasing debilities and pain.

"This farm is amazing, Rick," she said. "Everywhere you look in Canada, the farming mantra seems to be 'get big or get out,' and those big farms mostly are lonely places, run by one or two people indentured to bank loans. Your farm isn't big at all, and it's full of people, almost like a small village. There were ten cars parked over by the barns when I arrived, and other workers I know live right next door. It's a lively place. Bronwyn won't have to go far to find playmates."

"They're great neighbours, that's for sure," Rick said.

"This Gilles Comeau, your Uncle Gilles, somehow he was able to build up this farm successfully at a time when most farms in western Nova Scotia were going out of business. Do you think your uncle had some special insights or genius that made Lansdowne Highland work out so well?"

Rick pondered Anita's question for quite a while.

"I can only speculate," he finally said. "I didn't really know my uncle very well. Growing up, I only saw him once or twice a year, at family events. I think the origin story of Lansdowne Highland probably was a dream in Uncle Gilles's head, or maybe more like a vision, a vision of general happiness he'd held on to from when he was a child."

"What do you think that vision was?"

"Uncle Gilles and my mother grew up on a long, narrow strip of land in Meteghan Centre that ran inland from the shore of St. Mary's Bay through some cleared meadows and gardens, and on to a long two miles of forest. Their family was still part of the old subsistence economy, and the oxen and cows in the barn and fields were the linchpins of community and prosperity. Those animals turned poor grass and bushes into food, and fertilized the soil. Oxen tilled the land, cut and raked and hauled in the winter hay, brought firewood to the home and timbers to the shore to build boats and weirs. The neighbours all lived the same way, and everyone depended on everyone else in one way or another, year round."

"Do you think he was trying to re-create that way of life with this farm?"

"Well, I think that way of interdependent living was Uncle Gilles's model for happiness. When he found himself with a big bag of money in his hands, he must have set out to recreate a version of that happiness that would work in the 21st century. He was a do-it-yourself-er who worked things out as he went along. I think what he wanted was to live and work in a community of friends, and he set aside being a rich man in favour of building that kind of community."

"How do you mean?"

"Well, he invested his money in something that everyone involved could be a part of. Where he grew up, if a neighbour somehow made enough money to buy a new hay mower, then that mower would cut everyone's hay, not just the owner's. On his new farm, everyone got good wages with benefits and a pension plan, and he paid himself the same as he paid them. The farm still runs that way."

"Really! I bet there's not another business in the province that works that way, not in this age of greed. The fishery certainly doesn't; I've been talking to fishermen. I bet a good few wish it did."

"I never talk about this off the farm, if I can help it," Rick said. "It makes wealthy people angry and everyone else jealous."

"Does everyone on the farm get paid the same?" Anita asked.

"No, but there's only a small difference between lowest and highest salaries. Edgar, the master cheesemaker, earns the most. As farm manager, I earn the same as Jérôme Weaver, the dairy boss. The farm pays Zora for her veterinary work, but she does not get a salary. Zora and everyone on salary also are the directors of the company. We make all the big decisions together."

"What was the last big decision the directors made?" Anita asked.

"Pigs!" said Rick, "Come have a look."

He cocked an ear up the stairs in Bronwyn's direction, and then hurried Anita out the door and over to a quarter-acre of roughly-tilled ground surrounded by a one-wire electric fence. Four black and brown pigs came over to greet them and demand gentle scratching on noses and ears.

"They're Berkshire/Hampshire crosses that Zora got as payment for some veterinary work she did up the Valley," Rick said. "We're looking for some way to make use of all the whey left over from cheese-making. First, we tried making a Norwegian-style whey cheese and it turned out really well, but we couldn't find a market for it. So, now we're using it as feed for a few pigs."

Rick said that Lansdowne Highland produced enough whey to grow out quite a herd of pigs, but they needed other foods to go along with it. They'd estimated that the clean vegetable waste from all of their gardens and kitchens could provide all the additional food six pigs would need, so now they were trying to raise four of them on whey and vegetable peelings as a first experiment.

The pigs would become part of the meat side of Lansdowne Highland's business, half of which went to food banks and half to the same upscale specialty markets as their cheeses.

As they walked back to the house from the pigs, Zora drove into the farmyard and backed her truck up to the kitchen door. She came running over to say hello to Anita, and to ask if she and Rick could help her unload a few heavy items. She was practically bouncing off the ground with delight as she told them about the X-ray equipment she had just acquired, a gift from Dr. Proulx in Port George.

Fifteen years ago, Dr. Proulx had been a country vet like Zora, but gradually, his farm animal practice had disappeared, and he had gone to work in a nearby pet clinic. Zora's determination to make a country practice work had warmed his heart, and he had become a mentor and advisor to her from time to time.

Today, he had called her to ask if she would like to have the X-ray equipment he had brought with him when he had joined the pet practice, and which now they were replacing with the latest in digital radiography. Zora was ecstatic!

They lugged the heavy stationary table and X-ray generator right into the clinic at the back of the house, and retired to an outbuilding the small and feeble unit it was replacing.

"One day, I hope I can afford a digital sensor, too," Zora said to Anita. "But for us, this is a big improvement. The gift from Dr. Proulx included a big stack of unopened boxes of film, developing chemicals and an automated processor. Zora could hardly believe her good fortune.

Their storage room already was quite full of everything needed in the clinic and in the house, but by distributing the boxes of film into different corners, they got it all in.

Anita thanked Rick for this first interview and took her leave while Zora called Amanda, the new veterinary nurse, to tell her about the gift of equipment and to ask her if she could spend an extra half day tomorrow morning setting it all up, something Amanda could do far more expertly than could she.

Zora then headed over to the dairy and la fromagerie to take care of the weekly bacteria swabs and other public health checks.

Rick re-arranged the storage room to make sure the things he needed every day in the house were not buried under stacks of film and chemicals, and then went to the washer to retrieve and hang out the clean diapers. They came in an array of colours and Rick thought they made the clothesline look like the strings of coloured signal flags military ships decked themselves out with on formal dress-up occasions.

As the last diaper went on the line, Bronwyn sang out a loud and hungry greeting to the afternoon.

24: A dinner guest

Zora stopped in at the White's Cove fish farm on her way back from her bi-weekly satellite clinic at Freeport. Her contract with the Beluga Group called for a routine visit every two weeks, so this combination was perfect, easily done together on the same day.

Parker Churchill was the only person at the farm that afternoon. Johnny Tidd was on a two-week holiday, and construction on the new buildings and pens had halted temporarily so the carpenters could earn windfall wages doing urgent repairs to summer homes. The Beluga Group was in no great hurry to expand the farm, apparently, and this seemed like good planning to Zora.

The smolts in the active pens had done well so far, but still had many months to go before reaching market weight.

Parker said, "The Beluga guys tell me that all the computer stuff down in the tunnels has been tested and works just fine, but its not plugged in to the farm yet, so Johnny and me still do all the feeding and testing. Last week we had a problem getting the seawater up through the pipe in the bore hole, but Trudy got it figured out and fixed without having to go into the tunnels. Even she isn't allowed in there no more."

Zora looked over his test records and time sheets, then walked down the hill to the cove to check in with Trudy and report that all was well from the veterinary standpoint.

The *Wagamama* was just arriving, and she and Trudy watched it approach the wharf and tie up.

"I got a message this morning that someone from upper management would arrive on the supply boat today." Trudy said. "That must be her there."

A woman about their own age had popped up the ladder and onto the wharf. She was well-dressed, with an expensive-looking handbag from which she took a small pair of binoculars. She looked at a cormorant perched on a nearby rock, then made a note in a small book, and walked briskly up to the office trailer.

"You must be Miss Denton," she said in perfect upper-crust English as she reached the deck where Trudy and Zora were standing. "I am Juanita O'Grady, from the Beluga Group. And you?" she said, turning to Zora and scanning her quickly.

"I'm the farm vet, just making a routine visit."

"Are either of you twitchers, bird watchers?" Juanita asked. "Is that cormorant over there a double-crested cormorant?"

Zora glanced at the bird and confirmed that it was.

Juanita O'Grady turned back to Trudy. "We'll begin at once then, shall we? And I will need accommodation for three or four nights, so please arrange that also."

She opened the door and stepped into the office.

Trudy rolled her eyes, but Zora took the hint and walked back up the hill to her truck.

Trudy waved goodbye to her, and gave another energetic wave to one of the technicians, Anton, who was smoking outside the tunnel entrance. He tossed his head and waved back. Lately, Anton had been finding ways to spend time with Trudy. He seemed to have a crush on her, and she was inclined to encourage it, although she really was not sure her job would last much longer, despite it being 'permanent.' There really was almost nothing for her to do these days.

But Juanita was waiting. She told Trudy that the Beluga Group had made her responsible for all of its fish farms in Canada, and she had come to make a detailed assessment of the White's Cove farm and its plans for expansion. She wished to start immediately.

It already was five o'clock in the afternoon, but Juanita made it clear that regular working hours meant nothing to her.

Trudy spent two hours showing her, on blueprints, how the tunnels had been created with mining techniques developed on the hard rock of the Canadian Shield. She explained the final configuration with internal compartments, walls, barriers and security precautions. The one-of-a-kind patented electronic controls that eventually would fully automate the farm were in a series of inner refrigerated chambers and entry to these chambers required authorization she herself did not have.

She took Juanita to the tunnel entrance and waited outside with Anton while a technician gave her a brief tour of the future control room. She then took Juanita up to the fish farm building on top of the ridge. Parker had gone home for the day, but Trudy was able to give a general explanation of how it all worked, and Juanita seemed to find matters satisfactory.

When the fish farm tour was complete, it was 9:30 pm, an hour after sunset. "Please take me to the nearest hotel now," Juanita said.

Oh dear, Trudy thought. "The nearest hotel is quite far away, in Digby. It's 25 miles from here. You must be hungry by now, too, and no restaurant will be open by the time we get to Digby. Why don't you come to my place, just a few minutes away, for a drink and light supper, and I'll take you into Digby after that?"

Such a personal invitation seemed to catch Juanita off guard. She stumbled for words, but then stopped and simply accepted the offer.

Trudy's home was one of the old and modestly-elegant houses on the rise above the brook and harbour of Little River. They left Juanita's suitcase in the car. Trudy ushered Juanita in, pointed out the washroom and busied herself in the kitchen to organize some kind of a quick meal.

Juanita seemed momentarily captivated by the homey surroundings. There were photos on a mantelpiece, of parents and grandparents and nieces and nephews, and a striking painting of Little River harbour at low tide done with thick paint and a palette knife.

Trudy stepped into the living room. "Can I offer you a drink? I often sit down with a jigger of rum when I get home after a busy day, but I have a good collection of wine and beer too, and I made some raspberry juice the other day that is wonderful with soda water."

Juanita had to tear herself away from the family memorabilia and struggled to remember what Trudy had just asked. Then she brightened up. "I'd love a glass of wine if you have one. Do you have red?"

With an hors d'oeuvre of pickled herring on cream crackers, followed by some Lansdowne Highland bratwurst, new potatoes, a salad from Trudy's garden and the two pieces of left-over strawberry-rhubarb pie, it was a lovely meal.

Juanita seemed to come out of a shell as they sat together. She wanted to know about Trudy's life, and seemed a touch wistful as she listened to Trudy's account of her happy existence.

For her part, Juanita cautiously admitted she was raised in England, mostly in boarding schools and a stint at St. Andrews University. She did data analysis for a large company now, one that included the Beluga Group.

By the middle of her third glass of wine, Juanita had dropped some of the barriers she seemed to keep around herself, but a dark cloud passed momentarily across her countenance from time to time, as if she were struggling with something she did not want to share, but which she also did not want to experience.

Trudy decided to invite Juanita to stay the night at her place. They could look for a suitable local B&B the next day. Her best guest room was in a small suite she had developed for visitors in the old barn just behind the house, and she excused herself for a moment so she could make a quick visit to the suite, to ensure that it was ready for a guest in case Juanita were to accept her offer.

"There are more paintings and old photos in the bedroom just off the living room," she said. "Feel free to take a look. I'll be back in just a minute."

It had begun to rain quite hard. Trudy donned a rain coat and left Juanita perusing the walls.

The gun shots, two in quick succession, were muffled but unmistakable. Trudy had groped her way to the breaker box in the barn, and was about to turn on the power so she could look over the suite. Instead, she froze in place, gripped by fear. She cautiously moved to a place in the dark barn from which she could see the back of her house through a window.

A car she did not recognize was parked behind hers in the driveway, its lights on and motor running. Nothing happened for a minute or so. Then a person wearing a large, hooded raincoat came out of the kitchen door, got into the unknown car, and drove away.

Almost immediately, her house erupted into flames.

Trudy was horrified and terrified. Juanita was alone in the house. And now? Shot? Burned to death?

Trudy reached for her phone to call 911, but then stopped as she was seized by an even greater terror.

Those two gun shots almost certainly were not intended for

Juanita O'Grady. No one knew that Juanita was in Trudy's house. It had never been part of her plan. The bullets must have been intended for herself. The shooter had made a mistake.

Trudy herself might be dead soon, too, if they discovered that she was still alive.

Why would anyone want to kill me? She could not imagine.

She suddenly knew that she must hide, that she must disappear, somewhere, somehow and not be discovered alive.

She turned off her phone, then removed the SIM card so nobody could track it.

Juanita had left her suitcase in Trudy's car. The police and firefighters would find it, and they would be here in minutes, called in by everyone who saw the house burning.

Trudy stole out of the barn to her car and retrieved the suitcase. She had to get rid of it too, to delay as long as possible any suspicion that it was Juanita, not her, who was dead.

There was an old well in a back corner of her property. Trudy grabbed the suitcase and hastened along in the shadow of the forest edge the half mile to that well. She could see headlights arriving now on the road in front of her burning house, and sirens were approaching in the distance from Sandy Cove.

The well had a heavy wooden cover for safety, but no one could drown in it now anyway. It had gone dry a generation ago. She heaved off the cover far enough to make an opening for the suitcase, and dropped it in. She was rewarded by a thud from about 10 feet down.

She threw her phone in after it. Even without a SIM card, it could connect to a wifi router until the battery died. She heaved the cover back into place, and melted into the forest.

25: Space aliens

The light southwest wind that for four days had allowed the rowers to share their work with the small sail died down to nothing in the early morning of the fifth day, and was replaced, after a short period of calm, with a gradually strengthening wind from the north.

Surinder pulled in his steering oar and took down the sail and mast. The crew were asleep in various configurations around the dory, and he hesitated before waking one of them to begin rowing with him straight into the new wind.

The boat was surrounded by fog, as it had been since day one. But there was something new in the air, a sound that seemed to arrive with the north wind, a distant rumbling that rose and fell in a slow rhythm.

Surinder was so tired from furtive sleep and a long steering watch that he did not at first recognize what he was hearing. When he did, his heart leapt and all fatigue disappeared. It was the distant thunder of ocean swells on a shore: Sable Island!

"All hands on deck," he shouted, startling the crew into unwelcome consciousness. He said nothing more.

The men sleepily pulled themselves up onto seats, noting first the change in the wind and then the low sound. They snapped to attention. No Marshall Islander could mistake that sound. They gazed forward, straining to see through the fog in the dim light of dawn.

Then, with a great shout of joy, each grabbed an oar and, sitting side by side on the two rowing thwarts, they rowed like Olympians straight toward the ever-louder crash of breakers on a sandy beach. In twenty minutes, they began to glimpse the shoreline through the fog.

They paused offshore at the point where the waves steepened and began to crest. Landing on such a beach is perilous, drowning a common result. This crew had long experience of such landings, however.

The engineer took command. He asked Surinder to sit in the middle seat and to remain in the boat no matter what happened, holding onto rope loops the crew had tied onto the risings for him to use. The engineer inserted the steering oar again. Two men sat at the oars and the fourth stood in the bow, holding the rope attached to the bow ring.

The rowers moved the dory slowly forward into the zone of ever higher and steeper waves. Then, as they slid down the back side of a wave that had just crested under the boat, the engineer gave a shout like a starting gun, and the men at the oars began fast, powerful strokes.

The dory rose up the steep forward slope of the next wave, but this time was moving forward sufficiently fast to surf down its incline. The men rowed at maximum speed and the engineer wrenched his oar from side to side as needed to keep the boat perpendicular to the wave. It crested just behind them and hurled the *Liberdad* forward, up onto the sand beach, where it grounded in six inches of water.

The man in the bow leapt out and held the boat from being washed backward into the deadly surf as the water receded. Then everyone, including Surinder, jumped from the boat and, together, they hauled the heavy dory up the beach and out of the reach of the endless waves. With four long heaves, they pushed and pulled the *Liberdade* up and over the high tide line to safety.

As they reached the top of the beach, a heavy rain began to fall. They took their precious water and food out of the dory, flipped the boat over, and restowed the cargo and themselves under it, a perfect roof against the wet and wind.

The sand under the boat made a comfortable bed and they were asleep before any of them could even realize how exhausted he was.

~

"Hey, any of you space aliens alive under there?"

Surinder vaguely heard a sound, of a voice, coming, it seemed, from no comprehensible place, calling him to wake up. *But why? But where?*

He opened his eyes and could see a rim of light where the gunwale of the overturned dory curved upward a little above the sand.

In that rim of light, he saw the heels of a pair of boots, and beside them an upside-down beard and a face, its owlish eyes magnified by immensely thick wire-rimmed glasses. He remembered now that there had been another noise too, like a portable bilge pump or a lawnmower, but it had stopped.

The face disappeared and was replaced by a hand that gripped the gunwale and pulled it higher off the ground, while a second hand placed a stick of driftwood into the enlarged space to hold it up.

"The rain's over, boys and girls. Come on out and introduce yourselves."

Some muffled grumbling was audible from under the *Liberdade,* and one by one, the five castaways rolled out from under the dory and found themselves staring up at a rain-free sky and at the person of Morley Finster.

"I'm out here to count horses and seals," Finster said. "Which of those would you be?"

He pulled out a pack of cigarettes and a lighter, and offered them around, to the immense delight of the crew.

"Better take a few," he said. "Keep the lighter. We don't get many tourists out here. Actually, tourists aren't allowed. Were you rowing here direct from Ireland, maybe trying to get around the rules?" He winked. "Hey, I got quite a stack of sandwiches with me that you fellas might like to try. Just let me go fetch them."

Finster walked down the beach to the ATV he had arrived on, rummaged in its small trailer, and returned with enough food to feed a football team for a few days. The castaways could hardly believe it, and dug in.

"How about a beer?" Finster said, pulling out a six-pack. "I was down at the east end the last few days, and you always got to go there prepared to be weathered in for a week or two more than you planned on."

"Where are we now?" Surinder asked.

"You're about 12 clicks from the lighthouse and buildings at the west end of the island. We'll all get there today before dark. I got a radio down on the quad. There's some nice beds there, and a shower. I guess you probably know this is Sable Island, eh? in Canada, eh? Or maybe you don't."

Whoever this kind man was, Surinder wanted to repay him at least with an explanation as to who they were and why they were cast up on this beach. But how much did he dare tell? The *Nightingale* had not sunk in a storm. It had been blown apart intentionally, planned, it seemed to him now, weeks in advance, before he even had signed on as captain.

He and the crew were supposed to be dead. What if it became known that they were not? What had been the targets of the sabotage? Them? The ship or both? Were they really safe now, or would they be hunted down somehow? Whatever the case, he would have to say something, tell their story in some way.

"My name is Surinder Singh," he started slowly. "I was the captain of a small trading vessel, two days from Gloucester, in lobsters, headed for Lisbon. We hit something at full speed and the vessel sank so quickly we had no chance to call out a mayday. We just barely got off in the dory and rowed here in six days. No loss of life. This is my crew. They got us ashore alive, through the surf."

The crew nodded sufficiently, and at the right moments, to indicate to Surinder that his account worked for them too.

"Whatever we hit must have been just under the surface. We had all three radars going and there was nothing on the screens."

Finster listened to Surinder's account and was silent for a while. "Well, isn't that something," he finally said. "We always get alerts to comb the beaches whenever there's a shipping mishap anywhere nearby, but you seem to have disappeared without a trace. No alerts came our way these last four weeks."

He paused in thought again, then shrugged. "Hey, my name is Morley, Morley Finster. I'm here on Sable most of the year. I used to work out here with the Coast Guard; now the island has become a national park, and I'm with Parks. I mostly do beach surveys."

He pointed eastward down the beach toward a distant grey lump above the surf line. "Look at that monster seal way down there. He came ashore two weeks ago all tore up by a shark, deep gashes all in spirals. We thought he was a goner, but he's coming around now, probably be off to sea again within the week. Hey, I better call for some help. You fellas probably don't fancy a ten-mile hike down the beach to get to that hot shower."

26: Marching orders

Colonel Elisabeth Lindenmayer, US Armed Forces, was in her Washington office early, with a full day of urgent matters ahead of her, when the three military police officers in civilian clothing walked in unannounced.

One of the officers addressed her. "Colonel Lindenmayer, we have orders to escort you immediately to a secure room in the Pentagon for a meeting about which all further information is classified. These are your clearance papers for entry into the designated room. Please review them and sign that you will adhere to all the stipulations."

Lindenmayer was more annoyed than surprised. Being jerked around from above is the norm in every government service. She was not in uniform, but she hardly ever was, and she knew it would not be expected by whomever she was to meet with.

After she signed and handed over the documents, she removed her necklace and earrings, locked these, her phone, and her purse in her desk drawer, gave the key to the corporal at the reception desk, and fell in with her escorts, two in front, one behind.

The military police were dismissed at the outermost security level. The secured room, three levels further in, was just an average small conference room with seating for about twenty people. It was special because it was beyond any possibility of electronic or in-person surveillance. In the room, there were no brief cases, papers, pens or computers.

Lindenmayer recognized General Symons, responsible for her division on nuclear terrorism, at the head of the table. She was seated beside Lieutenant Johnson, the staff member she had sent to assess the manufacturing records of the missile guidance systems that somehow seemed to have made it to North Korea. *Perhaps this is the format of his report?* She did not know the others in the room.

The general spoke as soon as she was seated. "Lindenmayer, this meeting is to understand the security breach that caused you to instruct Johnson here to investigate the classified daily production records of our largest aerospace manufacturer. Why did you give that directive?"

Lindenmayer had been through many similar interrogations in her career. She explained her assigned duty as the U.S. representative to the nuclear terrorism division of the IAEA, and the surprising announcement by the technical expert from China that North Korea had acquired some number of American missile guidance systems. "I considered this an urgent security matter, and immediately sent Johnson to check the manufacturer and the military's inventories of the systems in question, and then also to determine if the production records of the manufacturer matched the inventories. I have not yet received his report on this second matter."

"China!" The general glowered. "Why didn't you report this information to me directly and immediately."

"Sir, you have made it clear to your staff that you do not want to be briefed with unverified information."

The general paused for a moment. "You're right," he said, "I have."

He paused again.

"Elizabeth, we've got a lot to figure out here."

His tone no longer was combative.

"Johnson, you may make your report to Colonel Lindenmayer now."

"General, Colonel: covertly, I gained access to the daily records of supplies received and products completed at the advanced electronics division of IRC Michesen, our military contractor. These did not harmonize with their or our inventories of completed guidance systems. Twenty-five guidance systems manufactured in recent weeks are not recorded in the inventories."

"Thank you, Johnson. You may go."

The general pressed a button on his console that opened the exit door, and Lieutenant Johnson left the room.

"Very perceptive of you to check out actual unit production after the inventories had matched," he said. "Johnson's a top-notch hacker. He really put the security systems through the ringer. He got into the most secure computer system in the aerospace industry without being detected, but he didn't know that the National Security Agency had been in there ahead of him."

General Symons explained that, a few weeks ago, US authorities had been tipped off by a whistle-blower that something might be going on with the missile guidance systems. The whistle-blower itself was a surprise – The Republic of Cuba.

"Cuba's arm was being twisted to serve as a clandestine transit site for some stolen American military equipment," he said, "and Cuba didn't want to do it. One of the arm-twisters was North Korea. Cuba got in touch with us through Canada because we aren't allowed to talk directly to them. Eventually, Cuba found out the equipment had to do with missile guidance in some way. This was huge! We called in the National Security Agency."

The NSA managed to get an operative inside IRC Michesen's production site and discovered that a small number of missile guidance systems were being set aside as they were manufactured, one or two every few days, and were moved to a verification testing space outside of the primary production area. These units were tested and approved, but were not placed back into the inventory of completed guidance systems.

"IRC Michesen is a big, top-secret contractor," Symons said. "Any corruption there has to be stamped out fast, and that's what we're doing now."

He said the Department of Defense planned to use this North Korean initiative to identify and neutralize all the players involved. As a first step, some internal components in 25 of the guidance systems already delivered to the Department had been changed so that any missile with one installed would fly erratically for a short distance and then directly into the sea or earth below. The units that had been set aside out of inventory were replaced with the neutralized units which bore the serial numbers originally assigned to the set-asides, a series from 3141593-1 to 3141593-25

All had gone according to plan until it was discovered that the 25 disabled units, kept under 24-hour-a-day surveillance, had disappeared from the testing room. How this was accomplished could not be determined. The boxes had remained in the room, but the missile guidance units had been removed from them.

Cuba was advised immediately to be vigilant for the arrival of these units by any possible means of transportation, and the full array of

American military surveillance routinely aimed at Cuba was focused intensively on all possible conveyances, public and private, by air and by sea.

Ten days later, Cuba informed the US, via Canada, that the units had turned up in a warehouse on the harbour in Santiago de Cuba two days previously.

They were discovered because of an alert issued to all shippers and couriers by Cuban authorities as part of the enhanced vigilance requested by the Americans. A local agent for an international shipping company had been engaged to collect a wrapped palette from the warehouse and to dispatch it by air cargo to that company's agent in Sana'a, Yemen. Cuba identified the cargo as the materiel in question only because the warehouse manager became suspicious and contacted authorities.

No one had seen the palette arrive in the warehouse or knew it was there until the shipping agent arrived to pick it up, identifying it by a number marked in several places on the outside: 3141593. The cargo manifest said the palette contained cantaloupe melons, but fruit seldom is packaged so securely.

"Those missile guidance units would have arrived in Yemen a day and a half before Cuban authorities learned that the palette even had arrived," General Symons said, in a discouraged tone. "Whoever is behind all this sure knows what they're doing."

From discussion that followed, Lindenmayer deduced that two or three people at the table already were in possession of this information, while the remaining five or six, like herself, were hearing it for the first time. These latter had the most to say. Their comments included expressions of mistrust of Cuba, proposed threats to Yemen, further sanctions on North Korea and dismay and condemnation that such a theft could take place from the United States military or one of its trusted suppliers.

After five minutes, the General had had enough. He signalled for silence and turned to Lindenmayer. "What do you think, Elizabeth? Where do we go from here?"

"We must do nothing that will cause North Korea to think that we have discovered this shipment. It will take some time for them to learn that the units are defective and then to determine what those defects are. Their possession of these defective units is not a security threat."

She proposed that three matters truly were urgent. "The first is to identify the other parties in this transaction. North Korea cannot have achieved this high-security theft on its own. Whoever has done this is an enormous security threat to the United States and our allies."

"The second is to determine what North Korea has paid for these units. It is unlikely simply to be money. It may be that the transaction was not initiated by North Korea, but by this other party. North Korea is very poor and is vulnerable to coercion. It is exceptionally important to determine what this other party has sought in exchange for the guidance units.

"The third matter is to determine how it is possible for a shipment of any object from the Unites States to Cuba to evade detection. What is the current state of military stealth technologies and who are the manufacturers?"

The General sat in silence for a long and uncomfortable minute, his eyes unfocused, as if he were alone in the room.

He then came to attention, swept the room with his gaze, glanced at the clock on the wall and turned to Lindenmayer. "Thank you, Colonel."

He turned to the others. "Offiers, ladies and gentlemen, you have your marching orders. Dismissed!"

27: Jeff or Lucille?

Henry and Rory had missed the May 31st deadline for their Walt Whitman birthday song by too many weeks to bother counting. There were just so many other things going on, including their wailing new Irish band, which so far had no name, no gigs and no firm intentions, but which was their favourite thing to do anyway.

They were determined to get that song written, though, and today each had carved out two hours to give it their full joint attention.

The café was the best place for this work. No one wanted to join their esoteric rants about what Whitman wrote or meant, so they always were left strictly alone.

As they took up seats at a corner table, Purley Jordan waved from another group in earnest discussion. "We're just as busy as bees over here complaining about potato beetles," he shouted. "Harold here says they shredded all his plants, and he'll have none to eat at all."

Purley turned back to his group. "The trouble with you, Harold, is that you only ever think about having new potatoes as early as possible, and those beetles think the same way. Forget about early. Hold off until the middle of June, until the acacia trees are in full bloom, and plant your potatoes then. By the time their leaves are above ground and good to eat, the beetles will have just about quit for the year."

Henry and Rory still were working on the main chorus and first verse of their song, in which Whitman sets out to find truth. They hadn't even gotten to the early, bloated grandstanding in *The Song of Myself*. They had a lot of work ahead of them.

Rory took out a notebook and began to read to Henry a new version of the three lines they had not yet been able to agree on, when his reading was cut short.

The café door burst open, and Anita St-Pierre rushed in and over to the poets' table, out of breath, wet eyed and barely able to speak. "Henry, Trudy Denton's house, in Little River, it burned down last night, right to the ground and everyone's sure that Trudy was caught inside! She, she's dead!"

Anita was too upset to say anything more. She and Henry had met Trudy several times in the past few weeks as they worked on their documentary about regional fish farms.

Greg spoke up from behind the counter. "They had it on the news this morning. Fire departments from Sandy Cove, Digby, Smiths Cove and Barton all responded, but there was nothing they could do except keep it from spreading. They said the owner might have died inside."

"Roger Laliberty was out on the 911 call," Anita stammered. "I just met him at the post office. He told me it was Trudy's house."

Anita felt she must tell Zora right away, so she and Henry drove out to Lansdowne Highland.

They found Zora in her clinic at the back of the house, cursing some big rectangular shadows that were ruining the radiographs she and Amanda were taking to test the new X-ray equipment. Anita's terrible news put an end to that.

Amanda could see how upset Zora was, and she offered to handle the day's last three appointments on her own and call for help only if she needed it.

Zora ran to find Rick and Bronwyn in the dairy, and they all gathered in the kitchen to cry and grieve.

Rick asked Amanda to join them for a supper cobbled together out of the fridge. Telling her about their friend Trudy helped them to move slowly from overwhelming grief to a muted but earnest celebration of who Trudy had been.

The extended Denton family and the whole of the Digby Neck and Islands community still were numb with shock and grief when Rick, Zora, Anita and Henry arrived in Little River to join them for a memorial service for Trudy two days after the fire. There were no remains to examine or to bury, and by then, a new blanket of fear and disbelief had been thrown over the whole event by evidence that Trudy had been shot before her house burned down.

Why? By whom? It made no sense.

A spot of melted brass that the forensic chemists said was from a parabellum handgun shell had been found among the cinders in the area where the kitchen floor had been. The shooter clearly was not a local person, because he or she had thrown the pistol off the harbour bridge into the water. It was lying in plain sight on the mud the next day at low tide.

That night, Rick found sleep hard to come by. He and Trudy had known each other right up through high school, and he also knew everyone in all those grieving families.

It was a relief when Bronwyn called for attention about 2 am. Zora finally had fallen asleep, and Rick crept softly out of the bedroom and closed the door so as not to wake her.

A laugh and a cuddle with Bronwyn were the emotional opposites of the funeral of a murdered friend, and Rick was grateful for the comfort. It was short-lived, however. Bronwyn soon was asleep again.

Rick went downstairs to sit by himself for a while. From the kitchen, he heard the distant ringing of a telephone and realized it was the landline in Zora's clinic. *What a time for an emergency call!*

He walked back to the clinic and picked up the receiver. "Cromwell Veterinary Services."

He could hear that the telephone line was live, but the caller did not speak. "Hello, can you hear me?" he said.

Finally someone spoke. "Ricky, is that you?"

It was a whispered imitation of the voice of Trudy Denton.

Rick first was shocked, and then was outraged that anyone would make a prank call to bereaved people in the middle of the night, and he started to say as much, but the caller cut him off.

"Ricky, I'm sorry. It's really me. I'm hiding, Ricky. I'm scared. Someone tried to kill me. They think I'm dead. I need help."

Rick desperately wanted to believe the voice, but he also knew it just could not be true. He thought for a moment, then spoke again. "Is your cousin Marianne a Denton or a Titus?"

"She's an Outhouse, Ricky. You know that."

"Did Marianne marry Jeff or Lucille?"

"She's a nun, Ricky! She's not married to anyone. She married Jesus."

"Trudy, where are you?"

28: Dark shadows

Trudy continued to whisper, apparently fearing to be overheard. She said she'd heard two gun shots from inside her house where she had left Juanita, seen someone run out of the house and drive away and the house go up in flames, and then realized the shots and flames were meant for her.

"I ran into the woods to hide. I got up and over the paved road and way up the hill. I knew Johnny Tidd was away on holiday, so I pushed through the bush the two miles down to his place in Tiddville. I knew he'd hide a key somewhere and I found it and locked myself inside. There's food here, and water, but there's people around a lot. I'm not safe here. I threw my phone away. I'm calling you on Johnny's land line. Ricky, can you come pick me up and help me hide somewhere?"

Rick looked at his watch. It was 3:30am. If he left now, he could get there and back before dawn. Bronwyn would sleep for 3+ hours more, and Zora was here if she didn't. "Okay. I'll come right now."

"Don't come to Johnny's house," Trudy said. "Someone will see. Before you get to Tiddville, turn your lights off, and your dome light, too. Nose into the old track used to go to the diatom sheds at the bog. I'll be in the bushes on the right side. I'll just open the door and slip in. Leave your phone at home."

Rick didn't know what to think. At 3:30 that afternoon, he and Zora had been at Trudy's funeral. Now, twelve hours later, he was leaving to pick her up and find her a place to hide. He had to tell Zora something, but what?

He wrote a note—*Called down the Neck for something urgent. Back by 7:00am at the latest*—and taped it to the coffee pot Zora had left ready to go for the morning. He snuck up to make sure Bronwyn was indeed sleeping, and sped off toward Tiddville.

At that early hour, and with no fog, it was only a thirty-minute drive if you considered the speed limits optional, thirty minutes to figure out how and where to hide Trudy.

Rick sped right through Tiddville, but slowed and turned around on the empty stretch before East Ferry, and crept back at a snail's pace with all lights off. He nosed into the old track as instructed, and a real, live Trudy Denton slithered in through the passenger door and hunkered down below the level of the dashboard.

Rick crept east on the Neck Road until well past Whale Cove, and only then switched on his headlights.

As they drove, Trudy released some of her pent-up trauma in long gasping sobs. She poured out the whole story of Juanita O'Grady's arrival, their dinner together, the shots fired, her house erupting into flames, hiding Juanita's suitcase and her own phone, sneaking down to Johnny Tidd's place in the dark through the woods and bogs.

"Where do you want to go now, Trudy?" Rick asked.

"Some place safe. Some place no one can find me. Some place I won't be a danger to others."

"Not at your place, Ricky," she said. "I don't want what happened to Juanita to happen to anyone else."

Rick didn't want that either, although he really could not imagine it.

They had reached Highway 101 and had to make some decision right away. Rick pulled off onto the Lansdowne Road and stopped on the shoulder to think while Trudy cowered down into the passenger foot space. *What to do?* He struggled to imagine even one possible option, and then it came to him: Jeremy!

"Trudy, would you feel safe in a cabin in the woods with no road to it and that no one ever comes near?"

"I would, at least for a while."

Rick had thought of Mel Prime's cabin on Crouse Lake. Mel would have to be told, but he could be trusted. Trudy could hide there for months, if need be, but she would need some kind of connection with the outside world, for supplies and communication.

That's where Jeremy could make it all work. Jeremy would not hesitate to walk to Mel's camp from time to time, unseen in the dark and through the woods, to carry supplies in and messages out. He would have to agree to do it, though. If he did, Marie would have to be told, too.

Rick started driving again, heading for Morganville by way of Clark

Road to keep out of sight as best he could. It was just after 5 in the morning when he pulled into Jeremy's driveway and around to the back of the house, where his truck could not be seen from the road. The kitchen light was on.

Rick coaxed Trudy out of her hiding place, opened the back door of the house and called to Jeremy, who soon came into the entry way, showing no surprise at so early a visit.

"Jerry, this is my friend Trudy Denton. We need your help," Rick said. "Someone tried to kill her. Everyone thinks Trudy died. Now she has to hide for a while. Would you take her out to Mel's camp and bring her groceries and stuff every so often for a few weeks, without being seen?"

Jeremy listened, stone-faced as usual, and did not move or say anything for about two minutes. Finally he said, "Marie."

"Marie and Mel will be helping out, too," Rick said. "We can get all the stuff Trudy will need and we'll look after Rosie, too, whenever we need to."

Jeremy stood silent for another minute and then nodded his head once. "When?"

They agreed that Trudy would hide in Jeremy's house for the rest of the day, and that Rick would talk to Marie and to Mel. Rick or Mel would take Jeremy and Trudy and some supplies out to the end of the Lake Joli Road after dark that night and Jeremy would guide her the long mile through the woods to the cabin and show her what she needed to know to live there. Then he would walk back home.

Rick drove across the road to Marie's house to explain the situation to her, and headed for home at 6:45. He would be home by seven o'clock, as he had promised. He hoped Zora's first appointment was not too early. He had a lot to tell her.

When Bronwyn awoke, Zora swept her out of her crib and down into the kitchen as usual. Bronnie shunned any notion of breakfast, however, and instead made several rounds of the floor and walls as if looking for something.

When Rick came in through the kitchen door, she squealed for a cuddle, and only then made gestures that she was ready to give full attention to the array of favourite foods Zora had organized for her.

As she alternately ate, squashed and showered down on the waiting cat her gourmet selection, Rick told Zora all that had taken place since the early-morning telephone call from the not-dead Trudy Denton.

Zora was both relieved and horrified. She had been one of the last people to see Trudy and Juanita O'Grady, standing together on the deck of the Beluga Group office at White's Cove. She was trying to process this flood of new and hardly-imaginable information when Amanda walked in from the clinic at the back of the house, carrying some X-ray films. It was a welcome interruption.

"I have good news!" she said. "Look at these perfect radiographs!"

Amanda had come in early to wrestle with the new X-ray equipment that seemed never to take a good picture. On her way to work, it had occurred to her that the film, rather than the equipment, might be at fault, so she had taken a new package out of the store room to try. Voilà! No black rectangle messing up the image of the frozen pork chop she'd used for a test radiograph.

"I wonder if some of this film got left in range of an X-ray beam at some point," she said.

Rick was looking at the X-ray images, too. He had never paid much attention to X-rays. "Aren't X-rays kind of like light? Wouldn't shining an X-ray beam onto the film make it brighter, or even white?"

"Nope," said Amanda. "It's a negative image, like the old black and white camera film. Where X-rays hit the film, it comes out dark. Put a bone that X-rays can't get through on top of the film and, under the bone, it comes out clear. Look at this chop I just zapped. Where the bone was over the film, it's white because no X-rays got through, but you also can see shadowy meat and fat because they block some of the X-rays, too. Don't worry, that chop is still good to eat. No X-ray ever made a pork chop radioactive."

Rick paused to think this through. "What could have exposed those bad sheets of film in the shape of a long rectangle?"

"Good question!" Amanda said. "Let's hope it happened just to that one package of film and not to any of the others."

Overcoming the stubborn X-ray problem, and Bronwyn's nearly-successful attempt to stand up in her highchair and leap to the floor after her breakfast, lifted the nightmarish cloud that had darkened Rick and Zora's recent days. Trudy was alive, the Frasers' donkey needed castrating, and Bronwyn needed a complete cleanup before she and Rick headed out to deliver cheese to local stores.

He and Bronnie would be back for lunch and a nap, and laundry and bill-paying and cooking the irradiated pork chop for dinner and a chat with Melvin Prime that would send him out on the road toward his camp in the middle of the night.

29: The captain's problem

Morley Finster was fishing for a chance to chat with Captain Singh. The castaways had eaten and slept their way through two days of Sable Island hospitality, making up for their week of hard labour on short rations. Morley was a Parks employee, so it didn't matter much to him what washed up on the Island's shores, so long as each was recorded in the day book and cleared away if deemed unnatural.

The five shipwrecked sailors were of uncertain category here, but they certainly would have to be cleared away, too, and soon.

They had spent their second day helping Morley trailer the *Liberdade* to the main station, where they turned it upside down on some wooden blocks and left it shipshape and ready for...well, who knew, but at least it would not be smashed up by winter storms and buried in the sand.

But five extra people were five too many for Sable Island and they would all be flying to Halifax tomorrow or the next day.

Morley was perplexed at the appearance of these mariners in a lifeboat. Surinder's explanation was credible as far as it went, but there was a big hole in it. Ship owners always are in contact with their ships. If they lose contact, they raise alarms, search and rescue teams surge into action: Coast Guard, Navy, Airborne. Regional shipping is alerted, and reconnaissance satellites focus on the area. Television reporters interview concerned family members. The Sable Island main station would be a hub for any search and rescue operation aimed at a spot 100 miles south of the Island. But no alarm had been raised, and no search was underway.

The Marshall Islanders had never been anywhere near real, live horses, and they spent much of their time on the edge of the dunes, watching and marvelling at the Island's feature attraction. Thus, after lunch on their second day at the station, Morley found Surinder by himself, leaning against the dory, lost in thought.

Morley hopped up and sat on the flat, upturned bottom next to where Surinder was leaning. "Out there, where you went down last week, there's nothing for a ship to hit would sink it in ten minutes. What really happened?"

Surinder jerked to attention.

"Don't answer that question," Morley said. "Let me guess. Don't tell me if I'm right. The owners of that ship must have wanted her sunk. They must have known it disappeared a week ago and they haven't made a peep about it. Either you scuttled the ship yourself or they sank it under you. If you'd planned it, you wouldn't have planned to spend a week in an open dory rowing for Sable Island in the summer fog and with only an old compass to guide you. So, you all were supposed to go down with the ship."

They sat in silence for a while.

"I think you've got a problem, Captain. What happens when they find out you five are not dead?"

Surinder held steady against this blast of detective reasoning for a long, silent minute and then slumped his head and shoulders as if in defeat. "Yeah," he said. "I do."

"I spent a few years on Coast Guard ships some time ago," Morley said. "Once I was on an icebreaker for six months straight. I was about the same age as the third mate, and we got along real well. 'Peach-fuzz McEachran' the older guys used to call him, 'cause his young beard was so scraggly no one would have noticed if he shaved it off. These days we all call him Commodore McEachran, Royal Canadian Navy. He's on shore duty now, naval intelligence. Somehow, we're still buddies. I stay at his home for a day or two when I go through Halifax for any reason. He needs to hear your story. You can trust him."

30: Sound analysis

At Lansdowne Highland, life gradually had returned to its habitual rhythms after two rollercoaster days of murder, fire and tearing emotions.

Rick had much catching-up to do on the domestic front, and the bouncing seat suspended in the doorway to the living room was a lifesaver of contained self entertainment for Bronwyn. Rick could see that it was starting to lose some of its magic, however. Like everything else, its days were numbered.

A month ago, Bronnie would enjoy a full 50 minutes of non-stop bouncing without fuss or complaint. That was enough time to prepare the fundamentals of family meals for two or three days and to get a load of laundry washed and on the clothesline. Now there were worrying pauses when she would stretch down her ever-longer legs to the floor, plant her feet and, with determination, stand herself up just above the support of the seat. Sometimes, after only ten minutes, she demanded release onto the floor and an ever-growing level of parental vigilance thereafter that slowed to a snail's pace everything else Rick needed to do.

He had just extracted Bronwyn from an overturned wastebasket and gotten her into her highchair for a pause and a snack when his phone rang. The call was from area code 780. *Alberta? Who do I know in Alberta?*

"Rick Robichaud," he answered.

"Hello Rick!" It was the familiar voice of Surinder Singh.

"I didn't know you could sail a ship to Alberta," said Rick, "or is this just your girlfriend's phone?"

Surinder paused, then said, "I wish I had a girlfriend, and that this was her phone, but it's not. This is the government's phone, Royal Canadian Air Force. I'm their guest right now, in Cold Lake. It's a long story."

He gave Rick the short version, that the *Nightingale* had been re-routed to Europe, had hit something in the water and sunk, and he and the crew had made it to Sable Island. For some reason, the military was interested in the event.

"They flew the whole crew back home to the Marshall Islands, on the government's tab. Those men hadn't been home in six years. They invited me to spend some time as a guest of 4-Wing in Cold Lake, a little holiday time away from the sea, I guess. I'm doing the first part of flight school here, just for fun. How are things with you?"

Rick knew he couldn't even begin to answer that question right now. Everything was fine, nothing much to report.

"I'm calling to ask a favour, Rick. My big old dory from Westport, that's what got us to Sable Island. The ship's life raft didn't work, so we rowed and sailed to Sable in the dory. There's a Coast Guard buoy tender at Sable right now and a man I met there has talked the captain into taking the dory as far as Digby if there'd be anyone there could pick it up. I wondered if you could do that for me."

"Sure I can," said Rick. "One thing we have here on the farm is space. It'd be nice if they could call me a day ahead. When are you going to get back here?"

"Right now, I don't know. The first round of flight school runs for six weeks. Maybe after that. Thanks so much, Rick, gotta go."

Rick collected up the fragments of pancake that Bronwyn had scattered just beyond her reach and reassembled them for her to have another go, incentivised with a few more drops of maple syrup.

Surinder's story made no sense. *How could a boat sink off Nova Scotia without it being big news? Why is Surinder having a vacation with the air force in Alberta?*

Rick decided he just would not try to make sense of it right now. If the Coast Guard really brought him Surinder's dory, he would think about it again. Right now, the experimental pigs needed whey, Bronwyn needed something to do, and he needed to get out of the house.

On their short walk over to the pigs, the sweet and somehow hopeful melody of a mourning dove in the old acacia tree floated down to them, some young flickers called raucously from behind one of the outbuildings, and there was a loud but chaotic burst of bird noise from a dense lilac bush beside the pigs' feeder. Rick was a passive bird watcher, but he tried to identify and appreciate all the birds he saw or heard during his daily work. *What bird sings such bubbly melodic chaos?* He knew he should know, but...

As he puzzled over what the bird might be, he remembered that he had a bird-song app that he never had actually tried to use. He'd gotten it free through a naturalist club about a month ago. Time to try it out!

He brought it up on his phone and set it going. The chaotic song burst out again and, bingo, "Gray catbird," the app reported!

As if on cue, the bird itself flew to a visible perch, gave its eponymous meowing cat call, and flew away.

Meanwhile, the app also identified the mourning dove and northern flicker, then a song sparrow, an American goldfinch and an American robin. When Rick listened with total concentration, he realized that, indeed, he could hear at least some fragments of these other bird songs himself. On the screen of the phone, the app showed a moving graph of intricate patterns of sound waves as it listened and analyzed the incoming data.

Rick was amazed. In his former life as a fish biologist, he had used sound recording as part of his research on noisy reef fish. It hadn't worked very well. The software to analyze the sounds just had not been up to the task. *This bird song app is something else! Sound analysis must really have advanced in the last decade.*

Rick tried to share some of his enthusiasm with Bronwyn by showing her a few bird pictures on his phone and playing their calls. She studied the pictures with some attention and then responded with a loud raspberry, which she repeated more or less continuously as Rick walked them across a small pasture, letting the app search for birds.

Somehow, the app could hear through the raspberries with ease, and picked out a passing blue jay and a red-tailed hawk through all the other not-bird noise.

Rick was delighted.

31: Ghost ship

Zora was in between farm visits that same day when she received a phone message from Johnny Tidd: "Please call back."

When she did, Johnny said he was at work again now and that both he and Parker thought some of the fish in the White's Cove farm weren't behaving right. They were partly off their feed and swam slower than normal. They wanted Zora to come have a look.

Zora had planned to be home early that day, for some extra time with Bronnie and to catch up on the never-ending paperwork. She called Rick to explain the change in plan.

"We need an outing," Rick said. "Swing by and pick us up. We'll come with you."

They arrived at the fish farm on the hill above the cove in the mid-afternoon. Zora went in with Johnny and Parker for her official veterinary inspection. Rick peeked in but decided he and Bronwyn could use a walk down to the wharf.

The *Wagamama* was unloading bags of fish food onto a truck with the assistance of Anton and another of the Beluga Group technicians. It was a fine August day, and no one was in a hurry.

The captain of the *Wagamama* waved Rick on board and sat him and Bronwyn down in the wheelhouse, intent on some conversation. The captain was from Tiverton. His dad had hauled weir-caught herring across the Bay of Fundy to Blacks Harbour for 30 years and he'd done it with him for a while himself. All the herring were gone now, fished out, and he'd switched to hauling fish food and farmed salmon back and forth instead. He and Rick knew the same island communities and had plenty to talk about.

Anton came up to the wheelhouse when the feed bags were unloaded. He asked the captain to remain at the wharf for another hour so some possibly sick salmon could be caught and put on ice for the

Black's Harbour folk to look at. Johnny and Parker would bring them down.

He turned and greeted Rick. "Things don't seem right around here now, with Trudy gone," he said. "Head Office told us their officer, that lady who came, was so upset she just left and went home. She never came back here at all. I feel like that, too."

He left and walked up to what had been Trudy's office trailer.

"Those ladies from Head Office are something else," the captain remarked. "I brought the boss-lady here one time and took her away again, and I brought that other lady here, too. Do you know how they get here?"

Rick surveyed the wheelhouse floor and walls up to about three feet, and decided it was safe to release Bronwyn into the journey of exploration she had been wriggling for.

"I suppose you bring them over from Blacks Harbour," he said.

"A person would think so," the captain said, "but I don't. I meet them half way over, right in the middle of the Bay, and in the strangest boat you ever saw. It just appears like out of nowhere. About five miles away, suddenly it shows up on radar. Then, when its about a quarter of a mile away, I start just barely to see it with my own eyes. It kind of looms up out of the sea even though it's big; it must be 150 feet long. It's painted some kind of ocean camo pattern, blues and greys and browns in big patches. It's an odd shape, too, angular all over and low in the water except for the wheelhouse. It looks to me like some kind of military ship, but the guys who bring the ladies over in a Zodiac wear white yachtsman suits."

Bronwyn had discovered the captain's rubber boots in a corner of the wheelhouse. She was pulling out the wool socks he kept in them and trying on each one as a hat. The captain seemed just a little bit pleased with the show.

"What happens after they come on board?" Rick asked.

"They tell me to head for White's Cove and then they go down into the crew cabin. About the time we are fully underway again and on course, I can't see that camo boat any more, not even with binoculars, and after a while I can't see it on radar, either, although there's plenty of fishing boats around that show up just fine."

"How do you know when you're supposed to meet up with this boat?"

"I get a call on my cell phone after we're already on our way over here for some other reason, usually when we're well out past The Wolves. I suppose the call comes from the camo boat, but I really don't know. I never recognize the voice. Then the boat just turns up. It's only happened three times so far. The boss-lady arrived and then she departed that same way, and this other woman arrived, too, but seems she went away on her own."

Bronwyn had shaken a leather-sheathed fish filleting knife off a high shelf, and the dull thud it made on the floor next to her convinced Rick that it was time for them to move on. They said farewell and began their walk back up to the fish farm.

Anton was on the steps of the office building as they passed by. Rick knew that some level of friendship had developed between him and Trudy, and he stopped to ask him how things were going.

"The farm runs good. Johnny and Parker, they keep it going. We don't have much to do yet, just watch the monitors for anything goes wrong. Head Office say Beluga Group is buying Trudy's burned-down place, paying double, to help out the family. They want me to sign the papers."

Anton's tone suggested he might not believe the Beluga Group's stated ethical motivation for acquiring Trudy's place. Rick had to control his urge to tell him that Trudy was still alive.

He said goodbye and, with Bronwyn, scurried up the hill to the farm building. Zora had finished her assessment and was on the phone with the company office in New Brunswick.

"All the fish I looked at have severe cataracts," she said. "I am sure the cause is not eye worms. I had a good look with a strong lens. Mr. Tidd and Mr. Churchill tell me the water quality in the fish tanks has been rock solid for months, so the cause must be something else. Have you changed the feed in the past month or two? The only other thing I noticed is that those young salmon are growing incredibly fast. I wonder if they might be growing too fast."

Zora listened for a few minutes while Rick exchanged greetings quietly with Johnny and Parker.

"How was your holiday, Johnny?" he asked.

"I could've stayed way longer on them P.E.I. beaches," Johnny said. "I like being home again, though. Someone got into my house while I was away. I could tell 'cause some things was put away wrong and a good bit of food was gone. No one around ever saw nobody, and whoever it was didn't steal nothing except what they ate."

Rick tried to look genuinely surprised.

Zora began speaking again. "Well, you know your salmon and your farms better than I do, but if these fish are a new genetic line and if you are making new feed with soy beans and palm oil in place of fish meal, I'd worry that these cataracts could be due to the feed or caused by the fish just growing too fast for the lens tissue to keep up and form properly....Yes, you're welcome. Call me if you need me again in between my regular visits."

She rang off.

They drove home in thoughtful silence while Bronwyn fell asleep, thereby guaranteeing Rick a long, long evening. *Palm oil!* Zora thought. *I'm not sure I want to eat farmed salmon any more. I'd feel like I was eating the last of the orangutans.* She tried to think about something else, like her dog and cat clinic tomorrow morning.

Why is Beluga Group buying Trudy's place? Rick wondered. *Juanita's suitcase and Trudy's phone are still at the bottom of that well. I better get them out of there, and soon.*

"Ricky, the manager on the phone asked me all kinds of questions about the water quality in the fish tanks. Parker had just given me their daily test records to look at, so I could tell him. But all that fancy equipment down in the caves is supposed to monitor that stuff automatically and adjust everything to be just right. If those technicians aren't monitoring water data, what are they monitoring?"

It was a good question. *What are they monitoring?*

32: Up to no good

Appointments at Zora's clinic began at eight o'clock the next morning, and the first patient was a young cat that suddenly had gone lame on one hind leg about two months ago.

She seemed to get better and better on her own, and now was neither lame nor sore. However, she couldn't jump up on high furniture as she had done before her injury. She still tried, but often would miss with her right hind leg and tumble back down. The owner was concerned that there might be more damage to the leg than he had supposed.

Zora examined the cat's hips and reflexes. The right hip joint could be moved around a small but abnormal amount, and the cat had no placing reflex on that side.

"What you describe is very typical of a fracture at the hip joint. The tip of the leg bone that sits like a ball in the hip socket gets broken off. The hip joint won't reform but a lot of tough tissue forms around it and the cat often does just fine without the actual joint. Sometimes there is damage to a nerve that runs close to the fracture site and that would explain why your cat's right hind leg isn't working 100%. We'll take an X-ray to see if a hip fracture really is the problem."

Amanda already had set up for the radiograph. The film drawer was empty, so she went to the storage room and grabbed another packet. In a few minutes, the image was coming out of the film processor. She groaned loudly and her face fell; the picture was useless! A black rectangle ran right across the image of the hip, making it impossible to read.

"I thought we were done with this problem," Amanda said in a discouraged voice.

"This is nuts," Zora growled. "Where did that film packet come from?"

"It was the last one in the box just inside the door on the right, on top of that carton of Rick's stuff."

Zora went to the store room, extracted a packet from a new box on a high shelf at the back, and asked Anita to try again. This time, the image was perfect and showed a space where the head of the right femur ought to have been. Diagnosis confirmed! It was not always that easy, and the cat would indeed be fine.

When the morning clinic was over, Zora went to the X-ray viewer, put the two images of the cat's hip side by side, and studied them together. The black bar that had ruined the first radiograph had a fuzzy general outline, but there was a sharp-edged long rectangle inside those fuzzy edges, about two inches wide. It ran at an angle straight across the entire film.

Zora went with Amanda to the storage room and picked up the now-empty box that had contained the ruined film. The box was on top of a stack of the steel bars Surinder had given to Rick to give to Mel, straight steel bars about two inches wide and two to three feet long.

"How can a steel bar leave its image on a piece of X-ray film?" Amanda wondered out loud.

"I guess it could if it were radioactive," Zora mused.

"Let's see if it really can," Amanda said. She took a film from the new packet, still in its light-tight envelope, and taped it down to the surface of the top-most steel bar.

"There should be some trace of exposure on that film by tomorrow morning if those steel bars really are the problem," she said.

From the store room, they gathered up all the supplies they might need for the next few days, then closed and locked the door.

Amanda would be running a vaccination clinic for dogs and cats that evening, so she left to spend a few hours at home before her workday resumed. Zora had a round of visits to some small sheep and goat herds lined up for the afternoon, but had two hours to spend with Bronwyn and Rick before hitting the road.

It was hodgepodge season, and each time Rick made that wonderful soup, there was some twist or surprise in its production that made it both traditional and inventive at the same time. Today's version was the usual milk chowder of new potatoes, carrots, turnip, and green and yellow beans, but also with a sliced and sauteed fennel bulb, handfuls of fresh Thai basil and some Lansdowne Highland feta to sprinkle on top.

Bronwyn was game to try any food at least once, but eating with a spoon was a challenge she had yet to meet. She insisted on her own spoon and bowl, however, and splashed and spattered the liquid on herself and her surroundings until the solid bits were revealed and could be eaten with her hands. It was total entertainment, and a fairly substantial meal as well. She had six teeth now, and more coming.

As they ate, Zora told Rick about the return of the mysterious black rectangle in the X-ray and her suspicion that it might be coming from contact with those steel bars in the store room. "We should have some evidence soon, one way or the other, from that film Amanda taped to one of those bars."

"This is getting weirder and weirder," Rick said. "Radioactive steel bars from the captain of the *Nightingale*? At least they have been sitting in a place where no one spends much time. How can steel be radioactive?"

"I guess it can happen," Zora said. "A famous horse vet from Poland gave a talk at Saint-Hyacinthe when I was studying there, and I remember his story about some steel recycled from a demolished nuclear power plant ending up in a batch of factory-made horse shoes. They caused terrible radiation burns and lameness in the horses that got those shoes. He said the steel had become radioactive from its long exposure to radiation in the reactor."

Lunch was over. Zora restocked her truck and headed out to her appointments. Rick extracted Bronwyn from her full-body bib and turned her loose on the floor while he washed down high chair and table. Bronwyn needed a nap but whether or not she would take one was anyone's guess.

A diaper change and a quick bath seemed the best route toward that goal, and an hour later, after a twenty-minute session with a favourite picture book, she drifted off.

Rick had at least one domestic occupation for every ten minutes that Bronwyn would sleep, starting with deep cleaning of the kitchen floor. He had just dumped the wash water down the drain when his phone rang, the very last thing he wanted or needed at that precious moment.

He grabbed his phone off the table, and scowled at it. The caller was from country code 54, wherever that was. *Spam!*

But he answered anyway, just in case, "Hello, Rick Robichaud."

"Hello, Rick." It was Wolf Wylie. "I'm off duty for a few hours so I thought I'd call for a chat. Can Bronnie spare us some time?"

"You caught her napping, Wolf, so she can be generous. Where are you now? Where is country code 54?"

"Argentina. We're about 50 miles off South Georgia, only two time zones ahead of you, but about 7,000 miles to the south. We're helping Argentina and the UK corral a fleet of supremely bad actors in the illegal fishery, with a little connivance from Chile and NATO. Argentina gave us a free phone for calls home. I figure you and Zora count as home for me."

Rick was delighted to have a conversation with Wolf. They had plenty to catch up on.

Wolf had heard about Trudy Denton and Rick did his best to tell Wolf how the family and community were coping without revealing how strange and complicated things really were.

Wolf recounted to Rick how he had been following the voyage of the *Cahow*-turned-*Nightingale* out into the Atlantic and how it had seemed just to disappear.

"You know, it really was there one minute and gone the next. I thought it might just be some failure of our equipment or of the ship's transponder, but the French officer who's working with us did some checking with her navy. That ship just plain disappeared. Wasn't there anything on the news about it?"

"Nothing that I saw or heard," Rick said. He thought he should keep Surinder's brief and questionable account to himself, at least for now.

"There's something going on there," Wolf said. "That ship sailed out into the Atlantic and disappeared, sank for sure. Dead men don't talk and neither do the people who didn't want them to talk. It's a bad business Rick."

A group of young crows that hung out in a tree near la fromagerie took offence at something and exploded in a loud chorus of dismay and harassment. The noise jarred Rick's memory.

"Wolf, can ships or certain kinds of fishing activity be identified by the sounds they make underwater? Do you ever record underwater sounds to analyze in that way? I have this new app on my phone that can identify every bird it can hear; it's incredible."

"Funny you should ask. We do, but it's a new thing for us. We don't analyze any of those data ourselves, but our navy partners are really into it. It seems that there are underwater microphones recording sounds all over the ocean floor now, everywhere."

"What do they do with all that information?"

"I don't really know. It's mostly classified, or, at least, not shared with an NGO like us. It seems like they can identify different classes of ships and also different kinds of armaments and explosive devices like mines, based on sound wave signatures. They must have a lot of fast computers to plow through all the non-stop data they receive."

Indeed they must, thought Rick. "What's next for the *Slocum Warrior*?"

"Our current mission either will succeed or fail in the next few weeks. Then we plan to work our way up the west coast of Africa over a few months, to help with some programs there. After that, we'll see where we are most needed."

"When will we see you back home again?"

"Well, I'm due for some leave, that's for sure. Getting to shore is the challenge. This new style of conservation battleship has a lot more cabin fever built into it than the old, wild-west version. I've been at sea for months. I'll need to take a break before too long."

An eager conversation between Bronwyn and her stuffed animals drifted down to the kitchen and Rick knew his time with Wolf had come to an end.

"Give my love to Zora, Rick. Keep an eye on that White's Cove crowd. They're up to no good!"

Rick just had time to get clothes in the washer and to organize a fulsome afternoon snack before Bronwyn's store of self-entertainment ran out and she demanded attention. The timing was good. A big feed of squeaky fresh cheese curds and a handful of grapes, with a banana held in reserve, would give them the two hours Rick needed for an important visit to Little River.

33: Seventy-two feet wins the banana

Rick did not know what would happen to Trudy's land if and when Beluga Group or anyone else bought it, but he felt sure he must retrieve Juanita O'Grady's suitcase and Trudy's cell phone from the bottom of the dry well before any change of ownership took place.

He had considered a stealthy 3:00 am visit as the best plan to avoid detection, but then decided that a visit during the day would be easier to explain, should he have to do any explaining. Plan B, then!

He put some old lumber and tools in the truck and enlisted Bronwyn as chief assistant and general declaration of innocence. For cover, he would say that he once had promised Trudy that he would fix her well cover, and he was determined to make good on that promise.

Rick's truck was hard to see, much less to identify, through the thick hedge of choke cherries and alders that separated the well site in Trudy's small back field from Denton Road. Bronwyn was content to sit near the well, admiring and dissecting the bouquet of brilliant yellow goldenrod and blue and white asters that Rick gathered for her.

Rick had come equipped with an old cod jigger on a stout line, and with this he easily hooked the handle of the suitcase and retrieved it.

Trudy's phone was another matter. He had a hard time seeing it at all, but finally located it using a flashlight.

There was nothing on the phone for the fishhooks on the jigger to catch. After some thought, Rick cut down a tall, thin chokecherry and stripped off all the branches except for a broom-like tuft at the top. He added a few late-season daisies to Bronwyn's dwindling bouquet to buy time, and grabbed the bucket he kept in the truck to lure wayward cattle back through broached gates and fences with the offer of some sweet feed.

The bucket he filled with enough soil to give it weight and stability.

He tied it onto the fishing line and, after several tries, managed to lower and swing it to a position on its side with the open end toward the phone. With the crude chokecherry broom, he gradually swept the phone over to the bucket and into it.

Rick manhandled the well cover back into place, and put everything, including the incriminating chokecherry pole, into the truck. Then he helped Bronwyn circumnavigate the now-safe well with its stone wall protruding from the ground to just the right height that she could hold on and see over the top. She went around the well three times.

"How far is that?" Rick asked himself.

The well was about eight feet across. Diameter x Π = circumference, he remembered, from maybe grade 10. 8 feet x 3.14, or maybe 8 feet x 3 was close enough = twenty-four feet each time around; seventy-two feet wins the banana.

He tucked Bronwyn into her car seat gave her the prize, and they headed for home. In the end, they had needed no cover story at all.

What with finishing the laundry, getting supper on the table, catching up with Zora, starting tomorrow's bread and keeping Bronwyn entertained and out of trouble while Zora got the wet laundry on the clotheslines and resupplied her truck for the morning, it was 9 o'clock in the evening before Rick and Zora had Bronwyn sleeping and could take a look inside the suitcase from the well.

Rick wiped it clean with a wet towel and hoisted it up on the kitchen table. He and Zora stared at it hesitantly, buffeted by strong feelings of guilt and conspiracy.

This was the suitcase of a woman shot and incinerated and believed to be Trudy Denton, Juanita from the Beluga Group whom Zora had spoken to very briefly a few hours before she was murdered, and whom no one seemed to have reported missing, like the *Nightingale*. Should they even open it?

Zora broke the spell with an unexpected giggle. "Wait," she said, and she disappeared off in the direction of her clinic. She returned with two pairs of blue protective gloves.

"Here," she said, "let's put these on. If we are going to do this, we should use proper crime scene technique."

The gloves gave them the costumes they needed to feel like actors just playing their parts in a drama created by others.

The suitcase was not locked, and it opened easily.

There was nothing unusual inside. The toiletries bag was thinly populated with bare essentials. There was an electric toothbrush with a charger attached to a device with many different plugs for the electrical outlets of different countries. Two dresses, a pant suit, two blouses, miscellaneous underwear, a pair of slippers, two-piece pyjamas, a light bath robe, and a small four-page photo album.

On the first page of the album was a photo of a man in a tweed jacket who was just beaming with life. In the lower right corner "Papa, 2003" was handwritten in white ink. On the next two pages were photos of this same man with a young girl who Zora felt sure was Juanita as a child, 10 or 12 years old, perhaps.

In one, they were clowning together, looking at each other through binoculars while standing along a stone wall beside the sea, a field guide to British birds evident on the section of wall between them. In the other, they were seated at a table on which was a birthday cake with candles, 13 by best count. They both were laughing energetically, as the girl had just torn off the wrapping paper to reveal her present: a massive book on analytical geometry.

On the last page, a carefully folded newspaper article was tucked under the protective plastic. Zora gently removed and opened it.

It was the obituary for a person named Rodrigo O'Grady, professor of mathematics, University of Reading, found dead in his home on Friday, March 14th, 2008 of unexpected heart failure, age 46. From the photo published with the obituary, it was clear that the deceased was Juanita's father.

"What should we do with this suitcase now?" Zora asked.

They agreed that, until Trudy decided what she would do next, there was no one to whom the suitcase could be given.

Rick repacked all the items they had taken out, closed it up again, and headed for the store room with it.

"Hold on, Ricky, the store room is locked because of those steel bars. I'll get the key."

As they went in, they saw the X-ray film still taped to the topmost bar.

"I forgot about this experiment," Zora said, "I'll go run that film through the processor right now."

She disappeared into the clinic while Rick put the suitcase in an out-of-the-way place and started doing the day's dishes.

The processor had to warm up and it was fifteen minutes later that Zora returned with the processed film. She held it up to the overhead kitchen light so Rick could see. The black outline of a 2"-wide rectangle extended from one edge to the other across the film.

As the confusing implications of this verification were sinking in, Rick's cell phone rang.

"Rick Robichaud"

"Good evening, Mr. Robichaud. I apologize if I am calling late in the evening. I'm the communications officer on a Coast Guard buoy tender headed your way from Sable Island, bound for Saint John. We have an item of cargo on board for you, a big dory originating from Sable. The harbour master at Digby has given us dockside time tomorrow morning from 10 o'clock to 11. Can you meet us on the Digby wharf at 10 o'clock tomorrow morning?"

Rick was relieved to have his thoughts diverted by something more pleasing than radioactive steel bars, even if it was equally inexplicable: the forewarned arrival of Surinder's dory. He checked the calendar to be sure the big flatbed hay truck was not booked for some other use, and said he would be ready and waiting tomorrow morning at 10.

34: Dead men don't talk

Bronwyn was delighted when Rick carried her out to the old hay truck and strapped her into her safety chair on the high front seat. Vintage *International* was her brand, loud and commanding in all its many gears, all parts having been replaced at least three times. From her high perch she could see out the back window far and wide over the empty flatbed.

As Rick started out on the Lansdowne Road toward Digby, Bronwyn alternately made full voice imitations of the engine's whines as its speed rose or fell with each gear change, and clapped her hands in applause for the truck, for herself, and for the good life of the moment.

As they arrived at the head of the wharf, the Coast Guard ship was just docking. Rick waited until the crew made it fast, and then drove down and parked beside it.

The crew already were busy with the ship's crane, and while one crew member directed Rick to manoeuvre the truck into the correct position, three others on board guided the big dory up into the air and over and down onto the truck.

As the crew repositioned the crane and secured everything back into seaworthy positions, a man of medium height and beard, with thick, wire-rimmed glasses stepped down the gangplank and came over to the truck.

"I guess you'd be Rick Robichaud," he said. "Captain Singh said I'd know you by the baby you work with."

He looked in the window past Rick and winked, and got a squeak and a smile in return.

"I'm Morley, Morley Finster. I was out on Sable when Surinder and the boys, uh, arrived. I got some family in Saint John and the Coast

Guard offered to take me there since the ship is headed that way. Otherwise, I'm mostly on Sable."

"Any idea what happened to Surinder's ship?"

"He says they must have hit something that made a big hole."

"Ever heard of the *Slocum Warrior*?"

Morley thought for a moment. "Must be one of those boats that try to chase down illegal fishing and whaling."

"They've gone all remote and electronic," Rick said. "Now they work with the military, and do surveillance. My friend is on the *Slocum Warrior*. He says Surinder's ship disappeared in less than fifteen minutes, and the French navy says there was nothing anywhere nearby for it to hit."

"What else has your friend seen?"

"He watched two other ships disappear in the same way a few months before, one off the Faroes, one south of Bermuda, neither of them illegal fishers, neither of them his business."

Morley thought silently for a long moment, then looked at Rick and said, "Dead men don't talk."

He turned away, then turned back and looked Rick hard in the eyes. "Bad stuff's going on. There's a man in the navy needs to talk to you, the same one who invited Captain Singh to Alberta."

He pulled a beaten-up notebook and a pencil stub out of his breast pocket and wrote a number on a blank page, which he tore out and handed to Rick. "Send a text to this number with no message at all, completely blank. Before long you'll get a call from someone in the navy. They'll ask you for your rank right away and make sure you say it's 'Master Seaman', nothing else. Then they'll ask for the name of your ship. Make sure you say it's the *Erebus*."

He pulled out his cell phone. "I'm sending you a text message, to the number Surinder gave me for shipping this dory. If something goes wrong between you and the navy, call me."

"All aboard, Morley. We want to have our dinner in Saint John tonight." It was the captain out on the port wing of the bridge.

The crew already had cast off all but one line. The bow thruster began to swing the ship out into the Annapolis Basin the moment Morley Finster scrambled aboard.

Rick and Bronwyn watched the ship pick up speed and head for Digby Gut.

The truck was too long to turn around on the narrow wharf, so Rick backed out all the way to the shore end. Bronwyn briefly was re-energized by the symphony of truck noises, but soon showed the signs of a nap coming on.

Rick kept her awake with the current menu of favourite songs and car games, and got her home, changed and in her crib before sleep took over.

Now what? He sat down at the kitchen table, took out the page from Morley Finster's notebook and stared at it for a while. He needed to think. *Where is all this going? How is it all tied together?*

He made himself a double espresso with an equal volume of milk heated in the microwave, a truly flat white, and sipped it slowly, hoping that the caffeine and other coffee magic might kick-start some insight.

Trudy had built caves to house a bunch of electronics to run a fish farm. The electronics had arrived in a container strengthened with bars of radioactive steel. Trudy was thought to be dead, but no one seemed concerned about the disappearance of the Beluga Group's Juanita. Surinder's ship was scuttled. Okay...

The Beluga people who came to White's Cove arrived and departed in the middle of the Bay of Fundy in some kind of invisible ship. Wolf Wylie had watched the *Cahow* sail to Bermuda from the Faroes and then make a voyage south from Bermuda and back again before it was hauled up for repairs and returned to sea as the *Nightingale*.

Despite the fancy controls down in the caves, the fish farm still was running on manual. *What really is in those caves?* Maybe Amanda's experiment should be run again.

Bronwyn was still in a deep sleep. Rick went to an outbuilding that had been Uncle Gilles' repository for useful things that somehow never got used.

After much heavy lifting, he found some old sheets of lead salvaged from somewhere long ago, probably with home-made fishing weights in mind. They were about a foot square and 1/8 inch thick.

He brought two of them out to the farm workshop. On one of them he placed a new, clean X-ray film in its light-tight wrapping. He covered the film with the other lead sheet, and sealed the edges with some pounding and a warm soldering iron. With a vice and a heavy hammer, he was able to roll the two lead sheets and sandwiched film to form a cylinder.

He taped a second X-ray film in its light-tight wrapper around the outside of the lead cylinder and sealed the whole thing inside a few sturdy plastic bags with some layers of packing tape. Perfect! Not quite four pounds.

Now, how to get this thing into those deep caves for a few hours?

In the end, it was easier than he could have imagined.

Zora came home mid-afternoon and learned of his plan.

"Piece of cake!" she said. "Trudy made a bore hole for a sea water pipe and the control cables that goes straight down from the fish building to the back of the caves. I'm due for a visit to the farm tomorrow. I'll just tell Parker and Johnny it's a device to make sure the cables are working properly. There's enough rope in the fish building to reach down to the cave."

Rick was sure that he never could talk his way through such a deception. Zora, however, had nerves of steel, and just enough chutzpah.

~

Parker was at the farm when Zora arrived and helped her get the lead weight down the bore hole without hesitation or question. The next morning, she took Bronwyn along with her when she went to retrieve the experiment.

As she was getting Bronwyn out of the truck and preparing to bring her into the fish building, Anton, the head technician, drove up the hill from the office trailer and hopped out of his vehicle.

"You were here yesterday afternoon," he said, "so I did not expect to see you again this morning. Is something wrong?"

"Nope, no problems with the fish," Zora said. "I'm just back to pick up a data logger I left running overnight. Here, can you hold Bronnie while I dash inside to get it?"

She thrust Bronwyn into his not-really-awaiting arms, and slipped into the building.

At first, Anton held Bronwyn awkwardly at arm's length, as if she were a fragile object that might break, and he looked around, as if fearing he might be watched.

Bronwyn stared at Anton's face, then reached out a hand, touched his cheek, and giggled.

A thaw passed through Anton's normally-stiff bearing. He shifted the baby to the crook of his arm and touched Bronwyn on her nose. He received a big smile in return.

They drifted away from the fish building door, and Anton began to sing Bronwyn a children's rhyme in Tosk Albanian.

Parker already was hauling up the lead weight when Zora walked in. She took it outside, put it behind the seat of her truck and went strolling after Bronwyn and Anton.

It was a beautiful, clear, August morning on the Bay of Fundy. Some young brown gannets were feeding close to shore, dropping straight into the water from a height about even with the ridge on which they were standing. Two cormorants were drying their wings at the tip of the White's Cove wharf. The wind was from the west and the tide was surging out from the east, opposing forces that kicked up tall, white-crested waves on the blue, blue water.

"Anything new, Anton?" Zora asked.

"Home Office is pretty quiet these days. Trudy's family is not so sure they want to sell her place, but Beluga is sending in some people to look over the property, just in case."

"What about the farm? More fish coming soon?"

"Not that we know of, but then we usually don't know until it happens. We just watch the dials, and they don't move much. Sometimes the chillers turn on when the tunnels get a bit warm. That equipment has to stay cool."

"This is a lovely spot, White's Cove, but it must get a bit lonely. Do you get any visitors or friends dropping by?"

"We have no friends here, and we are instructed to discourage visitors."

"Well, I'd better get Bronnie home. I have to go up the valley this morning to visit some pigs."

They strolled back to the vehicles beside the fish building, Bronwyn sticking with Anton until they arrived at the truck, when she reached for Zora.

Back home, while Zora got Bronnie a snack and off for a nap, Rick took the lead weight to the shop, cut loose the outer film envelope and, with some effort, got the two lead sheets apart sufficiently to extract the envelope inside.

Amanda ran them through the processor and the result was black and white. Whatever was in the cave where the lead shield experiment had spent about twelve hours was emitting a whole lot of radiation.

Zora packed a lunch while Rick sat at the kitchen table, contemplating the all-clear and all-black X-ray films and what it all might mean.

"Text that number, Ricky," Zora said.

35: The Bermuda petrel

She had seen his face just once before. That was fifteen years ago.

How strange, the things one remembers. He was in the driver's seat of a car parked almost in front of her home when she returned from school that day. "Vincent Van Gogh!" she had gasped to herself.

His face was a perfect likeness of her favourite painter, in all his self-portraits she had on her wall. At that moment, he had been busy rummaging in a bag in the passenger seat, and had not noticed her. She had stared as long as she dared.

He had seemed in a hurry, and soon sped away.

Now she was looking at his face again.

From the engineer's bedroom door, she could see his reflection in a large mirror on the living room wall. He had burst in through the kitchen door, a pistol in one hand and a parcel under his other arm, crouched, moving with speed and menace, like a hyena.

In that instant, everything had become clear to her. On that day fifteen years ago, she had entered her home and found her father dead on the parlour floor. Now in the mirror, she saw the assassin she had not known existed, hired again to eliminate an innocent but inconvenient person.

Juanita's sudden clarity exploded into rage.

Her pepper spray blinded the assassin before he had even seen her. With a dish towel, she picked up the pistol he had dropped. She shot him twice.

Four packets, attached together to a timing device by electrical wires, had spilled out of the assassin's parcel. She recognized them as military incendiaries manufactured by a family business, and which her mother delighted in using to set off a massive bonfire once a year. *So, the house was to be burned down around the engineer's body.*

This must still happen, or they will pursue the engineer again. She hoped Trudy Denton would understand that she was the intended victim, and find some place to hide.

Juanita put on the assassin's raincoat, gathered up the pistol and her handbag, set the incendiary detonator for 45 seconds, and drove away in the assassin's car.

She threw the pistol into the water from the little harbour bridge. It was raining hard, but the thermite in the napalm mix would ensure that only white ashes would remain where the house once stood, not a bone left intact.

All this had happened two weeks ago. Now, Juanita's shock and anger had lost some of their intensity, and she was able to think more clearly.

Up to the age of fifteen, Juanita had only a dim awareness of her mother's immigrant Russian family and their dark enterprises, a grandfather and various aunts and uncles pacing around their Sussex mansions, with guards and cameras and sharp wire fences, dour, sinister and rich. Her mother had kept her away from them, and their own home had been simple but joyful.

But then Papa died, and Mama turned to ice.

Juanita was starting to understand this now. Mama had loved Papa and her family had killed him to warn her that such love is forbidden, to force her to rejoin them. If she said no again? Her daughter surely would be next, a drop of novichok on her skin perhaps, or a messier accident of some kind.

Mama had gone back to them, her last act of love for her daughter. Soon, grandfather and the aunts and uncles, and many cousins, had met their ends in various ways. Mama took charge and took revenge, but Mama also became a monster.

Her mother had been gently pushing Juanita down that same path, but for Juanita that path had ended in the engineer's living room. Her new path now was to destroy the oligarch mafia that had murdered her father and that fattened on war.

I can do this, she thought. *I am better at chess than my mother is.*

Juanita was practised at living incognito in foreign countries. She knew codes to access unnamed bank accounts and extract unlimited funds from certain ATMs, leaving no transaction record. A bargain hair dresser in Halifax had eliminated all traces of her British stylishness, and a thrift store had furnished a clean and comfortable wardrobe to match.

However, after two weeks without any word from her, there would be growing suspicion within the family that the elimination of the White's Cove engineer may not have gone as planned. They would be looking for her. It was time to act.

The news media had reported the engineer's death, funeral and suspected murder, but there had been no further developments. She must have hidden herself well, somehow, somewhere. She would have needed help to hide so well. *Did she take my suitcase with her?*

Juanita decided that her first step must be to locate Trudy Denton. *Who might have helped her and knows she is alive? What about that black woman who knows birds, the veterinarian? They seemed to be friends.*

~

Rick was still at the kitchen table, puzzling over those radioactive steel bars from the shipping container. The *Nightingale* had come from Bermuda, not a major centre of world commerce.

Zora had sent him a photo of that ship with the container on board when they had been interested in the incorrect check digit. He looked through the photos on his phone and found it. There was not much to see, just one end of a rusty, old, half-size sea container with a bar code at one corner.

Just for interest, he walked down to the clinic and tried reading the bar code in the photo with the reader the clinic used to keep track of sales and inventory. On first attempt, the reader said the code was for a bottle of pediatric ampicillin, just right for kittens.

However, when he enlarged the image just enough, the reader consistently displayed a number not associated with any product in its data bank: 3141593.

Rick knew that number; it was the same as the *Nightingale's* IMO, which was lower down in the same photo.

What else do I know about that container?

Surinder said he had seen the Russian word for lighthouse on one of the inside walls, partially painted over. The Beluga lady was not pleased that the damaged container had been dumped overboard at the White's Cove wharf and had insisted that it be hauled up again and placed back on the ship, the ship that sank mysteriously a few days later in deep water. *Does any of this make sense?*

Rick was distracted from his confusion of numbers and containers and steel bars by a telephone conversation Amanda was having on the clinic landline. It had been going on for some time, but Rick had ignored it. Now, Amanda's voice seemed anxious and troubled.

She covered the receiver with one hand and turned to him. "This lady wants to speak to 'Dr. Zora Cromwell' about Trudy Denton. She says Zora cannot call her back and that it is urgent. She wants me to call Zora on her cell and have her drive back to the clinic immediately to speak with her. She says she will pay any professional fees required."

"Who is it?"

"She won't tell me her name. She's British. Here, you speak with her!"

At that moment, through the baby monitor, Bronwyn gave a great howl to demand immediate post-nap attention. Amanda quickly made signs that she would attend to Bronwyn, and hurried away.

"Hello, I'm Rick Robichaud, Dr. Cromwell's husband. How can I help you?"

The lady on the phone repeated her request for immediate access to Zora. Rick found her aggressive insistence annoying.

"It is not possible to contact Dr. Cromwell right now. She is with clients on farms."

"I need to speak with her about Trudy Denton. I believe she was a friend of Miss Denton's."

"Yes, we both were Trudy's friends. But now she is no longer with us; she died two weeks ago," Rick said, matter-of-factly.

The woman on the phone was silent for a moment, then said in a quieter tone, "Perhaps not...Where is the suitcase?"

Rick's mind grappled desperately to find some fixed point of reference within his total confusion. Only he, Zora and Trudy knew about Juanita's suitcase. And Juanita, too, of course, but Juanita was dead. Or...perhaps not?

He took a deep breath, slowly in and slowly out, trying to find an instant of calm, to think, to remember. "What is a cahow?" he finally asked.

"The Bermuda petrel. It is a small marine bird. I have never seen one," the woman replied.

"Can the Pythagorean theorem define a circle?"

"The square root of the hypotenuse would be its radius."

"What happened in 2008, on March 14th?"

After a pause, the woman replied, "My father died on that day."

"We thought you were dead."

"It was necessary that Miss Denton should believe so. You must tell her. There is more to do. You will hear from me."

Juanita rang off.

Bronwyn's cries had not abated and were getting louder as Amanda carried her down the stairs, through the kitchen and back into the clinic. They rose several decibels when she saw Rick, rousing him from his stupor of incredulity into parental action.

He had learned that the offer of some forbidden fruit was the surest way to break Bronnie out of such whole-body fits of petulance. With his free hand, he managed to dump a ration of kibble into Engelbert's empty bowl, which summoned the cat to the spot. He put Bronwyn on the floor beside him.

Her delight in sampling his kibble pellets and groping the food-focused cat at the same time was sufficient to break the spell. Soon she was in her high chair, happily occupied with eating and wearing a wake-up snack of rewarmed pasta with tomato sauce.

Rick sat beside her, still churning through his information overload from conversing with the not-dead Juanita O'Grady.

With a sigh he took out his phone and the note from Morley Finster. He keyed in the number and pressed SEND.

36: Bronnie does the rounds

Rick had run over in his mind many times what he could or should say if someone in the navy really did call him. When it happened, and when his coded sailor credentials were requested and accepted, he still hardly knew what to say or where to begin.

"What is your name?"

"Rick Robichaud."

"Where do you live?"

"On a farm near Bear River, Digby County."

"What do you wish to report?"

"I have evidence that radioactive material arrived at White's Cove on Digby Neck by ship in July of this year and now is stored in caves constructed as part of a new salmon farm owned by a business called the Beluga Group."

"One moment please."

The slight background noise from the caller's phone abruptly disappeared; a speaker phone now switched to 'mute,' Rick imagined. He waited a good two minutes before the voice returned.

The Commodore would like to speak with you in person. Would you be available at your home tomorrow afternoon at two o'clock?"

The navy arrived right on schedule, in an economy-size rented car and in civilian attire, two men and a woman, politely knocking at the kitchen door.

Rick ushered them in and to chairs at the kitchen table.

The Commodore began immediately. "Mr. Robichaud, I am Commodore Duncan McEachran, naval intelligence. This is my co-worker, Captain John Franklin, no relation to the explorer, and this is Colonel Elizabeth Lindenmayer, our colleague visiting from the United States."

Each of them placed their identification papers on the table so that Rick could verify they were who they claimed to be.

"We know you are who you say you are. You are well known to the RCMP, it seems. A Constable Laliberty from the Digby detachment has advised us to believe everything you say."

Bronwyn had no interest in a nap that afternoon, and had been absorbed with favourite objects in her kitchen playpen when the military had arrived. Gradually, she had turned her attention to the new arrivals, and by the time the introductions were finished, she was standing up along one side of the pen, insisting on inclusion.

Rick took her up and hoped she would put up with some cuddling and lap play while he spoke. He had plenty to recount: the new fish farm, the caves, the *Nightingale* and its radioactive steel bars, his lead weight test for radiation in the caves, the attempted murder of Trudy that had killed Juanita O'Grady instead but then, apparently not, Juanita's suitcase and Juanita's telephone call.

The captain and the colonel each had filled half of a large notebook by the time he was done. Bronwyn had lost patience toward the end, and was working herself into a serious fuss.

The commodore reached over and snatched Bronwyn onto his lap. She went rigid for a moment, but then softened and accepted the offer, at least for the time being.

"How do you know it was Juanita O'Grady who called you?" he asked

"I asked her some questions I thought she could answer but most other people could not," Rick said. "I didn't have much time to think of better ones."

"What questions?"

Rick explained.

"Very clever," McEachran said. "We know Juanita O'Grady. We have been trying to monitor her activities for a while. She is not easily traced. She has committed no crimes of which we are aware. We found a weak spot or two in her family's financial manipulations that allowed us to locate her recently in Halifax. We have her under surveillance. I wonder if a body really did burn up in the Denton house fire. O'Grady likely can tell us."

Bronwyn was becoming squirrely on the Commodore's lap and Colonel Lindenmayer offered to take a turn with her as she asked Rick to tell them everything he could about Surinder Singh and the *Nightingale.*

Rick told her what little he knew—the shipping container broken, then dumped overboard, then retrieved, its cargo placed in the caves, lobsters loaded for Boston then re-routed to Portugal, then a telephone call from Surinder in Alberta.

The Colonel's questions all pertained to the period between the arrival of the *Nightingale* in White's Cove in early July and its sinking on the 2nd of August. Rick wondered if they knew the ship's longer story.

"Do you ever work with the *Slocum Warrior?*" he asked the three officers.

Captain Franklin replied that Canada's navy provided some assistance with data and intelligence to the effort to curtail illegal fishing in international waters, but that it was a small component of naval intelligence. Colonel Lindenmayer said the same was true of the US navy.

"Wolf Wylie, the captain of the *Slocum Warrior,* is from Westport, like me," Rick said. "He was my childhood hero, and we keep in touch. Before the *Slocum Warrior,* he was on a boat that tried to chase down rogue fishers, and the last one he tried to catch disappeared into Murmansk. A few months later, he was on the Faroes and in sailed this same ship, but its name was changed to *White-tailed Eagle,* in Russian. It off-loaded some cargo onto a small freighter called the *Cahow.* Both boats had the same false IMO. The *Cahow* sailed all the way to Bermuda. The *White-tailed Eagle* sailed north a few hundred miles and then disappeared. NATO figured it hit something and sank. It was never reported as missing.

"A few months later, the *Warrior* was on station in the Sargasso Sea when the *Cahow* came sailing 500 miles south from Bermuda and met up with an ancient North Korean gill-netter seven weeks out of Sinpo. There was another boat of some kind nearby, but the *Warrior* crew could see it only with a special radar. The *Cahow* sailed back to Bermuda, the gill-netter sailed east a short distance and then disappeared, sank apparently. The third boat quickly became invisible to the *Warrior's* instruments.

"The *Cahow* went into dry dock. When it came out again, it was not the *Cahow* but the *Nightingale,* with new captain and crew. It sailed to White's Cove. It still had the *Cahow's* false IMO painted on the stern. The *Nightingale* sank in less than fifteen minutes in deep water off the continental shelf. The *Warrior* watched it happen on live-streamed satellite data."

All three officers seemed stunned by Rick's recitation. Captain Franklin retrieved Bronwyn from Colonel Lindenmayer, as if to shake himself free for a moment.

The colonel was first to speak. "Mr. Robichaud, we will have to verify the information you have just given us, but I am confident it will check out. Your insights are extraordinary. You have given a huge advance to our efforts to solve an urgent global issue that we have been focused on for months."

Commodore McEachran asked, "How did Captain Wylie know the IMO numbers of those first two boats you mentioned were incorrect?"

"The check digits were wrong."

The Commodore raised his eyebrows questioningly.

"The last digit of an IMO is calculated from the first six. It's called the check digit. I guess it's a kind of verification of the whole number."

"I see."

"I think that number was being used as some kind of code," Rick said. "The *White-tailed Eagle* and the *Nightingale* were painted with the same IMO: 3141593. I only remember it because it's the value of *Pi* without the decimal point, the ratio of a circle's circumference to its diameter. I guess we all learned about *Pi* in school at some point. The same number was in the bar code on that radioactive shipping container. It was in the background of a photo my wife took at the fish farm. I scanned the photo with the bar code reader in the clinic, and it gave the same number."

"What can you tell us about that nearly invisible third boat in the Sargasso Sea?" Captain Franklin asked.

"Wolf said the *Warrior's* regular radar could not see it at all, but a Swedish military radar they were given to try out, that was designed to pick up stealth aircraft, could detect it when it was less than about 40 miles away.

He thought for a moment. "You know, according to the captain of the supply boat for the fish farm, when management people from the Beluga Group come to White's Cove, they come into the Bay of Fundy on a boat he can't see on his radar. He meets it in the middle of the Bay and brings the passengers in to White's Cove. He says the boat is long and low in the water, and seems painted in some kind of camou-flage."

This information created further intense silence among the officers. Captain Franklin returned Bronwyn to Rick, although she was in no hurry to change handlers.

"Another puzzle piece," said Colonel Lindenmayer. "Maybe it explains Cuba."

Rick was remembering his chat with Wolf about underwater sounds. "Commodore McEachran, does our navy or NATO or any group like that collect and analyze underwater sounds for military purposes?"

"Yes, indeed. It's mostly classified work, but I guess it's no secret that there are listening devices all over the ocean floor."

"I was wondering if that kind of sound data could help explain the fast sinking of those three ships. Wolf Wylie told me that all three disappeared in a matter of minutes. If they were sunk intentionally, with explosives of some kind, would those classified listening devices pick up the explosion? Do different kinds of explosives have sound signatures that can be used to identify them, like my bird-watching app identifies birds by their calls?"

Colonel Lindenmayer listened intently to Rick's question and conjecture. "You know, they just might," she said. "I'm going to check into this."

Commodore McEachran was staring off into space, but then suddenly sat up straight and shifted gears, from information to action. "As you probably can see, Mr. Robichaud, this is a serious and urgent international matter. Morley Finster did well to urge you to contact me. I hope you will continue to help us. I also ask that you keep our conversation and the topics we covered confidential. If you agree, I would like to take with us Ms O'Grady's suitcase and those X-ray films showing radiation from the steel bars and the deep cave. Those steel bars seem rather hazardous to you as household items. I would like to take one with me for testing and, if you agree, to send a small hazmat team here tomorrow to remove the rest from your store room. They will be discrete.

"Whoever is behind all of this must have wanted Ms Denton dead and will be wondering why Ms O'Grady has disappeared. I would like to move both of them to a protected and safe location. To do so, I must communicate with Ms Denton and, eventually, know where she is. I hope you will help us with this also."

37: Someone's always watching

Sandy McEwan enjoyed the occasions when, as a courtesy, the armed forces informed Nav Canada in Halifax that one of its big Cormorant search and rescue helicopters at CFB Greenwood would be taking off. If his work permitted, he would track it and try to guess its mission.

Most of those flights went west, into his home area. Often, they went only as far as the Annapolis Basin off Digby, hung around for a while, and returned to base. Sometimes their destination was Digby Neck, or all the way down to Westport. Every once in a while, they headed off-shore on a real rescue mission that he would hear about on the news later that day.

Today the notification came at a good time; air traffic control at Stanfield International Airport was not busy. Sandy had time to watch the spot on his tracking screens move west out of Greenwood at a gentle cruising speed.

The chopper headed southwest, up over South Mountain, across Highway 8 at Milford, and on across Big Lake. It stopped then, over tiny Crouse Lake, of all places.

Sandy was alarmed. Could this be a medical evacuation from Mel's cabin? Had something happened to Mel?

At that moment, an incoming flight approached his control zone and Sandy had to shift his full attention back to civilian air safety.

At the end of his shift, however, he called Mel right away. He was relieved when Mel answered.

"Earlier today, I saw a helicopter fly out of Greenwood and stop at Crouse Lake. I couldn't follow where it went afterwards. I was afraid it might be you getting rescued for some reason."

"Not me," Mel said. "They must have been fooling around or practising something. I hope they didn't scare away my beavers. They're the workers who keep the water in the lake and in the brook high enough so I can get in there with my canoe."

"I'll be home for ten days starting this weekend. You got a few sessions organized?"

"Not now, I don't, but I will have before you get home."

~

Sandy's telephone call strengthened Mel's view that, whatever you do, someone is watching you. He was glad Sandy had not asked any more questions about that helicopter. He hated to lie to his friends.

The chopper had not come for him, but he was there when the rescue tech from that huge yellow hovering machine had come spidering down on a long cable to his canoe and had taken Trudy Denton back up with her. Rick had come to his place the night before, to tell him of this plan, and he and Jeremy had gone out to the camp to help make it happen.

Trudy certainly was ready to go. She had been in hiding, alone at Mel's camp, for almost two weeks, always by herself except when Jeremy brought her supplies. Marie had kept Trudy's spirits up at a distance by sending her some fine food and a constant stream of books—some of them shockingly dirty, in Mel's opinion. The books had kept away some of the terror. Mel hoped that being evacuated by the Armed Forces might make Trudy feel safe again.

~

Juanita was spending her days designing a chess game to bring down the oligarchs, a game in which, she knew, she herself was just a pawn. The players she faced drew great fortunes from the death and destruction that people of every stripe loosed upon the world, but those players themselves waged war only on each other, wars of dominance, pre-eminence and prestige. They thought of nothing else. It was their fatal weakness.

In chess, when all his other players are taken, a lone king sometimes can avoid capture forever. Each such game must end in a draw, for there never is a winner, only devastation of both sides. In some ways, Juanita thought, the prolonged survival of a lone king was her family's endgame, a game of passionate and brutal self-interest. She wondered if a lone pawn also could avoid destruction under certain circumstances. Could it ever prevail? Could a queen ever change her colour?

Whatever the game, Juanita would need some other players on her side. Thus, when a uniformed naval officer carrying her missing suitcase approached her at her favourite thinking spot at a table high up in the Halifax public library, it roused in her more hope than concern.

The officer had greeted her by name, had given her the suitcase, and had offered her a safe haven in exchange for her advice on some intelligence matters.

She considered the proposal for a moment and then accepted it, and she walked out alone to the car he had identified through a window, parked on a side street.

A late-night flight in a small propeller plane had taken her from CFB Greenwood to CFB Trenton, where she was able to catch up on sleep in a comfortable residence before boarding another, larger, plane for a second late-night departure.

As she settled into her seat, several more passengers arrived, one of them the officer who had met her in the library. He greeted her and shook her hand.

The very small passenger compartment soon was full except for the seat next to her, and there was much rumbling and shaking from further back in the plane, suggesting the loading of freight.

The aviator serving as flight attendant was announcing that the flight to Cold Lake would take approximately three hours, gate to gate, when a last passenger, a woman in a hoodie and sunglasses, came in, accompanied by two officers. They brought her to the aisle seat next to Juanita and helped her stow her suitcase in the overhead bin.

As the newcomer removed her jacket and sunglasses, Juanita recognized her as the engineer, Trudy Denton.

Trudy sat down in her seat and turned politely to greet her seatmate. She froze, stared for a moment, and screamed.

The plane had reached cruising altitude before Trudy had regained rudimentary control over her emotions. In those 20 minutes, she had relived the whole terrifying experience: the gun shots, the house fire, the hiding, the desperate certainty that Juanita had been murdered.

Juanita sat quietly beside her, her emotions, as always, invisible.

Finally Trudy turned to her. "I thought you were dead. I thought you had been murdered by mistake, murdered instead of me."

"I might have been, and you might have been. I am glad we were spared."

"I need to know everything. What happened in my house?"

"We will tell each other our stories. We must, and with nothing left out, but later, when we are alone. We must tell our stories also to the Canadian Armed Forces. We have been brought together again for this purpose."

Trudy relaxed back into her seat, trying to let this new reality soak in and relieve some of the unbearable anxiety of her past three weeks. Suddenly she felt an overwhelming need to hug Juanita, to hold her tightly and feel the reality of her being alive. She raised the arm rest between them and with a sob mostly of joy enveloped Juanita in her arms as tightly and as completely as she could.

No one had hugged Juanita for 15 years, and she stiffened automatically in resistance. Trudy did not pull back, however, and slowly Juanita relaxed. She wrapped her arms around Trudy also and allowed her head to rest softly on her shoulder.

They settled back into their own seats again eventually. Neither chose to replace the armrest and, as they drifted off into sleep, Juanita's hand found Trudy's and held it tightly.

38: Neutralize operatives

Trudy and Juanita had been together as guests of CFB Cold Lake for four days before anyone requested a meeting to ask them questions. At breakfast on their first morning, they were surprised to meet Surinder Singh, the captain of the *Nightingale,* and even more surprised to learn that the ship had sunk, and that Surinder and his crew had managed to reach Sable Island.

Surinder was deeply suspicious of Juanita, whom he recognized as from the Beluga Group, which, he surmised, had tried to kill him. For him, Juanita was part of the enemy, and he made no attempt to hide his distaste for her.

Soon, Trudy stepped in. "Juanita saved my life, Surinder, and she's a fugitive from the Beluga Group, too. She is a victim like the rest of us."

Surinder leaned his elbows on the breakfast table and stared down into his empty coffee cup, clearly not convinced by Trudy's declaration.

"You are right not to trust me, Captain Singh," Juanita said. "You were deceived and nearly murdered by members of my own family. I want to put an end to all of this. Perhaps you can suspend your judgment of me until I have tried."

This was enough to move Surinder's attitude from hostile to semi-cordial, and they managed to watch a few movies and the news, talk, walk outside where permitted, and play some board games quite enjoyably for three more days.

On day four, they were escorted to a building with impressive security fences, processed through three layers of security screening, and eventually brought to a small meeting room. Six people in uniform already were seated there.

Commodore McEachran was at the head of the table and, as soon as the three civilians were seated, he began introductions. "Welcome, and thank you for being here. May I present to you General Roger Symonds and Colonel Elisabeth Lindenmayer from the joint anti-terrorism division of the US Departments of Defense and Homeland Security, Commander Orm Løiten and Lieutenant-Colonel Marie-Pierre Domremy from the Joint Intelligence and Security Division of NATO. Captain Singh, I am Commodore Duncan McEachran, and this is Captain John Franklin. We both are with the joint security division of the Canadian Armed Forces."

He turned toward the military participants. "This is Captain Surinder Singh, most recently captain of the MV *Nightingale* which we believe was scuppered deliberately in international waters off Sable Island. He brought his story to my attention. This is Ms Trudy Denton, the civil engineer in charge of construction and maintenance of the White's Cove operation for the Beluga Group. An attempt to murder Ms Denton was made one month ago, and, at present, the general public thinks it succeeded. Only five people, other than ourselves, know that Ms Denton is alive. They helped her to hide. And this is Ms Juanita O'Grady, the daughter of the primary owner of the Beluga Group and of several much larger companies that manufacture military supplies and equipment. Ms O'Grady prevented the murder of Ms Denton, and has been in hiding ever since that event. Our civilian colleagues are here with us voluntarily. None is under arrest or is being detained against their will."

He turned back toward the three civilians. "One way or another, each of you has been caught up in a scheme of international nuclear terrorism. We have come together here better to understand that scheme and how to neutralize it. I believe your knowledge and experience can help us do this. Ms Denton, we believe the tunnels you constructed at White's Cove now contain stolen military-grade plutonium. Captain Singh, we believe your ship delivered this material to White's Cove. Ms O'Grady, we believe that arms manufacturers, including some controlled by your mother, organized the theft and storage of the plutonium. I hope this brief explanation will allow you to follow and contribute to our discussion. I now turn this meeting over to General Symonds."

The general stood up, went to one of the whiteboards on the walls, and began to write.

1. Stolen Plutonium – Russia – Маяк
2. Classified electronics to North Korea.
3. Sunken ships – Faroe, Sargasso, Sable
4. Radiation – White's Cove

"These are the four issues I think we need to understand completely," he said. "Do you all agree with this list?"

After a moment to study the list, Colonel Lindenmayer said, "I think we also must consider the attempted murders of Ms Denton and Ms O'Grady. These are police matters, but they also seem to link to the White's Cove fish farm."

The general added *5. Murder?* to his list.

After another pause, Juanita said, "Perhaps this already is understood, but the ultimate objective must be to destroy the forces behind all these actions. They threaten the whole world."

The general nodded and turned back to the board. At the bottom of the list he wrote *Neutralize operatives*. Then he drew a circle around the words and an arrow up to the top of the list.

"This is number one, of course," he said, "but it is the hardest to imagine right now. Let's start with item 1, the stolen plutonium. How much of this do we understand?"

"I think we know this completely now," Commander Løiten said. "The division of Nuclear Security of IAEA has worked quickly and effectively to discover and trace the missing warheads. While they may be on the ocean floor north of Faroe, it is most likely they were brought to Bermuda by the ship *Cahow*. We have learned unofficially from civilian contacts in Ozyorsk that much of the missing material is deteriorated and no longer is usable in weaponry."

Surinder had been scrutinizing the general's list. "What is that last word in item #1?"

"It is the name of the big nuclear materials plant in Russia where the plutonium was stolen; you pronounce it 'mayak.' I like writing that backwards 'R.'"

"That word was on the inside of the sea container my ship brought to White's Cove. It had mostly been painted over, but you could still see it. I've seen it on Russian navigation charts. I thought it meant 'lighthouse.'"

"You are correct," Juanita said. "It means a lighthouse, *маяк* or sometimes *световой таяк.*"

"You speak Russian?" the general asked.

"With my mother, I speak Russian."

The general put a check mark by item 1. "Okay, how well do we understand item 2, the stolen electronics?"

This was Colonel Lindenmayer's file. "These are produced by IRC Michesen, one of our most trusted and important contractors. Somehow, this part of the company has become corrupt. We are using financial information to identify who within the company may have profited from this theft. We have evidence that the units came to Cuba in a high-speed, military-style corvette equipped with the most modern stealth technologies. With help from French and Swedish naval intelligence, we have discovered traces of such a vessel in recorded radar and satellite surveillance data for the period in question. We are trying to identify this vessel. The manufacturer of these corvettes also sells non-military versions to wealthy people as yachts, so some are privately owned."

Commodore McEachran turned to Juanita. "Ms O'Grady, can you add anything to our understanding about this stealth vessel?"

"Perhaps," Juanita said. "I have been a passenger on such a vessel. My mother sometimes finds it convenient in her work to avoid immigration and customs officials. This boat brought me to the waters off White's Cove on my only visit there, a month ago. The boat itself seldom enters harbours. I do not know who built it or who owns it, but I expect that my mother owns both the boat and the builder. She takes great pleasure in this boat, and is skilled at operating it herself."

"The builder of such corvettes for our navy is a subsidiary of IRC Michesen," Colonel Lindenmayer remarked.

The general sighed and shook his head. He checked off item 2. "What about item 3, sunken ships?"

"This we now understand quite completely," McEachran said. "We are indebted to the farmer, Mr. Robichaud, for this. He proposed to me that underwater sound surveillance data could be analyzed the way bird songs are these days, and might be able to detect underwater explosions and identify the explosive devices."

Captain Franklin said, "It turns out that a coalition of NATO allies has been sponsoring highly-classified research on this very kind of analysis and the sound surveillance data required for it. This group agreed to address the issue of the three sunken ships. Commander Løiten is a member of that research team and can explain what conclusions the group was able to reach."

Løiten rose. "I can give no details regarding our methods, but the results of our analysis are clear. Each boat sank immediately after an on-board explosion. Four explosive devices were detonated simultaneously on the ship from Russia and on the *MV Nightingale*. The wave form profiles for these were the same, and they match those of devices based on an RDX-TNT mixture manufactured in western Europe by military contractors. The North Korean boat was out of range of NATO sound surveillance, but we obtained data from a conservation organization which has a ship that was less than 100 miles away. From those data, we can say that this boat experienced a single explosion, largely of TNT and with a very strong detonation signal. It is typical of explosive devices designed to be delivered by drone submarines and attached to a target vessel's hull."

Surinder's thoughts flooded with terrible memories. "I detonated those explosives on my own ship. I sent a text message and BANG."

"To whom were you sending that message?" McEachran asked.

"The Lisbon shipping agent, or so I thought. The owners told me to send them a message when I was in international waters and fully underway."

"Do you remember the number?"

"I wish I could forget it. It haunts me still: 3141593."

"Check." The general was back at his list. "All ships scuppered. What about item 4, radiation at White's Cove?"

"That is now fully confirmed," McEachran said, "and also, I think, fully explained. Mr. Robichaud and his wife, Dr. Cromwell, correctly identified some steel bars cut away from the container used to transport the nuclear material as being radioactive, and with considerable bravery devised and deployed an X-ray film probe to identify radiation in the rock tunnels constructed beneath the fish farm. Our Chalk River Laboratories have confirmed that the sample I sent them for assessment was of soft steel made radioactive by exposure to radiation over a period of time. Metallurgical analysis indicates that the steel originated from a producer in the Russian city of Novokuznetsk."

"What do you think all this means?" the general asked.

"It means the tunnel under the fish farm contains plutonium and whatever the Korean boat delivered," Trudy said. "I watched that cargo arrive and go in, 40 or 50 rusty barrels together with a few open boxes of electronics. If anything happens in the tunnel to crush those barrels together, some of the plutonium might go critical and irradiate all of the people in Digby County!"

"This is a very delicate situation," Captain Franklin said. "At present, we think the nuclear material is safe and secure in the tunnel. Any steps we might take right now to remove it would send the perpetrators into hiding and out of our reach. Our most sophisticated remote surveillance now is keeping watch on White's Cove."

General Symonds turned back to his board and checked off item #4. "And then we seem to have a murder," he said. "I'm a little confused about this. As I understand it, an attempt to murder Ms Denton failed and Ms Denton thought Ms O'Grady had been murdered instead of herself, by mistake. Ms Denton's house was burned to the ground, a melted shell casing was found in the ashes, and a pistol was found not far away. But Ms O'Grady is here with us now, so something else must have happened. Do we know what did occur?"

Trudy and Juanita looked at each other, wondering which of them should speak and what she should say. How might Juanita's actions that night be weighed on the usual scales of justice?

McEachran spoke before either of them could do so. "I think we can check this off our list, General. We know that an assassin was hired to kill Ms Denton. We also know that the assassin was neutralized and burned up in the house fire. It seems the assassin knew nothing of the presence of Ms O'Grady. Neither Ms Denton nor Ms O'Grady was murdered. My office will work through these details with the police once we are free to do so. At the moment, the police and the public believe that Ms Denton was murdered and burned in her house, and civilian authorities are focused on tracing the origin of the pistol."

General Symons shrugged slightly as he turned and checked off item #5, then stepped back to look at the board. He drew another large circle around *Neutralize Operatives*.

"Who has done all of this? What's the point? It seems like something only nuclear terrorists would do, but who are they? How do we find them and put them out of business?"

Juanita slowly stood up. "The enemy you seek is not terrorism," she said, "it is greed. It is the maniacal greed that affects all people who acquire vast wealth."

She turned toward the general. "It will be clear to you that this stock of stolen nuclear material has no actual military value. This operation is intended to raise the false spectre of nuclear terrorism, in the hope that some missing war heads will trigger another global arms race and enrich a small cartel of global manufacturers."

She paused to collect her thoughts, then addressed the military officers in a voice undaunted. "The military supply chains for weapons and munitions of all countries are dominated by a small club of vicious people, each of whom thinks only of being the richest among them. In this, NATO is no different from Russia or China or Yemen or Switzerland. Nearly all of your arms, planes, ships, electronics, bullets and explosives are produced and supplied to you by this cabal and their corporate networks of greedy and servile dependants. My mother is the dominant power among these monstrous people. She knows that I do not care enough about wealth and power to be a partner in her businesses. I am a mathematician, and I am employed by her enterprises for data analysis and creating models for complex financial transactions. However, I have learned to see through the data and the models. I understand far more of my family's businesses than they ever would imagine. They are fully focused on their money."

The general glowered with ever increasing anger as Juanita spoke. Finally he erupted. "I don't believe you for a minute when you say that the American Armed Forces obtain most of our armaments from criminals," he shouted. "What arms do we buy from this so-called cabal?"

"You must verify this internally for yourself, General, but you will find I am telling you the truth."

"Just give me one concrete example!"

"Consider the classified electronic systems sent to North Korea, the explosive devices that sunk the ships, the drone submarine that planted a bomb on the North Korean ship, the special stealth equipment of the invisible corvette and the corvette itself. All of these are produced by companies that my mother fully controls. For NATO countries, these businesses are legal and regulated, and follow western rules, but the same armaments are produced and supplied by these same companies under different names to all of the countries against which NATO arms itself."

The general glowered and began to pace, troubled and angry, glancing darkly at Juanita every few steps.

Colonel Lindenmayer stepped in. "General Symons, I think we need to give serious attention to what Ms O'Grady has just said. It is hard to accept that our most trusted suppliers could in any way be corrupt. However, our preliminary investigation of IRC Michesen reveals illegal payments to personnel from top to bottom in the guidance electronics division, and we are tracing some very large sums of money seemingly laundered through several of our other contractors for classified development of marine stealth technologies."

Everyone around the table was crestfallen at this intelligence update, especially General Symons. He sat down and leaned his elbows on the table with his head in his hands.

Finally he looked up. "What can we do? Can you help us, Ms O'Grady?"

39: "Lexie"

Olga Alexandrovna O'Grady sat alone, deep in thought, more deeply now than she ever could remember.

It was five o'clock in the morning, and a faint glow of dawn was just emerging on the eastern horizon. Below her hilltop perch, she could see a few lights coming on in the houses around Bath Bay. In the shadowy light, she watched the sleek black rats climb purposefully up the coconut trees to their daytime nests among the leaves, a sign that the day was arriving and the earthbound mongooses soon would begin their day of hunting.

Sometimes, a few monkeys would pass through her grove of trees, seeking food and mischief, but not this morning. Faint ceremonial noises rose to her from the Rastafarian whose bivouac was in the deep, narrow ravine just below her bungalow.

For the next 45 minutes, the dawn would slowly brighten until the sun suddenly would rise from the sea and flood Barbados' whole eastern shore with light. There was a soft tropical breeze coming from the sea, and a distant roar of ocean swells breaking far off on the outer reef.

This was her refuge, the place where she could pretend not to be who she was, the oligarch among oligarchs, the Godmother among those Russian expats who had invested their stolen wealth in crime. She'd bought a mansion on the west side of the island as a foil, with a staff, an address, a telephone and a constant parade of free-loading guests. This hillside cottage on the eastern shore had none of those things.

When she rose that morning and went to the balcony, she found a plate of sweet fig bananas on the table beside her chair. Justine must have brought these earlier that morning, on her way up the hill to her small shop on the paved road.

Tucked among the bananas was a small courier package that had been addressed to Justine at her shop. Inside it was a plain white envelope with "Lexie" handwritten on one side.

Olga held the unopened envelope now, as she was swept by emotions that long ago she had forbidden herself. Roddy had called her this, his pet name for her, a salve against the hated patronymic from her hated father. "Lexie, the red queen who stole my heart," he would say at introductions, and she and Juanita and everyone would laugh with delight.

So, Juanita was alive. To Olga's surprise, this was more important to her than anything else.

Juanita had disappeared when the engineer was killed. Olga had sent her to inspect the new fish farm, but really to be in place to take over its management when the engineer unexpectedly disappeared

Juanita might have been killed by mistake, or by intention, like Roddy. The contractor had disappeared also. He could not be questioned.

Olga opened the envelope. Inside she found only a yellowing newspaper clipping, the obituary for Roddy written by his many university colleagues and published in *The Guardian* on March 17th, 2008. She gazed at it for a while, touching the photo softly with her fingers. She had taken that picture herself, on a hilltop in Wales they had climbed together.

She refolded the clipping and put it back in the envelope.

Juanita was alive, but the message from her was much more than this. Juanita must have come to know why Roddy died, and the game was changed. Juanita had crossed the board, a pawn become a queen, and now she would defeat the family, or die trying.

Olga knew her daughter. Juanita had sent a message to the red queen, but Juanita was not playing at cards.

She placed the envelope in a small drawer in her bureau. She walked up to Justine's store to explain that she was leaving now, and then used three different taxis to reach her west-coast mansion.

~

Purley Jordan was just bubbling with the good news. Those Hollywood people finally had come through, delivered on all their "maybes" and "perhapses". The big movie was going to have its very first open public showing right here in Bear River!

"That movie did so well at that TIFF thing in Toronto, I thought they'd forget all about us," he said, leaning in the truck window far enough to be sure Bronwyn would hear the good news, too. "They're showing it in the Oakdene on Thanksgiving Monday, three shows, morning, afternoon and evening, all free of charge. The Oakdene probably hasn't got enough chairs, so you'd better bring your own."

Purley raced off to spread the news and Rick and Bronwyn headed for Digby. The big, old, luxury hotel that everyone called "The Pines" usually closed each year about the end of September, but yesterday they had phoned in a big cheese order, and Lansdowne Highland was glad to oblige.

As Rick and Bronwyn were leaving the hotel to walk back to the truck, they met Anton from the fish farm, heading into the hotel and looking flustered.

"Is the farm giving you a little vacation weekend at the Pines?" Rick joked.

Anton shook his head dismissively and looked at Bronwyn, who returned his look with a smile and a squeak. Rick looked at Bronnie and then held her out to Anton to see if this was what they both wanted, and it was.

Bronwyn turned back to give Rick a big smile and then reached up to touch Anton's nose.

"Head Office called me two days ago," he said. "They want me to organize a stockholders' meeting for the farm, here in The Pines. There's lots of stuff they want, quiet and privacy and no one around. I don't know what these rich people need."

"Well, they'll get good cheese," Rick said. "Or somebody will. Here, we'll go in with you. I bet the managers here know exactly what rich people need, and if the money is coming through you, there is nothing they won't do for you." They headed into the hotel, Bronwyn playing with Anton's ear and giggling.

40: Checkmate

It was time for the partners in the nuclear stockpile at White's Cove to meet again. However, their security contractor in Vaduz recently had reported disturbing activities around their traditional meeting place, suggesting new and unwelcome interest by Interpol. Thus, the meeting had been arranged in an unexpected location, in remote and unheard-of Digby, Canada, a town of 2000 people 150 miles from an airport. From there, they also could view in person their clever achievement at White's Cove.

Arranging this meeting was easier than the previous one by 16%. Only last week, Evgeniy of the Verdi Group had fallen from a very high window in Dubai after making an unauthorized sale of bombs to Myanmar. There were only seven partners now.

Arrivals and departures would have to be discrete. Seven private jets arriving anywhere at the same time might rouse unwanted interest. Three would fly to Portland and two to Saint John. The corvette, with Olga O'Grady on board, would pick up partners in Portland and meet the Beluga Group supply boat, sailing out from Blacks Harbour with the others. The corvette was Olga's private yacht: *Perestroika*, Cockburn Town, IMO 2178214. She was looking forward to showing it off and fanning fires of jealousy in the other cartel members one more time.

Juanita leaned against the western breakwater of the tiny harbour at Victoria Beach on the Annapolis Basin, watching birds swirl on the tide surging in through Digby Gut. It was a sunny afternoon on the first day of October, and there was much to see. Scoter ducks and a few loons from the Arctic had begun to arrive for the winter, while the local cormorants had not yet completely departed, and grebes and phalaropes were still passing through. A group of porpoises was milling around close to the breakwater, pursuing fish.

The leaves of the maple, oak, and poplar, ash, birch and beech, had begun to show their fall colours. The background greens had brightened to a mosaic of yellow and orange, including some bronze-brown oaks and a few bright-red maples. Stands of dark-green spruce among the larger patches of colour made striking contrasts. Looking across at the towering canvas of the western facade of Digby Gut, Juanita was immersed in a tableau in which art and nature, abstraction and realism, were inseparable.

A peregrine falcon suddenly swooped in and plucked a plover out of the air.

In Cold Lake, Juanita had proposed to the military a strategy, a design for an earnest game of chess with the cartel, and they had accepted. She had been flown back to Trenton, was taken to the train station and was left on her own, with no further surveillance, connected to them now only by the plan and by trust.

Only a few moves remained to be played in this game. She was waiting for one now.

At three o'clock in the afternoon, the *Perestroika* sailed in from the Bay of Fundy at about 20 miles per hour, a third of the speed its 16,000 horse power turbines could deliver. It hugged the Victoria Beach side of the passage, and the roar and whine of its engines dropped in volume as it drew even with the breakwater and nearly stopped. It then turned 90 degrees and surged across to the western shore in a burst of speed, where it slowed again and headed south toward Digby.

Check. This was the penultimate move.

Juanita watched the corvette move away with a heavy heart. Like the trees on the far shore, the queen had chosen to change colour and also to fall to the ground.

The *Perestroika* discharged its seven passengers at the Digby wharf, where a van from The Pines was waiting. The ship then motored east a few miles and anchored in deep water, where it was sheltered by Bear Island from the seasonal southwest wind.

At dinner that evening, Olga reviewed their agenda.

"Tomorrow morning, we will go in the yacht to view the White's Cove facility. The Verdi Group mercenaries at the site believe they are guarding a stockpile of sensitive electronics. Nothing must be said to the contrary. We will return to the hotel for our business meeting, which will include lunch and dinner. All aspects of security for the meeting have been assessed and confirmed by our usual contractor. We will depart the following morning as we arrived, in the yacht. At tomorrow's meeting, each partner will present their plans to extract profit and advantage from our White's Cove project."

The corvette was at the wharf at 8:30 in the morning to pick up its passengers. With Olga at the controls and engines at 60%, they covered the 32 miles to White's Cove in 40 minutes.

The tour there was short. There was nothing much to see, and none of the partners was interested in nature, farmed fish or exercise.

The *Perestroika* returned to Digby at impressive speed, surged in to a stop, and made a gentle approach to the wharf.

To Rick's annoyance, the drive into Digby that morning for a short meeting with the Lansdowne Highland accountant took far more time than he had planned. First of all, some kind of road work was being set up on Highway 101 just east of Digby, with big machines nearly blocking the road. Two police cars seemed to have pulled over a big tour bus at the same point on the highway, and it was an obstacle to traffic as well. He and Bronnie had to wait a good ten minutes to pass through.

There was another road construction site at the Flat Iron corner, with traffic slowed to a snail's pace. Rick and Bronnie waited behind four more big tour busses, with their hostile-seeming one-way glass windows, as each was stopped, then let through the road repair zone one at a time. Every year, the fall colours of the tree leaves attracted some bus tours to the area, but five all at once seemed like a lot to Rick, and the leaves were only just starting to really colour up.

Two of the busses turned north onto Victoria Street, heading for The Pines, Rick supposed, but the other two lumbered slowly ahead of Rick all the way to the accountant's office on Water Street, where they then veered off toward the commercial wharf.

Rick and Bronwyn were late for their appointment, but were forgiven, and soon were on their way again. They were just leaving the accountant's office when the *Perestroika* roared into the harbour.

Rick had never heard or seen such a boat before, so he and Bronwyn drove down to the wharf to have a look at it. The road was partly blocked by the busses, which had parked close to the head of the wharf and were taking up part of the wharf access road. A big transport truck was parked in front of them and its trailer's long loading ramp protruded part-way into the road, all the handier for loading in fish from the fish plant just across the road from it, Rick supposed.

He threaded his way around busses, truck and ramp, and drove out toward the strange, noisy vessel that was just then docking at the outermost spur of the wharf, its engine noise now reduced to a deep purr. When he and Bronwyn had driven part way along the wharf, a passenger van from The Pines drove up behind them and flashed its headlights to signal Rick to move out of its way.

There was no good place to pull over where they were, so Rick hurried along ahead of the van all the way to the corvette, and then beyond it. The van stopped at the boat.

As Rick and Bronwyn watched, a small group of people, three of them in white yachty uniforms, walked down the boat's gangway and got into the van, which turned around and drove back up to the head of the wharf.

Then the whole scene suddenly became totally bizarre. At the head of the wharf, the van did not thread its way around the ramp, the truck and the busses, but drove right up the loading ramp into the trailer of the truck. Out from the busses swarmed heavily-armed and armoured men who entered the trailer and formed a cordon around it.

The RCMP arrived at the same moment, with sirens and flashing lights, moving people away and re-directing traffic. Two military helicopters zoomed in and circled over head. It all made for an amazing and unanticipated spectacle.

As he and Bronwyn sat and watched all the drama from their excellent vantage point, Rick noticed that the corvette, which was close beside them, was drifting slowly away from the wharf, pushed by the wind. The ropes that should have held it fast had been cast off from the boat's side and were floating in the water.

The *Perestroika*'s engines suddenly roared into action, and the corvette sped away from the wharf at maximum speed, its engines screaming. Bronwyn gave a startled look at Rick and seemed about to cry, but then looked again at the corvette accelerating away and turned back with a big smile, clapping her hands.

A military vehicle came racing down the wharf to where the corvette had been. An officer jumped out, radio in hand, and seemed to be giving excited instructions into it.

One of the circling helicopters tilted suddenly and sped off to the north, seemingly in pursuit of the corvette. The officer jumped back into the vehicle, and it zoomed away.

Juanita was seated on a bench near the Point Prim lighthouse. The sun was bright, but the air was cold. She had lit a small fire of twigs and driftwood on the rocks in front of the bench, partly for warmth, but mostly for amusement. She was pretending to watch birds, but really was steeling herself to carry out her mother's wishes one last time.

Half an hour earlier, she had watched the corvette return from White's Cove along the Bay of Fundy shore and turn south into Digby Gut. It would be soon, now.

A big grey seal was lolling about in the near-shore water, and Juanita was watching three purple sandpipers prowling along at the edge of the seaweed when she heard again the thunder of those engines.

The *Perestroika* raced into view, heading west across the Bay at full speed. A helicopter off to one side was keeping pace with it. Checkmate.

Juanita held her phone at the ready, waiting. The text message soon arrived: "сделай это"— "Do it".

She keyed in the code number, and pressed 'send.'

The *Perestroika* erupted into a ball of fire.

The helicopter veered away, rose high and then returned to hover over the spot where the boat had been. Soon a second chopper joined it.

Juanita's small fire was burning strongly now. She dropped her phone onto it and watched it melt, burn, and disintegrate while her personal confusion of emotions did the same.

When the fire had done all it could, she picked up the phone's burnt-out remains with a stick, and from a high rock she flicked them into the sea.

The helicopters still were hovering a long mile offshore when she walked back to her car and drove away.

41: The report of my death...

September was a busy month for Commodore McEachran and his team. Captain Franklin had to secure the hidden nuclear stockpile while keeping the intense military interest in White's Cove undetected. Juanita had provided Colonel Lindenmayer with a large and detailed chart of interconnected ownerships, codes, bank accounts and commercial transactions to keep a few hundred national and international security agents busy gathering evidence of crime in the global arms industries, and developing arrest and extradition dossiers for the major players. McEachran had to organize a sting operation for the top criminals that would neither fail nor cause harm to civilians. There had to be a backup plan, too, on the US side of the border, just in case, with air and sea deployments in the Gulf of Maine.

In the end, there was only one surprise. The corvette had gone to the bottom of the sea in fragments and Olga O'Grady had gone with it. She was not among the passengers in the van when it was unloaded under tight security in a hangar at CFB Greenwood. Olga O'Grady had collaborated in the dismantling and destruction of her own cartel, and then had chosen suicide over captivity. The military would leave the matter there.

There was much they could do now that secrecy no longer was required. The armed forces had swarmed into White's Cove only moments after the van and its prize of VIP prisoners had been secured and escorted in a military convoy toward Greenwood. The fish farm now was under heavy guard and nuclear specialists had been called in to determine what really was in the tunnels.

Coordinated arrests of over 100 industrialists were made in the United States, and of 100 more in Europe, with several also in China, India, Israel and South Africa. Simultaneous press conferences by defence secretaries and ministers were held at six o'clock in the evening that same day in Ottawa and Washington, and at midnight in Brussels, to explain the exceptional intelligence and security operation that had just been completed, and to assure the world that it was safe once again.

The four mercenaries at the fish farm tunnels had offered no resistance. They were unarmed and had no illegal possessions. Captain Franklin put them on a military flight to a NATO base in Latvia and, after a brief interrogation there, they were flown to their homes in Albania and Serbia.

The Denton family, and the whole local community, deserved a full explanation of all the events associated with the White's Cove fish farm, and McEachran felt he should provide that explanation in person. A week before the sting operation, his staff had reserved the gymnasium of Digby Neck Consolidated School in Sandy Cove for a private event on October 3rd, and now posters in local stores and on community social media groups announced a community meeting there at one o'clock in the afternoon that day, open to everyone.

At eight o'clock in the evening of the day of the operation itself, McEachran drove Trudy Denton to her parents' home in Little River, and watched her walk in through the kitchen door. He remained in his car, but twenty minutes later, Trudy and her parents burst out of the door and swirled him into their home and their emotional tornado.

Rick was in the vegetable garden, spreading manure on the patch where he soon would plant next summer's garlic, when his phone rang and bannered him that Wolf Wylie was calling. Bronwyn still was asleep, and he was happy to take the call.

"Where are you now?" Rick asked.

"Fogo Island."

"What, back in Canada! In Newfoundland!?"

"Nope. Cape Verde. We're tied up at Sao Filipe for a few days. We all need some time off the ship! Just one person on board for security. I'm calling with a question."

"Shoot!"

"What the hell is going on around Digby? Yesterday, I made a virtual visit home with a hi-rez satellite feed, and I saw a boat leave Portland, Maine going really fast and head into the Bay of Fundy all the way to Digby. It was easy to follow because its transponder was on. The marine registry lists that signal as from the M.V. *Perestroika.* That boat was just whizzing along. I put a special watch on it. Today, it motored fast out of Digby to White's Cove and then back again after about an hour. A few minutes later, it took off out of Digby like a bat out of hell! It zoomed out into the Bay a mile or so and then—poof!— it disappeared. What's going on? I bet you know."

"I think the military finally connected all the dots," Rick said, "starting with the ones you gave them about ships with false IMOs. Watch the CBC news on line tonight, or any good news channel. There will have to be some kind of announcement. I'll be watching, too."

Wolf recognized cautious and incomplete information when he heard it. "Okay, I get it. I'll call back in a day or two. I want the whole story!"

By one o'clock in the afternoon the next day, every chair in the school gymnasium was filled, and at least fifty more people were standing at the back. From Westport to Rossway, everyone who could do so had made their way to the meeting. On the news, they'd heard or seen the Minister of Defense announce the capture of international criminals, and the discovery of a nuclear arms stash at White's Cove!

The press had swarmed to Digby Neck, too, and to the meeting, but the reporters and their crews were diverted into a classroom with a video feed from the gymnasium and asked to await a press conference just for them to be held at four o'clock. The RCMP had taken charge of managing the traffic and the meeting, ensuring that the Fire Marshall's rules were followed and trying to accommodate all comers.

Two chairs in the front row were reserved for Trudy's parents, who would not be separated from their daughter for any reason and were with her in the side room where Commodore McEachran, Captain Franklin and two staff members also were waiting.

Captain Franklin had called Rick the previous evening and had asked if he and Zora would be willing to have Trudy and Surinder, and perhaps one other person, as overnight guests following the community meeting in Sandy Cove, and if he and McEachran also could join them that evening for an hour or two. Rick and Zora had agreed and had insisted that they all come for supper as well. They decided they would skip the big meeting in Sandy Cove in order to get ready for all their guests.

At one o'clock, Constable Roger Laliberty stepped to the microphone, greeted the crowd, pointed out the exits and washrooms, and said there would be a brief presentation from the Armed Forces followed by an opportunity to ask questions.

From a side door, Commodore McEachran emerged, followed by the others.

As they mounted the few steps onto the small stage, there was an outburst of gasps and muffled screams. A living Trudy Denton stood before them, leaning on her parents, all of them smiling and crying at the same time.

As the intensity of shock and emotions began to subside, Captain Franklin ushered the Denton parents to their seats in the front row, and he and Trudy moved to chairs on the stage as McEachran went to the microphone.

"I am Duncan McEachran from the Canadian Navy," he began. "I'm here with some coworkers to share with you what has happened here in the past few days and weeks. It has touched all of you in one way or another. We are here to tell you what we know and answer your questions as best we can."

He began by describing the Beluga Group, its murky ownership, vast resources and purchase of the regional salmon farm industry as a cover for hiding stolen nuclear material for ransom or extortion. "The global cartel that controls the Beluga Group has been ruthless," he said. "It destroyed at least three ships and murdered the crews of two. We believe it also attempted to murder Trudy Denton. For many weeks, we all believed that Trudy was gone, but happily, that assassination failed."

A wave of muffled mumbling passed through the audience, and someone shouted, "What *did* happen?"

As the commodore started to answer, the door at the back of the gym opened and Juanita O'Grady stepped into the room.

Johnny Tidd and Parker Churchill stared at her with surprise and loathing, and Johnny blurted out, "It's that Beluga Group lady!"

People standing near Juanita quickly stepped away from her, and another dark rumble passed through the crowd.

Trudy leapt to her feet. She jumped off the front of the stage, ran to Juanita and threw her arms around her, sobbing. "I was afraid you were in that boat!"

She took Juanita by the arm, and walked with her onto the small stage. Then, Trudy quickly walked to the microphone.

"This is Juanita O'Grady," she said. "Her mother ran the Beluga Group, but Juanita did not. Juanita saved my life. If you love me, you've got to love Juanita, too. That murderer burned up in the house fire. I thought he'd killed Juanita by mistake and would kill me if he found out I was still alive, so I ran away. Johnny, I snuck into your house to hide for a few days when you were on holiday. I guess I owe you some for all the food I ate. Then Ricky Robichaud rescued me and found me a safe place to hide."

Trudy went back to her chair beside Juanita, grasping her hand as she sat down.

McEachran said, "We all owe a great deal to Juanita O'Grady. She provided the key information and strategies that led to yesterday's arrests all over the world. We also owe much to Mr Robichaud, whom Ms Denton just mentioned. He was able to see patterns in events that we and others did not, and he went looking for evidence when he thought that people he cared about might be in danger. It was Mr Robichaud who alerted the military to the presence of radioactive material at White's Cove and to its probable origins."

The commodore gave a summary of the criminal acquisition of nuclear material from sources in Russia and North Korea; the intelligence gathered by the Canadian, American and French armed forces, by NATO, and from Captain Wolf Wylie of the *Slocum Warrior*; the classified stealth technologies used on the high-speed corvette to move people and materials undetected; and the cartel of expatriate Russians and other criminals who, until yesterday, had dominated the global manufacture of all conventional weapons, and were now in high-security detention at various locations across Canada. All but one.

"I want to clarify for you the role and outcome for Ms Olga O'Grady in this munitions cartel. She was the dominant personality in the cartel, but it also is clear that she herself had decided to destroy it. Her collaboration in this operation was extensive and was essential to the success of yesterday's arrests. It also is clear that she had decided to end her own life. Yesterday, she was to have been arrested with the other six cartel members. However, she stayed on the corvette and sent her crew into the passenger van, which confused counting and delayed detection of her absence. She piloted the corvette out into the Bay of Fundy and detonated explosives on board."

McEachran then invited questions, and answered them as best he could, with Captain Franklin's help, until there were no more, and it was almost four o'clock.

The hardest question came from a woman from Little River who wanted to know how the man who had come to murder Trudy had ended up dead and burned in the house.

To McEachran's great relief, Constable Laliberty stepped in to answer that question. "This was investigated by the local detachment, the homicide unit in Halifax and by the coroner's office. I have been authorized to report to you that the would-be assassin of Ms Denton was neutralized by Ms Juanita O'Grady in an act of self-defence, and that the house fire appears to have resulted from incendiary material he brought to it. There will be no criminal charges, since the accused is dead."

As the audience slowly departed, McEachran invited the press and other media personnel to move into the gym and set up for the news conference. Trudy Denton's parents tearfully greeted and embraced Juanita as they all walked back to the side room, and Constable Laliberty took charge of the gym once again.

At that moment, a large military helicopter swooped in overhead and landed noisily on the main road in front of the school, at a spot cordoned off by police. Eight people emerged from it, some in uniform, some not, and were escorted into the school through a side entrance.

McEachran and Franklin were greatly relieved when they heard the chopper arrive. It meant that the top brass would indeed hold the press conference, and that they would not be needed.

The commodore turned to Juanita. "I was hoping you would join us today. The community needed to meet you."

"I had to come," Juanita said.

"Dr Cromwell and Mr. Robichaud have invited us to gather at their home this evening, for supper and to spend a few hours together before John and I head back to Halifax. They have offered beds to anyone who may wish to spend the night. Will you and Trudy join us? I really hope you will."

42: You'll need an engineer

Rick had made enough butter chicken to feed a small army, and he and Zora had brought a second table into the kitchen to make places for everyone.

Surinder had appeared mid-afternoon in a small truck he thought would be just the right vehicle to fetch all the material he would need to repair his house in Westport. He went out immediately to visit his dory.

Juanita and Trudy arrived from Little River at about the same time that McEachran and Franklin drove up in a chauffeured military car. Zora had insisted that Amanda stay after work and join in, and she invited the military driver in for supper, too.

It was a happy moment, with all formalities set aside. Conversations went in many directions and there was no program.

Bronwyn reigned over a good two feet of space at the head of the table. With concentration, she managed to scoop a small piece of chicken out of her bowl and into her mouth with the proper end of her spoon, at which triumph she rejoiced loudly and threw the spoon to the floor.

As Bronwyn began to crash, Zora whisked her away for a bath and bed, and the others moved into the living room, where a small fire in the wood stove was giving comfort against the cold fall night.

McEachran said he needed to be formal for a few minutes now. He took a folded piece of paper out of an inner pocket. "Everything has happened very quickly in the last few days," he said. "In the next week, the police, the courts, government leaders, parliaments, and international bodies will take over everything we have been working on together for two months or more. We will be out of the loop completely, or far off on the sidelines. But what we have done together, mostly what you have done, is a very big thing, and the highest levels of government recognize this."

He looked at the paper and passed it to Surinder, who was seated beside him. "Here are two thank-you notes, one from our Prime Minister and the other from the President of the United States. Neither is signed, of course, but both are genuine. Both governments fully recognize and appreciate your contributions, and one day this case will be declassified and become part of the historical record."

The statements were short and quickly read, and the formalities ended.

McEachran accepted a shot of scotch from Rick, and looked around the group. "Surinder, you have been harmed personally by this affair. Your ship was blown up under you, and you nearly died. Trudy, you were harmed, too; you were targeted for murder and terrified, and your home was burned to the ground. And, Juanita, I can only imagine what you have gone through. Each of your lives has been completely disrupted. It's none of my business, really, but do you have plans, paths forward of some kind?"

"I sure do have a plan," Surinder said. "Tomorrow, I am going to Westport to make my house there into my home. I've been at sea ever since I was a teenager. I may have had enough of that. I've got fifteen years of salary I never had a chance to spend, so I can take a few years to decide what's next. I'm off to Westport, and I want to meet that Wolf Wylie."

Zora had rejoined the group and sat down beside Trudy. "What about you, Trudy? What will you do now? Will you rebuild your house?"

"That I'll never do," Trudy said emphatically. "I don't think I can ever live on that spot again."

She glanced over at Surinder. "I don't want to be far away, though." She giggled nervously. "I've been invited to try making my home in an old house in Westport," she said, "and that's what I'm going to do. The old house needs some work. I think Surinder could use an engineer."

Well, now there's some news, Rick thought. *Two months holed up in Cold Lake together, clouds with silver linings. Wow! Jenny Thurber's old place! It sure needs some genuine love and attention, just like they do.*

Surinder was beaming.

"Juanita, what will you do now?" Trudy asked. "Do you have a plan? You can always stay with us until you figure things out."

Juanita sighed. "I am like that Lisbeth Salander in the books, just without all the tattoos. I have a few rare skills, plenty of money and I don't know how to make sense of my life or what to do." She turned to Trudy. "I think I want to start a new life for myself here. If you would let me, I want to build a house where your house was, where you saved me from myself with kindness, and where I escaped from—from emptiness. I could anchor a new life there, I think. I want to try."

"Then you're going to need an engineer, too," Trudy said, and kissed Juanita on the cheek.

43: Knowers and Lovers

The day had arrived, and Bear River was in a frenzy. The village had been on TV once before. They'd loved it, lies and all, but *this* was HOLLYWOOD, the big screen, with famous actors!

Purley Jordan had stirred everything and everyone into full celebration mode. When the carload of producers, the director and their assistants had arrived on Saturday, they were welcomed with flags and special signs of greeting.

A few members of the press arrived at the same time, not to report on the film, which already was widely praised at film festivals, but to capture the excitement and reactions of the little country village.

The film company had brought along high-end projection and sound equipment, and the big screen needed to show the film in the gym of the Oakdene Centre at theatre quality. Every hotel and B&B from Bridgetown to Meteghan was full, as village friends and family from all over the Maritimes streamed in for the showing.

The morning and afternoon showings that Thanksgiving Monday were standing-room-only and well-attended by the travellers, many of whom would drive back home that same day. It was anticipated that the evening show would be attended mostly by people who lived in the village itself, or nearby. A village party had been organized for this evening crowd, to start immediately following the show.

Rick attended the afternoon showing. Zora had been recruited by Anita St-Pierre to help out with the after-show party, and this required some sort of sewing bee with Lisa and Marie. Zora could look after Bronwyn while this was going on, and Rick could then keep Bronnie entertained while Zora took in the evening show.

Rick was blown away by the film. He had borrowed the Louis Penny novel from Rory and knew the story, but on screen he felt its depth and power all over again. It was not a light story with a feel-good ending. It gripped you and made you look into yourself.

As the audience filed out afterwards, it seemed to Rick that nearly everyone was moved, introspective and hopeful at the same time.

Whatever Zora and friends had been up to was finished by the time Rick returned home. He got Bronwyn up from a slightly-too-long nap and had a bath with her while Zora laid out an early supper. Then she headed out to the evening show and her work at the party afterwards. Rick stayed home with Bronwyn for another two hours.

Bronwyn was especially keen these days on an old push-cart toy Rick had found at a thrift store. This was the toy Bronnie had been waiting for, it seemed. She quickly had discovered that she could stand up using it for support, work herself around to the sturdy handles and then walk two-legged across the floor, pushing it in front of her like a walker.

When she reached a wall, she would come to a halt and collapse on the floor, look around at Rick, laugh with delight, clamber to her feet again, and head across the kitchen in another direction.

Twenty minutes of walker practice, a stroll with Rick out among the cows, a visit to the pigs, a snack, a diaper change and some presentable clean clothes, and they, too, were off to the Oakdene.

Rick found Zora sitting near the back of the gym, together with Lisa, Marie, Anita, Rory, Sandy, Henry, Mel and Jeremy. The movie had just finished, and the credits were scrolling by.

Bronwyn reached out for Jeremy, and they went wandering around the back of the room as the audience applauded or sat thoughtfully for a few minutes.

The lights flicked on and Purley Jordan went to a microphone in front of the screen. He called on the film director, producers and assistants to come up on stage and thanked them on behalf of everyone for honouring the village with the film showing.

"I'd like to give you the keys to the village," he said, "but the village doesn't have any keys. But we're all here tonight and you are here with us, and we hope you will stay with us and dance the night away."

Purley turned back to the audience. "We've been as busy as bees getting tonight's party set up. Don't nobody go home. We'll need some space to dance and some space for food tables. Let's get about half these chairs stacked up at the back and everything cleared away from that wall. Mel, get your kitchen party band up here. We need some music right now! Jeremy, I need your help with the tables."

Mel, Henry, Rory and Sandy headed for the stage with their instrument cases, and Zora, Marie and Lisa disappeared back stage. Anita went off in the direction of the projection crew, taking a tablet computer from her bag as she went.

Rick was standing beside Jeremy and Bronwyn when Purley hustled up to them, took Bronwyn from Jeremy, gave her a little toss and a whole-face smile, and handed her to Rick. "I need this strong young man," he said.

Jeremy followed Purley over to the stack of folded tables and began unfolding and carrying.

The music started. Rory had his fiddle out and they began with some old-time reels. Sandy and Henry were solid on rhythm and harmony, and Mel's fingers on the accordion never fell behind.

They switched to some Irish jigs, and Lisa stepped out from behind the curtain with her flute to join in on that set. They moved on to some polkas and some of the people gathered close to the stage began to dance.

Henry stepped to the mic and belted out "I'll Tell Me Ma," and the dancers just kept going.

Purley announced that the lunch was ready, and there was a pause in the dancing while people enjoyed some of the food on offer. While they ate, Rory sang an amusing Buffy Sainte-Marie song about infidelity that made the women laugh out loud and the men look embarrassed.

And so it went. Rick sat off to one side with Bronwyn, in delightful and never-ending conversation with everyone. Gerald and Becky Cheever and family arrived part-way into the festivities, and Millie came running over to see Bronnie.

Millie was big enough to hold Bronwyn now, and she took her away on a tour of the party, sometimes carrying her, sometimes holding her hands so Bronwyn could walk along herself.

The music and dance had been going for about an hour when, to some general surprise, Mel put down his accordion and stepped up to the microphone. "I'm not gonna sing, and I got nothing serious to say, so don't look so worried. Some of you who spend time at the café likely heard Henry and Rory trying to write the world's greatest song about this old American poet called Walt Whitman. They were supposed to have it done long ago, but I happen to know they finished it last week. I told them they had to sing it here tonight. I hope you're ready for it, 'cause here it comes."

There were some whoo-hoos and ululations from the crowd, then quiet expectation. The band members looked at each other a bit nervously, and then jumped into it. Henry and Rory together stepped up to the microphone, Mel sat down again with his accordion and Sandy took centre stage with his Irish drum. He began to beat out a steady 4/4 rhythm with a slight swing to it: boom-a-diddy, boom-a-diddy, boom-a-diddy...

Henry spoke over the drum beats. "Rory and I like Walt Whitman. He started out as kind of an arrogant S.O.B., but he ended up more like Moses. I heard an old Gospel song a few years ago, from the 1950s, by the Staple Singers. They called it *Don't Knock*: 'you don't have to knock on heaven's door.' I thought the tune was just perfect for Whitman. We kept a few of the Staple Singers' words, too, because they fit so well."

Rory stepped in as the drum continued. "This song puts Whitman's big poem, *Leaves of Grass,* in a nutshell, the whole thing evaporated down, like barrel-strength whisky. We're going to have some help singing it, too. Let me present to you *The Oakdenes.*"

From behind the curtain at the side of the stage, Marie, Zora and Lisa emerged. They were encased together in a single, one-piece, body-clinging dress with neck and arm holes for each of them. The gown was deep pink and flowed to the floor. Each of their arms emerged through a festoon of rainbow chiffon. Their large earrings and shoes matched the gown, and their hair was piled high.

The Oakdenes took a haughty Motown pose, and the audience burst out with laughter and applause.

Sandy's steady beat had never stopped. Now on the movie projection screen above the band, large words appeared: 'You Don't Knock.'

Mel squeezed out a long chord in the right key, and Henry began to sing. In all the right places, *The Oakdenes* cooed and chorused in classic 50s style.

> *You don't knock, you just walk on in*
> *That door to everything.*
> *There's love and joy for you,*
> *And hope to carry us all time through.*

There's a vast similitude to guide us to infinitude.
You don't knock, ring, pay out gold,
The rolling earth is just a-waiting for your soul.
You don't kno-o-ock, you just walk on in.

Rory sang solo on the next verse, and Mel joined in with rhythmic chords. *The Oakdenes*, who had been doing oos and oh-yeahs in the background, now started to wave their arms and sway to the beat, first to one side then to the other.
Henry and Rory sang on, sometimes solo, sometimes together.
There was a verse about religion:

Every creed and religion and philosophy
Boils down to "love your neighbour," and that's you and me

There was one about your life being better than the bad dream you might mistake it for, and another about compromise winning out over war and violence.
The Oakdenes really started to rock now, gyrating and adding short echoes as Henry and Rory sang together.
The last verse was a celebration: heaven is right here on earth, right now, and it can last forever if we want it to.

It's the knowers and the lovers who make it all run,
Soon there'll be no priests because their work will be done.
We're a-learning and a-loving round this
*   rolling earth with pride.*

Henry cried out, "Everybody sing!"
The top of the projection screen flashed to blue, and the words of the main chorus were projected in big white letters, line by line.
The drum, the accordion, the singers and *The Oakdenes* went wild.

You don't knock, you just walk on in
That door to everything...

The audience started to sing along, and the band repeated the chorus, then repeated it again, and then one more time, as everyone in the room stood up and sang and clapped and swayed. Even Lillian Cromwell, Zora's mother, and the Hollywood crowd were into it.

As they started into the chorus for the last time, Millie came walking over to Rick, holding Bronwyn up by her hands. As they got close, Millie let go, and Bronnie walked the last six steps to reach Rick all by herself. She looked up at him and back to Millie with a happy squeak.

The song ended, and the audience burst into applause.

Everyone took a break for refreshments at the food tables. *The Oakdenes* disappeared back stage and re-emerged as three separate people.

Soon the band was back on stage, now joined by Lisa with her flute. The dance tunes rolled out: reels, hornpipes, jigs, waltzes, a Country classic mixed in here and there. The dancers danced whatever way they wanted.

Jeremy came to sit beside Rick at the back of the room and Bronwyn quickly squirmed onto his lap. Marie, Zora, Zora's mum and Becky Cheever were sitting at a table together, talking, gesturing and laughing. Anita and Henry were out on the dance floor.

One of the film producers walked over to Purley Jordan. "Who are those guys?" he asked, pointing to the band, "The two guys who sang that song?"

"Henry and Rory, the village poets."

"My boss is working on a biopic about that Whitman guy," the producer said. "He's looking for a theme song." He took out his phone and found the notepad app. "Just give me those two names again."

Rick was thinking about the song, too. He had never read *Leaves of Grass*. A kind of secular bible, Henry said it was. As he thought about it, the messages of the simmering movie they all had just seen and of Rory and Henry's song seemed pretty close to each other: hubris and greed lead to misery for everyone, and there are better ways to live.

Bronwyn had crawled back onto Rick's lap and was nestling in with exhaustion. It was way past her bedtime. He looked around the happy crowd. The party was not even half over, he figured.

But it was over for him and Bronnie. Zora would catch a ride home with someone.

He zipped his big, woollen, flannel jacket around himself and his sleepy daughter, and headed out into the crisp cold night.

You don't knock

You Don't Knock: Walt Whitman at Barrel Strength
Lyrics by Rory Willson and Henry Wambolt
(Set to the tune of *Don't Knock,* by Roebuck Staples & Wesley Westbrooks, 1959)

You don't knock, you just walk on in
That door to everything.
There's love and joy for you,
And hope to carry us all time through.
There's a vast similitude to guide us to infinitude.
You don't knock, ring, pay out gold,
The rolling earth is just a-waiting for your soul.
You don't kno-o-ock, you just walk on in.

Well Walt Whitman he walked this road
To help us see and shed our load.
He travelled both low and high,
Through the earth and through the sky.
Like Woody did 50 years later on,
He found where truth was hiding and sang his song.
He was a walking not a knocking round this rolling earth with pride.

You don't knock, you just walk on in
The door to everything.
Walt said each and every part of us is part of him,
And friendship is the dynamo that makes us spin.
Every creed and religion and philosophy
Boils down to "love your neighbour," and that's you and me.
Don't stand like an oak shedding leaves all alone,
Let the efflux of your soul just carry you along.

Ted Leighton

You don't kno-o-ock, you just walk on in.

Do you think we're in a world of woe?
Well, Walt says, "No, no, no!"
We got a wild bird hovering high up over head,
To guide us through that murky old cloud of dread.
You may think it's just a dream that life can be good,
But evil is the dream, get that understood.
We're awake and not a-dreaming round this rolling earth with pride.

You don't knock, you just walk on in
The door, to everything.
Walt thought there could be glory in a righteous war,
But he ain't gonna study war no more.
You've got to reconcile instead of fight,
And keep away those siblings: Death and Night.
Oh Captain, My Captain, fallen cold and dead,
There can be way better lilacs in the days ahead.
You don't kno-o-ock, you just walk on in.

Well there's way more future than past,
And it's guaranteed to last.
The play goes on and on;
You sing your verse and time moves along.
It's the knowers and the lovers who make it all run,
Soon there'll be no priests because their work will be done.
We're a-learning and a-loving round this rolling earth with pride.

You don't knock, you just walk on in
That door to everything.
There's love and joy for you,
And hope to carry us all time through.
There's a vast similitude to guide us to infinitude.
You don't knock, ring, pay out gold,
The rolling earth is just a-waiting for your soul.
You don't kno-o-ock, you just walk on in.

Acknowledgements

I am greatly indebted to Andrew Wetmore of Moose House Publications for his expert and insightful editing of this novel. Every chapter has been made better in numerous ways by his close attention.

The stunning cover design by Rebekah Wetmore uses part of the wonderful 2023 diptych painting, *The Ghost of Loss (Under a Bruised Sky)*, by Eva McCauley, to magnificent effect. I thank them both for this beautiful application of their artistic talents.

Comments several readers of early drafts made to me also helped me to shorten, lengthen, clarify, and altogether improve the manuscript.

Eva McCauley provided version-by-version review and commentary, and constant enthusiasm and encouragement.

About the author

Ted (Frederick) Leighton, OC is professor emeritus at the University of Saskatchewan and professeur associé at Université Sainte-Anne. From 1984 to 2015, he was a professor of veterinary pathology at the Western College of Veterinary Medicine and was the founding director of the Canadian Wildlife Health Cooperative. Since retiring from academic science, he has focused on creative writing.

His first novel, *A Ring of Justice*, was published in 2022.

He lives in Bear River, Nova Scotia.

9 781998 149667